the prosecco fortune

the prosecco fortune

STELLA WHITELAW

ROBERT HALE · LONDON

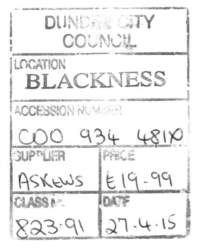

To
Diana and David
who would love Venice

one

The number 25 red London double-decker bus trundled by, totally full.

It didn't even stop at the bus stop. The driver shook his head.

'Damn it,' said Emma, rain dripping off her umbrella and down her neck. She could feel the wet trickle down bare skin despite her fawn Jaeger raincoat and Hermès scarf. When it came to clothes, she bought classic.

December was not her favourite month despite the Christmas and New Year festivities. It was too cold and too wet and Christmas left Emma feeling more alone than ever. She had no family and a microwaved Christmas dinner in her Brixton flat was a depressing thought. She'd seen all the repeat old films.

This morning at Irving Stone Accountants was going to be different. One of their most important and long-standing clients was to grace their doorstep. Emma had to be on time. She was now a junior partner in the old-established firm, working her way up, but it was vitally important that she should be there. She had the figures.

She hailed a rogue taxi, stepping out into a puddle. Water splashed right up and into her boots. 'Taxi,' she shouted.

She must have looked desperate because the taxi driver stopped. 'Where to, miss?' he asked, leaning across to open the door.

Emma gave him the West End address of Irving Stone Accountants. Goodbye to any lunch and probably dinner. Even her legs were wet from the splash. No chance to change her tights.

She sank down in the back seat, grateful to be out of the rain, grateful to be moving in the right direction. She knew this client was one of their oldest. She knew that his grandfather had been an esteemed client. The man was Italian. He grew grapes to make wine somewhere in Italy. She knew nothing about wine but a lot about his accounts.

When the taxi reached the offices of Irving Stone Accountants, an old red-bricked nineteenth-century house, hemmed in by tower-block buildings, Emma was in a slight state of panic. She had less than a minute to get to her desk and look efficient. She gave the taxi driver several notes, not counting, which was against the grain for an accountant.

'Thank you, thank you, so much,' she gasped. 'You're a star.'

'Slow down, miss,' he said, grinning. 'There's always tomorrow.'

She ran through reception, waving her identity pass, and squeezed into the lift as the doors were closing. She leaned against a wall, getting her breath back, only then aware of one other person in the lift.

'*Mi scusi*,' the man said. 'Your umbrella is raining on my leg.'

Emma froze. Her life was about to change. It was the most beautiful male voice she had ever heard, like soft brown treacle, deep and dark, but with the slightest accent and an element of amusement. She had never in her life heard a voice that was so magnetic. It was if his voice took her into a soft and slow embrace.

'I'm so sorry,' said Emma. She pulled away her umbrella and tried to close it. It was one of those automatic, extending umbrellas that were so difficult to get back into their fold-up shape. This one had no intention of being folded up. It had enjoyed its morning in the rain and was determined to continue the adventure.

'Allow me to 'elp you,' said the gorgeous voice.

'Thank you,' said Emma, desperate.

As he took the umbrella from her, Emma allowed herself to look at him. Then she wished that she hadn't. He was unbelievably good-looking. She drank in his masculinity. Tall with short, thick dark hair, chiselled cheeks and firm chin, a mouth curved and warm with amusement. And his eyes. She dared not look into them. They were a dark, velvety brown, like cascades of mountain water against rock, glittering with gold lights, fringed with dark lashes too long for a man. She looked away before he could see the sudden hunger in her eyes.

'There, I have fixed your rebellious umbrella,' he said, handing it back as the lift stopped at her floor. He was obviously going up further to the executive floor. '*Ciao, signorina.*'

Emma got out, legs unsteady as she took her first steps. She had seen the most beautiful man in London and already she was leaving him. Her life had been like that from day one. She never got dealt the best card. She always got the joker.

'Late again,' her colleagues shouted, as she raced through the open-plan office to her desk in the far corner. At least she had a window and a view. It was one of the perks of being a junior partner.

Emma gritted her teeth. Late by a minute was not exactly late again. She hung up her raincoat and examined her boots. The rain had splashed inside her boots and trickled down onto her feet. She eased off the boots and turned them upside-down to dry. She peeled off her damp tights and stuffed them into a drawer. Her fine, tawny-red hair was a tousled mess, but it would dry quickly.

She turned on her computer and brought up the file for Marco Angelo dell'Orto Vineyards. This was the man she would be meeting soon. She had to have all the information at her finger-tips. His accounts were in a mess. Even overnight, there was news from the Stock Exchange. Dell'Orto Vineyards were being pursued in a takeover bid by a giant American firm of wine importers. Dell'Orto grew grapes in their Veneto vineyards and brewed the prestigious sparkling Prosecco. Emma had no idea what that was. She'd never heard of Prosecco. All she knew, from Google, was that Veneto was in Northern Italy. And now, that Dell'Orto had no funds.

Her phone rang. She picked it up. 'Miss Chandler? Would you come into the conference room, with your files? We are waiting for you.'

Emma stood up. Her heart was beating wildly. She tried to calm down her breathing. It was not far to the conference room, but it felt like the green mile. She was followed by ribald comments. She had to survive this moment if she was to keep her job. She needed to earn enough to pay the mortgage on her high-rise Brixton flat.

She smoothed down the slim skirt of her grey suit and made sure the nipped-in jacket sat on her waist. The buttons were all fastened on her crisp white shirt, no wardrobe malpractice. She ran her fingers through her hair. That was all she had time for. She was, after all, employed for her accountancy skills, not her looks.

She picked up the bulky file she had prepared the day before and tucked it under her arm. This was not going to be an easy meeting. She had discovered many discrepancies in the figures sent to her from Italy. In fact, large sums of money had disappeared.

The conference room was a big corner room with tall windows on two walls. The furthest windows faced the river Thames, the other windows looked down onto the busy London street. The oval mahogany table was highly polished and laid with pads of lined paper, pens, water carafes and tumblers. There were already eight people sitting round the table, arm's length apart as if they were infectious. Emma saw her empty place on the far side.

'Good morning, gentlemen,' Emma said as she entered.

The gathering was intimidating. Irving Stone nodded a greeting. His son, Harry, looked at her with disinterest. He had not approved of her appointment. Maybe he thought she was a rival with her clever brain. Maybe he knew that she was not interested in him and that piqued his masculine vanity.

One man stood up. He was tall and lean, wearing an Armani suit in the finest black worsted material. His shirt was cream with the faintest pinstripe, a narrow grey tie knotted at his throat.

'Buongiorno, Signorina Chandler,' he said. 'Come sta?'

Emma did not understand a word of Italian but even if she had, she would have been speechless. It was the same deep and grave voice of the man in the lift, the man who had already shaken her composure with his devastating good looks. She could not take her eyes off him. He stood with an easy air of authority, his ebony brown eyes amused by her reaction. Her head jerked up.

'Buongiorno,' she said.

Marco dell'Orto was used to women falling for him on sight and this slim young English woman was no exception. But usually it was some glamorous woman in expensive couture clothes and immaculate make-up, straight from a hairdressing salon, every strand in place, reeking of expensive perfume.

But this young English miss had not bothered to make an impression on him. Her grey business suit was neat and service-able, her hair needed a comb or a brush, and there was the faintest shine on her straight nose.

Then he saw her lips and her eyes. Her lips were the most

perfectly curved shape with only a touch of gloss and asking to be kissed again and again. Her eyes were the most beautiful he had ever seen, the clearest hazel green, like summer pools of Monet water, her lashes long and silky, fluttering like butterfly wings.

He wanted to drown himself in those eyes. But Marco dell'Orto did nothing of the sort. He sat down abruptly, annoyed with himself that some young English accounts clerk should have this effect on him. Every young woman in Venice wanted to be with him, attached and unattached. There were even older women who would flatter him with undisguised desire. He could take his pick.

'To business,' he said, reverting to English. 'I am flying back to Venice this evening. This matter must be settled now.'

Irving Stone, the senior partner, had been briefed on the situation. Emma had given him all the facts that he needed.

'To be brief, Signor dell'Orto,' he began, adjusting his spectacles. 'The accounts for your business are in a mess. Large amounts of money are missing. And unless they are sorted out to our satisfaction, we feel we can no longer act for you. The situation is a delicate one, especially if you are considering this American offer.'

'The American offer is nothing,' said Marco dell'Orto dismissively. 'The vineyard is not for sale. It was my grandfather's before me and it is not leaving the family. I have worked all my life in the vineyards since I was a boy of eleven. No American company is going to trample over my name, change it to something smart and trendy.'

Emma could see him as eleven years old, working in his grandfather's vineyard. He would have been tall for his age, bronzed by hours in the sun, muscles hardening as he toiled in the terraced fields. Had he carried brimming baskets of grapes on his shoulders?

'Emma, would you like to give us some of the details?' said Irving Stone.

'Emmer, that is your name?' asked Marco dell'Orto, leaning forwards.

'Emma,' she corrected him.

'What a small name,' he said.

'No smaller than Marco,' she replied.

He laughed. It was a warm, rich sound. She wanted to make

him laugh some more but these figures were no laughing matter. She was about to destroy him with the figures. The Prosecco fortune had disappeared.

Everyone round the conference table had copies. It was an hour of relentless questioning and probing. Marco's face grew grim, all amusement gone from his eyes. He was still a rich man but his vineyards would collapse if he did not discover where the income of the past two years had gone.

'My accountant in Italy is an old man, Signor Bragora,' he said. 'I know there have been health problems. Macular degeneration, I believe. He is losing his sight. But I have always left the money side to him. I trust him implicitly. I ran the vineyards, day to day, and he saw to the bills and the accounts.'

'It is not a happy situation,' said Irving Stone, polishing his glasses. 'The money is not there.'

'I could sell my palazzo on the Grand Canal,' Marco went on, drawing on the pad of paper. 'And my villa on Lake Garda. They would fetch millions of euros. The winemaking plant. There are many assets.'

'It might be enough, Signor dell'Orto, to stave off bankruptcy,' said Irving Stone. 'But you really need to find out where the money has gone to satisfy the revenue authorities.'

Marco dell'Orto looked shaken by the events but he was drawing on some inner strength, his eye steely and stubborn. 'I shall find the money. I shall get it back. No one is going to take my vineyards from me, even if I lose everything else.'

'Emmer,' he said, turning to her suddenly. 'What do you think of this situation?'

His voice pierced right into her. It was if he was speaking to her alone in the room.

He had realized by then that she was no little accounts clerk, but a clever, efficient accountant in her own right. She knew what she was talking about and could see paths through a maze of figures.

He was not used to clever women. His women friends had lithe, supple bodies, not brains.

'Emma,' she said, making time. There was power in his bearing. If he stood up, he would tower over her. She was trembling, searching for her usual composure.

'Emma,' he repeated gravely.

'I think someone should go through every piece of paper and follow every transaction that has taken place in your office recently, maybe even going back several years. I'm really sorry, Signor dell'Orto,' she added, her voice softening. 'I can understand how much you care for your vineyard. We shall try to save it.'

'Vineyards,' he corrected her, his eyes glinting. 'I have more acres than you can imagine. They stretch to the horizon.'

He stood up, gathered the papers with rough movements. He had been touched by the sympathy in her voice. Not many women in his life cared about anything more than the money he could spend on them, the jewels he could give them, the hours of rough loving in his big bed.

'Gentlemen, I have a proposition to make. Give me one month to sort out this chaos. I will get to the floor of it, I promise you.' He felt suddenly awkward about using the word *bottom* in Emma's presence. He had already noticed the pert shape of her body as she walked round the conference table. His hands had tingled with longing to touch her.

'But I need help. I propose that this clever Ms Emma Chandler comes with me to Venice and takes charge of my accounts office. Let those lucid green eyes do some detective work. She is already a detective. I will pay her salary and all expenses. There will be a bonus at the end. Do you agree, gentlemen?'

Marco knew he was in serious trouble. He was also being foolish to trust a young woman, simply because she had beautiful eyes. He would go to the Questura as soon as he returned to Venice and speak to the Commissario di Polizia. He wondered if his old college friend, Claudio Morelli, was still working there.

'Someone more senior should go,' said Harry, drumming his fingers on the polished table. 'Emma has little experience and I don't think she speaks Italian. I know some Italian. She would be lost without the language.'

Emma gasped. No one bothered to ask her. They were talking over her head as if she was part of the furniture. She was indignant, her eyes dimming, blurred. She put her rimmed glasses back on. She knew they made her look officious.

'Excuse me,' she said, interrupting. 'But I do not wish to go to

Veneto, wherever that is. I have my job here and my home here. I don't speak the language and I would know no one.'

Marco came round to her side of the table. 'You would know me,' he said. 'And I would teach you enough Italian.'

He was leaning far too close. She could scent his aftershave, the cleanliness of his body. She wanted to reach out and touch him as if he was still eleven years old. There was a touch of mockery in his voice.

And that was the real reason for Emma's panic. This man was dangerous. A few minutes in a lift and she was ashamed of her wanton feelings. A month with him would be a nightmare. She would be the one sent home with a broken heart and nothing to show for it except perhaps a few moments of ecstasy.

'Emma,' said Irving Stone, ignoring Harry's objection. There was an edge of steel to his voice. 'We should like you to go to Venice and sort out this situation. The police may be involved. I know how much you like your job here. It will still be here for you, of course, when you return.'

There was a veiled threat in his words. Emma wanted to keep her job. She wanted to keep her flat. She was on a career ladder.

Marco bent down, his breath fanning her cheek. A wisp of her hair blew into her mouth and she raised her hand to remove it. Marco saw the softness of her inner lips and wondered if he would ever have the strength to keep his hands off her.

'It is only a month,' he said so that only she could hear.

'That's four whole weeks.'

'You need never wear any shoes, signorina.'

They both looked at her bare feet. Her feet were cold now. Emma felt exposed, almost naked. Marco was smiling. 'I will send a car for you at four o'clock. The plane for Venice leaves at six. Please be ready.'

Emma did not realize that she might lose her heart or that she might also lose her job. This was not simply misplaced money, this was hacking, cybercrime. Her life would be at risk. But she knew she would take the risk.

two

Later Emma rushed home, by bus, snatching a quick sandwich lunch of tuna and watercress. She had all the files she needed. Her colleagues had been envious, curious.

'A palace on the Grand Canal, a villa on Lake Garda? You've fallen on your feet, girl, this time,' they said.

Emma pretended not to hear as she took a few personal items from her desk.

'Mind you stay on your feet,' they teased. 'Not on your back.'

'I intend to,' said Emma. 'I know Italian men are very amorous but this is strictly business.'

'I wonder if you'll still be saying that when you come back. If you ever come back.' They tittered among themselves.

Emma had had no time for their banter. There was too much to do. She had to pack, put her plants in the sink and hope they'd survive, and empty the refrigerator. Not that she had much in it. She did not spend a lot of money on food. The flat, council tax and heating ate up her salary.

If she could keep her head, she might return to England with some savings. That would be a pleasant change. And set her up for the decorating she wanted to do in her flat. Her plain bedroom would be the first.

When she opened her wardrobe door, she realized how little she had in the way of suitable clothes for the office of such a wealthy man. She had three business suits which she wore in rotation, grey, navy and black; and several good white shirts. The usual selection of jeans and sweaters. Nothing swish or glamorous. She was going to work, not to be entertained so the three suits would have to do.

She had an up-to-date passport, mainly because everyone

needed identity proof these days and she didn't have or need a driving licence.

She was downstairs and waiting when the car arrived to pick her up, a small wheelie suitcase at her feet. It was a chauffeur-driven limousine with pale-grey leather upholstery. The chauffeur opened the door for her.

'Heavens, I've forgotten an umbrella,' she said, making to go back up to her flat.

'They have umbrellas in Italy. It rains a lot there,' he added, as if he knew.

He drove through the heavy evening traffic with skill. He was taking her to Gatwick Airport. It was like a dream. She could not believe that she was going to Italy with the best-looking man she had ever met. A man who set her pulses racing. A man who could also make her laugh. A man who even seemed kind and generous. It was almost too good to be true. No man could be that perfect.

They passed the Christmas shops with their snow-filled windows and endless Christmas reindeers and baubles. She suddenly realized she might be away for Christmas. No microwaved dinner then, all alone. But maybe she would be alone if Signor Marco dell'Orto had a family.

She knew nothing about his circumstances. He might have a wife and a brood of dark-haired children, waiting at home for him. It was a sobering thought. It would be easier to simply concentrate on her work, if he had a family. She was no home-breaker.

'Mr dell'Orto will be waiting for you in the first-class lounge,' said the chauffeur, unloading her small suitcase, which seemed to have shrunk on the journey.

She found the desk for the Italian flight and there was a boarding pass waiting for her. She made her way up the escalator to the first-class lounge. It was good to get away from the noise and bustle of the airport. Perhaps she would get some sleep on the flight. Her endurance needed strengthening if she was to survive those searching dark eyes.

The first class lounge was indeed a haven of civilized comfort. It had deep armchairs, newspapers, phones, WiFi, food and drink. Marco rose up from an armchair. His knotted tie was loosened now. He was reading an Italian newspaper.

'Ah, Emma. You see I am pronouncing it right now. I have been practising all day. Would you like some coffee or something stronger? There is a bar.'

'A coffee please, black.' She was feeling too sick with nerves to eat or drink anything. Seeing him again had brought back all her tingling feelings. She felt a wave of apprehension. Going to Italy with Marco was suddenly a bad idea.

'There will be some light refreshment on the plane. It is only a short flight, a couple of hours.'

He brought over a cup of coffee, always the gentleman, returned to his newspaper and left her alone. Emma was immensely grateful. There was no way she could endure small talk with this man.

Marco, too, was glad to hide behind his newspaper. Emma was even more disturbing now that she was travelling with him, all his for four weeks. It was a long time since he had wanted any woman. He knew he would not be able to resist her and that somehow he had to bring a gleam of happiness into those beautiful eyes.

He wondered why she looked so wistful and sad. Some man had hurt her perhaps. It was always a man. Some stupid moron who was foolish enough to let her go, to break her heart. Marco hoped he would never hurt her. Although there was a chance that things could go wrong. His lifestyle was complicated and this English miss would be feeling strange and homesick.

Suddenly he leaned forward and touched her hand. It was like an electric shock. A tidal wave of feeling engulfed her. Emma almost dropped her coffee. It was as if he caressed her body.

'Do not worry, Emma. You will be 'appy in my home,' he said. 'I will make sure you are 'appy.'

Emma smiled and the radiance lit up her face like a burst of sunshine. Marco was astonished at the change. She was an angel, she was perfect, she was made for the medieval splendours of Venice.

'Thank you,' she said, keeping the amusement out of her voice. 'I'm sure I will be very 'appy.'

A hostess escorted them to the plane when the flight was announced. There was no hurry. First-class passengers were the last on. They did not have to sit for hours on the flight deck, listening to announcements.

There were eight big, comfortable armchairs in pale uphol-stery in first class, each with its own swinging television set and a retractable table. There were extending foot-rests for catching up on some sleep. No beds. It was not a long-haul flight.

Emma hesitated in the doorway to the cabin. 'Which is my seat?' she asked, looking around for seat numbers.

'You can sit where you like,' said Marco, waving his arm. 'Choose one.'

'Doesn't my ticket have a seat number?'

Marco led her down the centre aisle. A white-coated steward was waiting with a tray of champagne and canapés, ready to serve them. The champagne was already poured and sparkling. It was Prosecco champagne, of course.

'Take a window seat and you will see the Alps,' he said. 'It is a magnificent sight. All that snow.'

'Which window seat?' Emma was thoroughly confused by now.

'Any window seat,' said Marco. 'I have bought all the seats here in first class. The whole cabin. This I always do. I buy my privacy.'

Emma slept on the flight. A glass of champagne, a few smoked salmon canapés and she was soon dozing off. A blonde hostess brought her a monogrammed blanket and a pristine white pillow. She also brought a dish which contained folded hot towels.

'Would signorina care to refresh her hands and face?'

Emma wondered who she meant, not used to the Italian word. She smiled at the young woman. She was slim and smart in her uniform.

'Thank you,' said Emma, unfolding a hot towel. She ought to try this at home.

She missed the Alps and Marco did not have the heart to wake her. She looked so peaceful, her wild hair in disarray on the white pillow, the blanket tucked round her legs. He wanted to slip into the wide armchair beside her and take her in his arms. He wanted that softness near to his body, to breathe in the scent of her pale skin.

As the plane descended to Marco Polo International Airport, Emma woke up. Her ears were popping and they hurt. She

clamped her hands over her ears. Even first-class passengers were
not immune to this pain.

'Keep swallowing,' said Marco, obviously not troubled. He sat
in the seat beside her, as near as possible. She had taken off her
jacket and the white shirt barely covered her breasts. She had
twisted while sleeping and the material was tight, outlining her
swelling shape and the pert rise of her nipples. 'Suck a sweet.'

'I don't have any sweets.'

'I 'ave sweets,' he said, producing a bag of highly coloured fruit
drops.

'Almost there. We will be landing soon.'

The lights of the airport were brilliant below. Emma saw strings
of light for motorways. But everywhere else was dark, so dark, like
a black sheen over the landscape. She did not know where she was.
She was suddenly frightened. She was in a strange country with
a strange man. The language was foreign to her and she had little
money, only a few euros.

'There's no point in this. I am not a detective,' she said.

'But you have a good brain. Maybe you will spot the discrep-
ancy in my accounts.'

Marco seemed to know what she was feeling, as if he had direct
connection to her thoughts. 'Do not be afraid, Emma. We shall soon
be at my palazzo. A car ride to Venice and then in my launch along
the Grand Canal. You will next be in bed, ready to sleep. I have
spoken to my housekeeper and she is preparing a special room for
you. Not so big that you will be lost.'

'You have a housekeeper?'

'Maria. A good, kindly woman. One of the old – what is it, you
say?'

'One of the old school?'

'That is it. She has been with the family for years. And her sister,
Paola. She will treat you like a daughter. And probably tell you off
if you do not eat enough of her good cooking.'

A bump and screeching reverse engines told Emma that they
had landed, and she had not really noticed. Marco helped her into
her suit jacket, refusing to let his fingers touch the softness of her
neck. The desire was almost too much to bear. He wanted to sweep
her into his arms, to carry her away, anywhere.

The hostess brought her raincoat, which had been on a hanger in a cupboard, and her briefcase.

'Your coat, signorina. Welcome to Venice,' she said.

'Thank you.'

Emma followed Marco in a dream through the brightly lit halls of the airport. Marco seemed to know everyone. She did not know where they were or where they were going. Somehow her small case was retrieved and a porter was wheeling it. Marco had no luggage.

A big black limousine was waiting for them outside the airport, similar to the one that had driven her to Gatwick. Perhaps Marco dell'Orto had a fleet of cars too. She could see nothing of the mainland countryside as they drove away. It was far too dark.

'So you grow grapes,' she said, struggling with pathetic small talk.

'I grow grapes,' he said solemnly.

'And make champagne?'

'No. Champagne comes from France. My wine is the best Prosecco. This is Italy's sexy cousin to champagne. You will love it. It is crisp with a slightly bitter finish.'

'And your vineyard is near Venice?'

'North of Venice, in the Trevisco province of Veneto. Venice is a floating city on several hundreds of islands, built on thousands of timber piles driven into the clay. I don't know how many. No one has ever counted them. You have never been to Venice before?'

'I've never been anywhere before.'

'Everyone should see Venice, at least once in a lifetime. It is the most beautiful city in the world. It will blow your mind away. It is sinking, so now is the time to see it.'

She stayed as far away from him as possible in the back of the car. They were driving over the bridge which connected the mainland to Venice. She felt she might fall asleep on his shoulder and that would be disastrous. Then she heard the sound of lapping water and realized that they were near the Venice Lagoon.

'To arrive this way along the Grand Canal is always the best way to approach Venice. Better in daylight. But the lights are still magic. You will see. This way, here into my private launch.'

He helped her out of the car, across a paved quayside and down into his launch. The driver was smartly dressed in dark blue. Marco spoke to him in rapid Italian.

'I told him to drive slowly so that you can view the palaces,' he said.

It was a magical journey. She almost forgot that Marco was standing beside her. He now had a light wool coat slung over his shoulders. But when he felt her shiver as the wind blew in from the sea, he removed the coat and put it on her shoulders. It still held the warmth of his body. His warmth added to the magic.

'It is cold in the winter in Venice. But in the summer it is so hot, one can barely breathe.'

The palaces were a parade of perfection. Emma could not believe that such elegant houses had been built so long ago, water washing up the steps to grand front doors. Many were lit with outside lights. No falling into the Grand Canal in the dark, not like Byron. She glimpsed crystal chandeliers twinkling in tall windows.

She was enchanted. There was the sound of music from somewhere. She felt their hips touching. She wanted to turn to him, to say how beautiful everything was.

But her voice had gone. Venice was as magical as his presence.

The air was scented. Spices, coffee, the sea, incense. She was in a different world. Every palace was perfection, delicate tracery and carvings, balconies, columns, arches and portals. They seemed unreal, like some exotic James Bond film set built on water.

'In the summer it does not smell so good,' said Marco. 'It is a problem.'

The launch drew alongside some steps, awash with water.

'So here we are. This is my house. Palazzo dell'Orto. Mind the step, Emma. Do not slip. It is often slippery. My palazzo is also sinking. But not tonight. I forbid it to sink tonight.'

She could not see his palazzo, but she sensed it was smaller, tall and narrow but still elegantly beautiful.

She followed Marco's tall figure, but she knew not where, into a sinking palace. The hall was huge, high-ceilinged, the floor tiled with black and white tiles. A naked statue at the bottom of the stairs shot arrows of love into the skies. She followed Marco up the marble stairway to the first floor, half-dead with exhaustion. She could barely collect her wits.

They went into a large room with tall, brocade-draped windows that looked out onto the canal below. It was furnished in a modern style, nothing over-elaborate, had several wide white sofas, coffee tables, a flat-screen television, bookcases brimming with books, thick white carpet. It was a bachelor room. No family, no kids, no scattered toys.

'Would you like some refreshment?' Marco asked, his eyes devouring her. But he knew it was the wrong time. Her delicate face was drawn, eyes dimmed. She was not ready for love. The accountant needed good sleep.

Emma shook her head. The day had drained all her energy. Her feelings had gone underground. She was ready to sleep, alone.

'I'm sorry,' she said. 'I'm so tired. There's a lot to do tomorrow.'

'I understand. Maria will show you to your room. Sleep well, signorina. Tomorrow is another day. Then we will work to find if my business is housing a cyber-criminal.'

Maria took her to another floor, up another flight of marble stairs. They passed walls hung with paintings, some oil, some watercolour, elegant statues in alcoves. It was as if Marco came with her, showing her his treasures. She hated him for making himself so appealing. The man was dangerous. She did not think the work would be dangerous. She would only be dealing with figures.

Marco turned on his phone, sat on a sofa and crossed his legs. He was also tired but this could not wait until the next morning.

'Commissario Morelli? *Come sta?* Do you remember me? Marco dell'Orto. *Si*, it is a long time ago. But I need your help. Someone is stealing my fortune. *Domain? Grazie*, Commissario.'

When Emma awoke, a wintry sun was streaming in through a gap in the cream brocade curtains, and she did not know where she was. It was not a large room, but it was twice the size of her bedroom in Brixton. She had slept diagonally across a double bed, not used to so much leg space. The linen sheets were pristine white and uncreased. The padded quilt was cream, matching the curtains.

She saw a figure standing by her bed. For a second, she was

alarmed but then she realized it was the portly figure of Maria, the housekeeper. She was a kindly woman, in her fifties, greying hair in a bun, neatly belted black dress. She was carrying a silver tray.

'The signorina would like tea? The English always like the tea to start the morning. Signor Marco, of course, prefers coffee,' she said politely, but she was smiling.

Emma struggled to sit up, her M&S floral nightdress slipping off her shoulders. She knew she was dishevelled but it was early and she had fallen into bed the night before, not caring about anything.

'How lovely,' she said. 'A cup of tea. Just what I need. Thank you, Maria.'

'The signor asks that you join him for breakfast on the balcony at eight o'clock,' said Maria.

'Breakfast at eight, on the balcony.' Emma nodded. 'I'll be there.'

'Is there anything you prefer to eat? The fried eggs and bacons of the full English breakfast?' Maria asked. Her English was good, only slightly broken.

'No, thank you. I'd like to have an Italian breakfast. I'll eat as you do while I am here.'

Maria beamed. '*Grazie,*' she said. 'That is good, signorina. My cooking is ver' good. I hope you will be 'appy here.'

Did all Italians have trouble with the word *happy*?

'Thank you,' said Emma, smiling. 'I'm sure I shall be very 'appy.'

three

Commissario Claudio Morelli was already up and walking the short distance from his small flat to the Questura. He had work to do before he went to meet Marco dell'Orto. He knew his old friend was one of the wealthiest men in Venice. They had little in common now. Marco probably spent in a day what Claudio earned in a month.

But he recognized the annoyance in Marco's voice. It was serious. He knew Marco was a good employer. If someone was cheating him, then it would cause pain.

He bought a bag of figs on the Rialto Bridge. This was breakfast. He would turn on his computer in his office and scan the internet, learning what he could about the business matters of his friend. But first he needed a black coffee. He was out of coffee at his flat and to start the day without a coffee was unthinkable.

Emma was seduced by the impressive en suite bathroom. She could have stayed in it all morning, sampling the bottles and jars of sweet-smelling toiletries. Thick cream towels of several sizes were piled on a padded basket chair. The walls were cream tiles edged with a gold Roman pattern. Even the taps and shower fitments were gold. Not real gold, she felt sure. Gold coloured. But still classy enough.

She sank down into the deep water, letting the fragrant scent relax away her tense feelings. She would be seeing Marco again soon. She would be sharing breakfast with him. It was all intimate, too close, as if they had spent the night together.

Her desire for him swept over her in a great wave of emotion. It was unbelievable. Rivulets of heat tore through her veins. She had never felt like this for any man. She would not be able to bear to look at him, knowing that her skin longed for his touch, her lips longed for his mouth. She had never felt so wanton, so out of control. It had been such a long time.

She stood up quickly, turned on the shower, and let the tepid water cool her thoughts. A cold spurt made her jump. That's what worked in boarding schools, wasn't it? She could see herself having a lot of cold showers.

Her hair dried quickly into feathery wisps and she ran her fingers through it, shaping the strands into her usual disarray. The only money she ever spent on her hair was for a good cut. She always went to Vidal Sassoon's salon and was never disappointed by their expert work.

She looked out of the window onto the Grand Canal below. It was misty, adding mystery to the elegant and decorative palaces that edged both sides of the canal. The canal was already busy with vaporetti and high-prowed gondolas churning the water. Even though it was December, it didn't look cold outside. Boots and scarves were being worn, yes, but they were more of a fashion statement, not a necessity.

Emma went downstairs and peered into several rooms, each high-ceilinged with extravagant carvings and cornices. But the rooms were not museum pieces. They had modern furniture. One was obviously a study with a partner's desk, several computers, a printer, fax machine, and wall-to-wall books. The dining room had a long rosewood table, high-back carved chairs and seating for twelve. Perfect for a buffet party, Emma thought, suddenly wishing she could throw a party in such opulent surroundings.

She saw that the balcony led from the dining room. The weak winter sun was shining through the glassed-in roof. Marco was standing with his back to her, watching the river traffic, shutting out everything. He was wearing dark slacks and a dark cashmere polo-necked jersey, his thick hair still wet from his morning shower.

He turned. For a moment he basked in the wonder of her, the untamed hair, the gorgeous eyes, the enticing feminine figure. She was wearing a plain navy jacket and skirt and another crisp white shirt. So businesslike and so English. But it did not prevent him obliterating that demure material and seeing the shape beneath.

'Emma. *Buongiorno*, signorina. You have slept well?'

She had momentarily forgotten the power of that deep voice, the grave tones, the delightful accent. It burned like a brand, again almost rendering her speechless. She was acting like a teenager.

She nodded. 'I slept very well, thank you, Signor dell'Orto. The room is most comfortable. Everything is perfect.'

Not quite perfect, she wanted to say, because this man was not for her. He must belong to someone else. Her heart steeled itself to this thought.

'Please call me Marco. As we are to be thrown together for four weeks, we should address each other as friends. But if you are actually thrown, I shall certainly catch you.'

Emma was not sure if this was a joke. She smiled, in case it was.

'This is breakfast, Venetian style, prima colazione,' said Marco, drawing out a padded cane chair for her. 'Cappuccino and plain, cream or jam-filled croissants. But if you are even more hungry, there are rolls, ham and cheese. And, of course, always fruit in my house.'

She could not believe she was sitting in this sun-filled balcony, having breakfast with this perfect man. Perhaps he was not so perfect in every way. Perhaps she would find out when she started work in his office. Her composure slipped another notch when she caught sight of his teeth as he bit into a croissant. They were white and even, but his right eye tooth was so slightly crooked. They were as nature made them, not the work of an expensive dentist.

'So today we are going to your vineyards?' she said, as she finished her second croissant, dabbing her mouth with a linen napkin.

'No, my vineyards are many miles away,' he said. 'But I will take you there one day soon. My offices are at the back of Venice, before the factories and smokestacks of Marghera start, past the Central Venice district.'

'Factories?'

'It is a big problem here. The pollutants, phenols, cyanides, detergents. But the worst is sulphur dioxide, which when mixed with the damp and salt air of the lagoon, eats away at the stone-work. You will see the damage to my own palazzo. The stone face is crumbling. Even I can do nothing.'

Emma could feel the love Marco had for his city. It was in his voice. For once he was not looking at her. She felt an urge to convey her understanding. But she dared not touch him. There were only trite words to say.

'How awful,' she said, bleakly. 'What a problem.'

It was early morning but already Venice was crowded with a stream of tourists. Every campo, bridge and walkway were thronged with people. Some hurrying, some with their noses glued to guidebooks, determined not to miss a single wonder.

'Are we walking?'

'Not today, my launch will take us to the end of the Grand Canal to the main station where a car is waiting for us.'

Now that Emma saw the Grand Canal in daylight, she could not contain her delight. It was Marco's pleasure to watch the joy on her face as each exquisite and lavishly ornate palazzo came into view along the winding waterway. She clapped her hands, like a child, as they went under the Ponte di Rialto.

'It's like in a film!' she said. 'I love it. I love it.'

'We will walk Venice,' he said. 'I promise. I will show you every corner of Venice someday, maybe the four hundred bridges. When we have some time.'

Emma remembered why she was here. It was not a holiday or a romantic liaison. She was here to work. She was here to find out why Marco dell'Orto was in such trouble. To find out why millions of euros had disappeared from his accounts. She was determined to help him. It was the least she could do.

At the far end of the canal, the quayside began to change, became more commercial, crates of vegetables and fruit waiting to be delivered to the hotels, bars and restaurants. Baskets of freshly caught fish from the sea, frozen carcases of meat, piles of loaves from the nearby bakeries. Emma wrinkled her nose.

'Food does not happen by magic,' said Marco. 'Restaurants need supplies for the hungry tourists. This is a way of life.'

The Venezia Santa Lucia station was a huge building and dominated the area. Trains ran to all the cities on the mainland. Marco's car was waiting for them, parked discreetly away from the commerce.

'You are looking prim-and-proper English in your plain navy

suit. So drab. And you look cold. It is enough to depress me,' he said. 'Wait here.'

He disappeared into a small boutique, one of a row hugging a waterless side street. He came out with a tissue-wrapped parcel. But as he neared her, he tore off the paper and shook out a scarf. It was gold and red silk. He draped it round her neck, his fingers now brushing her skin with unbelievable tenderness.

'Now you are wearing the colours of Venice,' he said. The closeness was almost his undoing. He was grappling with a very real desire to cup that beautiful body close to him. He wanted to hold her in his arms for a few brief seconds.

Emma read the conflict in his handsome face and drew back. He was watching her. No way. She was no trophy.

'Thank you,' she said. 'A lovely souvenir of my visit to Venice.'

'Where is your raincoat? You must wear a coat. It is winter here.'

Emma shook her head. 'I don't know where it is. I remember having it when we landed and were walking through the airport. But I didn't have it when we reached your home. Somewhere along the way I lost it.'

'It was stolen,' said Marco grimly. 'The airport has many light-fingered boys and girls. Someone lifted it when you were not looking.'

'Never mind,' she said. 'I'll manage without a coat.'

'I will get you a coat.'

'Another souvenir of my visit?'

She emphasized the word *visit*. She would be gone in four weeks, back to soggy London and her Brixton flat. Marco got into the front of the car, beside the driver. The driver's name was Enrico. She sat at the back, fingering the scarf.

The morning went by in a confused jumble of impressions. The dell'Orto accounts office was in chaos. It was housed in a modern brick building with no character. They had taken delivery of a new computer system earlier that year to make life easier for Signor Bragora, who was still a ledger-and-paper man. But the terminals kept failing. They had called in a series of so-called computer experts to sort them out. His two assistants, both pleasant young men, Rocco and Luka, were willing to learn but were as yet not ready for a complex system. Two female secretaries, Tina and

Rosina, had electric typewriters and were learning to do emails on the computers. The whole accounts office was out of date for such a profitable organisation. It was unbelievable.

Emma tried to put them at their ease. She was not there to accuse anyone of malpractice. They understood some English and seemed reassured. They brought her relays of aromatic coffee in mugs.

Fortunately the Italian words for the various aspects of computers were the same as the English. So no language problem when discussing their system.

Emma had her laptop. She unzipped the case and took it out. Luckily it ran on a battery and did not need recharging yet. She wondered if the electric sockets in the office worked.

Signor Bragora was a charming man in his sixties with masses of white hair. He wore thick glasses and it was obvious that his eyesight was failing. He seemed to have peripheral vision and could get about, but anything close up was a blur. He used a torch with a strong beam and a magnifying glass to read.

He spoke little English. It was impossible for Marco to keep translating every exchange. Emma could see he was getting impatient, his mouth changing into a stern line, his dark eyes growing darker.

'I think it would be best if you left me here on my own,' said Emma. 'First I'll go through all the paper transactions and see if they tally with the ledger entries. Figures are figures. I don't need an interpreter for that.'

'Thank goodness, at last, some sense. I have to go to the plant. It has a mechanical problem.'

Marco strode out of the building, obviously relieved to get away. He did not even look at her. She did not know how far he was going. Perhaps he had a luncheon appointment. Perhaps he was keeping a beautiful woman waiting.

Later, one of the assistants went out and came back with a box of snacks.

'Pranza,' Luka said. This was obviously lunch. Emma was happy to have a snack lunch of cheese and ham paninis and fruit. She declined the strange-looking fish pieces, though Venice was famed for its fish.

By four o'clock, she was almost cross-eyed with pouring over columns of small figures, even with her glasses on. How long was Marco going to leave her here? But even as thoughts of rebellion and escape entered her mind, Marco returned, a jacket slung over his shoulder.

'Finish for today,' he said, brooking no argument. 'Time for a Bucintoro,' he said. 'Or a Bellini, if you prefer it, but Bucintoro is definitely superior if lesser known. It is made with my own Prosecco so it must be far better.'

Emma closed down her laptop, not looking at him. She tidied everything into neat order, ready for the next day's work.

'Please do not touch,' she said to the staff.

'No touch,' they agreed. The men liked having such a pretty woman around. A woman who smiled a lot and took off her jacket so that they could glance at her breasts. Signor Bragora had already gone home. Half a day was enough for him.

Marco held out her jacket. She was still wearing the gold and red scarf, draped on her shoulders. 'So?' he asked.

'Do you expect me to have solved all your financial problems in one day?' she said, stepping back.

'No, but I expect progress.'

'You are getting progress,' she replied. 'There are discrepancies that I can't explain.'

'Then we will go to the Café Florian in Piazza San Marco to celebrate this progress.'

'I have heard of the Café Florian. And I saw it in a film.'

'Is all your education from films?' he mocked.

'No, not all of it.'

He raised an eyebrow. 'So which of it is not from a film?'

Emma was now out of her depth. Marco was making fun of her which was not fair. But she covered by saying goodbye to the staff in her newly acquired Italian. They were all packing up to go home.

'Buona sera,' she said.

'Buona sera,' they replied, grinning.

The reverse journey was by car then vaporetto. Emma loved all the new sights, shrugging off the chill wind. She wished she had brought a coat. Venice was a bustling city, so many people in such a small space. No cars and no buses and she loved the lack of traffic noise. The vaporetti were noisy, but it was a water noise and seemed acceptable. It was like coming home when they reached the palazzo.

Later, Marco was waiting in the hall. Emma had changed into jeans and put a thick sweater over her shirt. He had a long black cardigan over his arm.

'For you,' he said. 'You must keep more warm.'

'Thank you,' she said. She wondered if it was his but it did not seem masculine. It seemed feminine with gold buttons. But Italian men wore quite stylish clothes.

They walked to the Café Florian in Piazza San Marco. The crowds were horrendous, even in winter. San Marco was the number one tourist spot with so many cafés and shops, and the magnificent Doge's Palace and the famous Campanile nearby.

The Doge's Palace was a symphony in pink and white Verona marble, perched on lace-like Istrian stone arcades. The Campanile towered above everywhere, its famous five bells ready to toll the end of the day.

'Would you like to sit inside?' Marco asked. 'There is an orchestra playing inside. I believe it is too cold for outside in the evening.'

There was an immense forest of small tables in the piazza. Yet everyone was occupied, people drinking and talking, waiters hurrying with trays of drinks and small snacks.

But it was evening and Emma felt a chill from the sea. 'Inside, please,' she said. 'It's a cold wind even with this cardigan.'

'Of course, we have a lot of visitors now, even though it is winter. St Nicholas Day is on 6 December. You will be here for the celebrations? All the children have gifts, whether they have been good or bad.'

'A carnival?'

'Oh yes, no work. Everything closed.'

'But I shall still work,' said Emma firmly. 'I have my laptop.'

'Sometimes we have no electricity. There are many cuts. Does your laptop work on a candle? Always keep it charged.'

A waiter recognized Marco and ushered them to a table inside. It was not easy, following Marco's tall figure through the café, wanting to clutch his sleeve, ask him to slow down, wait for her. She hid the lurking hunger deep in her eyes.

'Now I will explain,' he said as they sat at a small, white-clothed table. There was a fresh carnation in a vase. 'Bellini is the most famous cocktail. It is made of champagne, maybe French, often Prosecco, and peach juice.'

'Sounds delicious,' Emma murmured. It might warm her up.

'But Bucintoro is a mixture of Prosecco and strawberry juice. It is remarkable. It is a cocktail that you will never forget. It is my champagne, Italian grapes from Italian soil. You will always remember your first taste. Believe me.'

As if she would ever forget anything of this first time in Venice. It was like an unreal world. A million miles from the greyness of Brixton.

She nodded, wishing everything was different. Wishing she was here in this magical café with a lover of her own. Not this powerful but gorgeous millionaire, who only wanted her to solve his money problems so that he could return to his customary life-style, buy a few more villas.

'Bucintoro, *grazie*,' she said, trying to pronounce it correctly.

'*Sì.*' He waved the waiter over for their order.

It was the most delicious drink. As Marco said, his champagne was crisp and slightly bitter, taking away the over-sweetness of the strawberries. Emma wondered if she could order it for breakfast. The taste flowed over her in waves of purity.

She didn't know the word for wonderful, but it was there in her clear hazel eyes and her voice. She was no good at hiding her feelings. Marco was delighted by her reaction, his eyes darkening as they locked with hers. He wondered when he could cross this strictly-business-only bridge and find the real Emma.

'So, Emma Chandler, when are you going to take off this so orderly prim face and tell me about yourself? It is warm in here, is it not?'

It was warm inside the crowded café. The orchestra was playing Gershwin tunes which Emma recognized but could not name. She slipped off the cardigan and jersey and hung them over the back of the chair. She knew her white shirt fitted, but it was not that reveal-ing and now she had the Venetian scarf. It fell round her shoulders in a cascade of colour.

'What do you want to know?' she asked.

'Where did this girl learn about complicated figures?'

Emma laughed. It was a sound he loved. 'I always liked maths at school. I could do it. Figures made sense. I always got top marks in every exam, but I couldn't go on to university. There were too many problems, money especially. My foster mother worked and there was never much money to spare.'

'But your father?'

'He'd walked out many years before. A sailor, I think.'

'Then it was not easy for you and your foster mother?'

'No. But I went to evening classes, got some useful accreditation and was accepted into Irving Stone Accountants' training scheme. It was a stroke of luck.'

Emma remembered the joy of that day. And she was so glad her foster mother had been alive to share that joy. They had shared a special meal together to celebrate.

Marco could see the look on her face. It was a mixture of pride and sadness.

She was sipping her Bucintoro. It was a spirit-reviving drink. But the gold flecks in her hazel eyes seemed to have dimmed.

'So now you are going to tell me sad things?'

'Yes, she died four years ago of cancer. So she never knew when I become a junior accountant at Irving Stone. She never knew when I moved out of our council house and could afford to buy my own flat in Brixton, with a mortgage, of course. It would have been perfect if she could have stopped going to work, taken it easy, enjoyed some life. But it didn't happen.'

Emma seemed broken with remorse. They didn't know who reached out for whom. Marco knew he could comfort her, but when and how? They were both so guarded. He reached across and clasped her hand.

'Sweet Emma. Grieve no more. Venetians know that the spirit lasts. Look around you. Your mother knows all of this. She is everywhere, here with you now, enjoying your joy. Not a whisper away. Do not despair.'

His words, in that gravelly voice, dug into her driving hunger. He was saying words that she wanted to hear. Emma closed her eyes, breathing in the sound of his voice. Not a whisper away.

'I do hope so,' she said. 'Oh, I do hope so.'

Back at the Palazzo dell'Orto, they found that Maria had taken the evening off. It was like that. No one had remembered it was her evening off. Marco did not seem worried. There were so many alternatives.

'We will eat out,' he out. 'A good Venetian restaurant, not touristy, not terrible menu with bad tourist prices. Somewhere ver' special.'

'That's fine. Anywhere,' said Emma, not caring.

'Put a dress on,' he said.

It was a command, not a suggestion. Emma was curiously unmoved. Her courage had returned. 'I don't have a dress. I only brought office clothes and a pair of jeans.'

'I am not taking out a pair of jeans,' said Marco, flatly.

'That's all I have,' said Emma. She respected his power, his strength, his masculinity but he wasn't going to dictate what she wore. 'I didn't bring any dresses.'

They were climbing the central marble staircase of the palazzo. At the top, Marco took a key from his pocket. It was quite a large key, not modern, from some time ago.

'There is a room on the next floor,' he said. 'This fits. You will find many dresses, unworn, still with price labels from the shops. Find something foxier to wear. Take anything you like. I will see you downstairs at seven o'clock. I will book a table.'

He turned abruptly on his heel, down some corridor. Emma was left holding the key. She turned it over in her hand. It felt unused.

She climbed up to the second floor. It was one of the locked bedrooms on the same floor as her own. But this room was at the back, maybe no view, somewhere lost and forgotten.

She hesitated at the door. It seemed like a forbidden place.

She turned the key and the door creaked open. It smelt musty and full of stale perfume. The curtains were drawn so she had to switch on the lights. The room was flooded with light and Emma gasped.

It was a big corner room with rose draped curtains over windows on two walls. A canopied bed against one wall, velvet curtains drawn back, a crimson satin quilt on the bed, huge cushions tumbled in rows. There was a dressing table opposite, the glass top crowded with cosmetics and bottles and jars. The crystal bottles were dusty, powder spilt, perfume dried to a sediment.

Two large wardrobes flanked the last wall, doors closed. A pair of fluffy slippers lay askew on the floor. Silk stockings hung over a chair. No one had been in the room for years. It was indeed lost and forgotten.

Then she saw the paintings and the photographs. They were everywhere. A beautiful young woman, dark and laughing, her long curly hair shining and lustrous, her skin glowing. She was vital and sexy. This woman as seen at parties, at the races, swimming. A woman who would have attracted every man in sight.

Then Emma noticed a man in the background of many of the photographs. It was Marco, a younger fresh-faced Marco, looking at the dark woman with adoration and devotion. There was no doubt. This woman must have been his wife. And that explained so much.

And Marco wanted her to wear one of his wife's dresses. It was weird. Emma did not know what to do. The room had been locked up for years. Maria had not been in here with her polish and duster. Emma opened the wardrobe doors and the scent of old perfume wafted into the room.

The rails were crowded with clothes, day, cocktail, evening dresses. There were dozens of them. It was like a shop. Emma could see that most still had their price tags attached. The price tags meant nothing to her but the labels did. They were famous designers she had heard of, but had never in her life been able to afford.

She had never seen so many couture clothes. She touched them tentatively, tempted beyond words to do as Marco said and wear one of them. They were unworn. It was not as if she would be wearing one of his wife's cast-offs. This woman had bought them, paid for them with Marco's money, his credit card. Maria had hung them in the wardrobes. But the woman had not worn them.

Emma took out several of the hangers, letting the dresses drape against her. Many looked too big, too voluptuous. But there was one which would fit because it was cut straight, a plain black silk with a fringed hem. The sleeves were long and straight, the neck a plain cowl. It was a beautiful dress, so simple and elegant. And with the cardigan, she would be warm enough.

Emma took the dress into her bedroom, locking the other door behind her. She wanted to look glamorous and desirable for Marco, but what would he think of her, wearing one of his wife's dresses?

In his study, Marco was on the phone.

'I could not come to our appointment,' said Claudio Morelli. 'I am sorry, my friend. We fished a poor girl out of the canal. I had to be there. She came first.'

'I am sad about the girl,' said Marco. 'A love affair perhaps that had gone wrong?'

'A love affair that hit her on the head and fractured her skull?'

'That is bad,' said Marco. 'Do you know who she is?'

'No, no identification on her. But she was wearing a fawn raincoat, a Jaeger raincoat. This is from a London shop, *si*? And in the pocket were several London bus tickets and a receipt for a tuna and watercress sandwich, dated yesterday.'

'I don't understand,' said Marco. 'Why are you telling me this?'

'Because we believe this raincoat belongs to your visitor. The girl was killed because they thought she was your English accountant.'

four

Marco was waiting at the bottom of the stone stairs. He was all in black, like some devastating James-Bond-type hero. Black silk shirt and tie, black trousers, fine wool black jacket, his thick hair unruly.

'Snip,' he said. 'As you say in your country.'

'Snap,' said Emma.

'You look very beautiful,' he went on, taking in the black fringed dress and the high-heeled black shoes. Emma had found the shoes in the back of the wardrobe, still wrapped in tissue paper. They were a little large for her but she had tightened the T-straps to the last hole so that they would not slip.

Marco approved of the cardigan Emma had on her shoulders. He would have to buy her a wool coat tomorrow. It was cold in the evenings in Venice when the sun had gone down.

'Are you hungry?'

'Not very,' said Emma. 'Your staff kept feeding me delicious snacks. And we had cakes this afternoon.'

'But I am hungry so we will eat. Perhaps your appetite will return.'

Emma had forgotten there was no street outside. It was quite a shock to stand on the steps outside the panelled front door, water washing over the lower ones, leaving a film of green algae. A long, black, flat-bottomed boat drifted to the steps, poled by a man in flamboyant black and gold clothes. It was a gondola waiting with its owner, a gondolier. He came forward, helped Emma into his gondola. There were fewer customers in the winter. It rocked enough to unnerve her.

'He's not going to sing, is he?' she asked.

'No singing,' said Marco, hiding his amusement as he sat

beside her on the red upholstered and cushioned seat. 'Unless he is asked to.'

She had seen pictures of gondolas but the ornate splendour surprised Emma. So much carving and gilding everywhere. The mysterious, multi-pronged *ferro* in the front of the boat, its six prongs facing forwards, was slightly disturbing. She did not want to ask Marco what it symbolized.

The waterway was even more magical by night, lights gleaming on the water, the sound of laughter and music coming from both quaysides. Even the great white churches were floodlit at night. Vaporetti swished by, laden with workers wanting to get home or diners wanting to eat, always in a hurry. Private launches sped by in all directions, their wash sweeping a line, out to the other islands or along to the hotels on the coast.

The gondola was leisurely, taking its time, negotiating the shallow mudflats, the sharply-angled canals and under bridges. This was a far cry from picking up a microwave supper from M&S on her way home from the office. Emma began to relax, even though Marco was uncomfortably close, his thigh brushing hers. Close to, the water of the canal did not smell so good, but Emma realized that Venetians had to get used to it. Collecting garbage from the hotels, shops and bars was a rising problem.

'My vineyards smell a lot better,' said Marco, reading her thoughts. 'Soon I shall take you there. You will see and smell my good grapes.'

A warm feeling swept over Emma. He was showing that he was interested in her as a woman. But then she thought of the room full of unworn clothes. Did they belong to his wife? Marco was not going to tell her. He had said nothing about the black dress. Perhaps he did not recognize or know it existed.

The soft material felt good on her skin, though Emma knew she was going to be cold. How could she have forgotten it was winter in Venice? If only she had her raincoat.

Another thought hit her. Perhaps it was not his wife's room. Perhaps this was where he took his mistress, or mistresses. Maybe they were all invited to choose an unworn dress, still with its price tag dangling.

But the photographs in the room had been of this one glamorous woman. The dark-haired beauty with luminous eyes. And the cosmetics had been standing on the dressing table for some time, gathering dust and congealing.

Emma wanted to ask him. She wanted to know. She wanted to know who was this mysterious woman, whose presence still occupied a room in his palazzo. Her heart came up into her throat as she realized how desperately she wanted to know.

'I shall take you to Harry's Bar, upstairs, now that you are dressed up. It is a legendary place for visitors. All the celebrities go there. We may see some famous faces. It was once an old storeroom.'

'You are taking me to eat in an old storeroom?'

'It's where Americans love to go and talk. You will feel at home. I thought you would prefer it to one of the big glitzy hotels in Venice.'

It was a thoughtful, if misplaced gesture. Emma did not want to eat American or listen to transatlantic accents. She wanted to eat Italian and absorb herself in everything Venetian. It was casting a spell over her. Marco was casting a spell over her. She had never felt this way about any man before.

They were heading south and as the waterway widened, so the wind freshened and Marco put his arm round her, to shield her lightly covered shoulders. For a few moments, they were fused physically if not spiritually. Her heart began to race, but then there was a cool withdrawal as they reached the quayside.

'Be careful,' said Marco. 'I am not dressed for fishing you out of the water.'

'I can swim,' said Emma.

'In this water? Even the fish think more than twice.'

Harry's Bar was on St Mark's waterfront. Marco guided her through the glass-paned doors. Inside, Emma immediately realized why Harry's Bar was so famous and so friendly. It was the ambience.

The downstairs area of Harry's Bar was thronged with early-evening customers, drinking and eating snacks and sandwiches. Upstairs was the restaurant for serious diners. They sat at a comfortable banquette with butterscotch wood trim, the table linen a subtle pale yellow. There was only one knife and fork at each place setting. The menu was elaborate and expensive.

'I really don't want much,' said Emma, shocked by the prices, for which by now she could calculate the exchange into pounds. No pence needed.

'Shall I order for you?' said Marco, not waiting for an answer. 'Cavatappi with cinque wild mushrooms and salad with a bottle of sexy Prosecco, the finest sparkling champagne in Italy. And I will have scampi all'Armoricaine. That's a tomato, herb and wine sauce. Ver' good. I usually have the same thing. I am regular here. Not everyone is tourist. Some of us dine every week, even every day.'

The cardigan had slid away from her shoulders and Emma lost track of where it went. She was entirely engrossed in the atmosphere of Harry's Bar, colour coming into her cheeks as she sipped the champagne. No famous faces tonight, but she could imagine Humphrey Bogart and Kirk Douglas sitting at a table.

'Ernest Hemingway, Maria Callas, Orson Welles and your Nicole Kidman, from today's films that you go to see much often,' said Marco, again reading her mind. 'The list is as long as the menu.'

'Thank you for bringing me here,' said Emma, in a rush, as the champagne trickled down her throat. 'It makes a change from an M&S microwaved meal.'

'What is this m-and-s microwaved meal?' said Marco, bemused. 'Is this a new dish? I have not heard of it. Explain how it is made.'

Emma laughed delightedly. And again, Marco was struck by the radiance which came into her eyes when she laughed. The wistful look and the sadness fled. One day, perhaps, Emma would tell him who had hurt her.

But she was here to work, he reminded himself. Her private life and her feelings were nothing to do with him. Yet he could not stop himself from imagining what it would be like to run his fingers slowly down her arms to her fingertips, even down her spine to the soft roundness of her hips.

He shook off his thoughts. He could not waste moments in daydreams. This was not a time for daydreaming. Emma was here to work. To find out where two years' income from his vineyards had gone.

'So what have you discovered today, clever-headed English accountant?' he asked as his scampi arrived, hot and succulent.

The plate of pasta was not too big or overwhelming, the perfect size for the dish, plain white china with a discreetly decorated edge.

'I have gone back many months, checking everything. Nothing seems amiss. Your staff are entirely trustworthy. They have done nothing suspicious. Every transaction, in and out, is properly accounted for,' said Emma, suddenly finding she was hungry after all. The freshly made pasta was delicious, so different from a microwaved supper.

'So it is me?' Marco said drily, his eyes hardening. 'Am I the one to blame? What have I done, to ferret away all these many millions of euros? Is it to some offshore account so that I don't pay the tax?'

'I don't know,' said Emma honestly. 'But I don't think you are to blame in any way. Nor Signor Bragora. He can barely see anything. Your staff tell me that you rarely come into accounts, you are always at the plant or the vineyard.'

'That is true.'

'Unless you sneak in at midnight,' Emma said.

'I have better things to do at midnight,' said Marco.

It was a true arrogance without a care how he looked, saying it. And at this moment, Marco was every inch a tall, striking Italian, who could have any woman he wanted. He was as sensuous as a panther. Emma felt an undercurrent of excitement and then despair crept into her bones.

Marco would never feel that way about her. She was even wearing another woman's dress. He would never know the real Emma.

'I'm sorry,' she said. 'I didn't mean ...'

'I know,' he said. 'Your eyes always speak the truth. That is what I like about you, Emma. I have only to look into your eyes and I can read them.'

It was not that reassuring. Emma did not want him to read her thoughts. They were wanton and stomach-clenching. She was drowning in her need to be closer to him. Perhaps a little more Prosecco would dampen the flood of warmth that was tingling her limbs.

They both said no to a dessert, however mouth-watering the selection. But Marco ordered Bellinis.

'This is the home of the Bellini. They were invented by Guiseppe Cipriani, the hotel barman who opened Harry's Bar in 1931,' he said. 'So you must have your first one here. Peach juice and champagne. It will warm your heart.'

Her heart did not need warming. 'Long before I was born,' said Emma.

'And also before I was born.'

It was only fruit juice, Emma told herself. Her five a day. And pasta was filling. It was not as if she was drinking on an empty stomach.

The restaurant was very warm, despite the chill outside.

'Tell me how you travel to work in London?' Marco asked unexpectedly. 'You take taxis, *si*?'

'No, I go to work on the bus. The Underground station is quite far from my flat.'

'And yesterday, before my car picked you up, did you have a lunch?'

Emma looked at him in amazement. 'Is my lunch important? Why do you want to know?'

'Was it a tuna and watercress sandwich?'

Was Marco clairvoyant? 'Yes, it was. But how do you know?'

'Because your raincoat was found in the canal and the receipt was in the pocket, also bus tickets.'

He did not say that a girl had been wearing the raincoat and that she had drowned. That the girl had been hit on the head. He did not want to frighten Emma. Perhaps tomorrow she would identify the raincoat as hers.

'My raincoat? But why?'

'So soon there will be the feast of St Nicholas,' said Marco, changing the subject. 'And we will party and go to festivals. You will like it. Small English accountants lead very dull lives in Brixton, I think.'

'No,' said Emma firmly, but not as firmly as she hoped. 'I don't lead a dull life. I go to films, the theatre, exhibitions, that sort of thing. My life is extremely busy.'

'Exhibitions?' Marco snorted. 'These are fun, these exhibitions?

You meet many handsome men and they take you out to dinner, make love to you?'

Emma's heart plunged, unable to unscramble her brains. The rose and purple of the evening seemed to overwhelm her. It was more than the absence of sound because the restaurant was as noisy as ever.

'No,' she said. 'They do not make love to me. I don't allow it. We have a different approach to life in Britain. It's more reserved, slower.'

'I could be very slow,' said Marco, finishing his drink. He stood up. The evening was over. Emma had forgotten the black cardigan, it was the last thing on her mind. It had slipped behind the seat.

But outside, the night chill caught the flimsy silk of her dress, whipped it against her body. Emma shivered despite the drink and the warmth of the meal. Marco took off his wool jacket and draped it round her. Again, it held the heat and scent of his body. They began to walk.

'But we came in a gondola,' said Emma.

'It was a new experience for you. We could have walked. It is not far.'

The walk was along narrow pathways, up and over bridges, along the quayside. Marco held her hand. He said it was in case she fell in a canal. Emma didn't care. All she cared about was the warm clasp of his fingers and the way his thumb rubbed over the soft skin of her wrist.

It seemed that they walked for miles but it was all twists and turns and over bridges.

She did not know when they reached the Palazzo dell'Orto. It was the back door to the world. It was plain and ordinary at the back, although the face of the palace rose three storeys high to the crenulated roof. They were going in by the tradesman's entrance, where Maria received her deliveries of groceries and food. It seemed strange to go into a modern kitchen with counters and tables and ovens. Emma went straight to the tap and poured herself a glass of water.

'Ah,' said Marco, disappointed. 'I wanted to taste the Bellini on your lips.'

Emma let out a long, despairing sigh. Marco had a depth and

power that frightened her. She knew he might blot out years of anguish but this was not the time, nor the place. She was here to work. Her job came first.

He came close, pushing her against the counter. He did not want it like this. He wanted to steer her towards the soft white sofa upstairs, to put on some music, to feed her grapes. But the desire was so strong that he could not stop himself.

Marco wrapped his arms round her, his mouth coming down on hers in a deepening kiss. He was crushing her with a passion that made her cry out with a harsh sobbing cry. Their thoughts were running swiftly out of control. Emma could feel his hardness against her thigh, through the thin silk of her dress.

This was not what she wanted, although her body longed for him. His hands were learning the contours and shape of her back. She could feel the fierce warmth in his fingers. She was tasting his mouth, the texture of his tongue, the smoothness of his skin.

He went for the zip at the back of the dress and Emma stiffened.

'No,' she said. 'Not that, please.'

'Let me take you upstairs,' he said softly. 'Let me unzip your dress very slowly so that you will not be afraid. Whoever hurt you before will be forgotten. This will be so different.'

Emma could barely control her terrible, aching need. His cheek was close to hers and she could feel his breath fanning her face, her hair. She wanted to cling to him with fierce abandon, to let him heal the past. To let him give her body what it needed, what it wanted. To feel him against her, if not with love, at least with genuine care and desire.

But she couldn't. The past was too strong. She pushed Marco away.

'I can't. I won't,' she cried.

'Please, *cara*,' he urged. 'It will be good. I will make it good for you.'

'It's the wrong time,' she said abruptly.

Marco stopped. 'You mean, the wrong time ... of the month.'

It was not what she meant, but she let him think it. It was a way out that had not occurred to her before. She stood back, her breath ragged, her breasts heaving.

'I'm sorry,' she faltered.

'But I don't mind,' he said. 'Italians are different to the cold English.'

'But I do mind,' she said.

Marco took her hand and kissed the tips of her fingers. 'Then I will let you go to your bed and to sleep sweet dreams. It has been a wonderful evening, showing you my Venice. We will not spoil it. *Buona notte*, Emma.'

'Goodnight, Marco.'

Tomorrow he would tell her where the raincoat was found.

five

Emma wondered why she had said anything so stupid. It was not her so-called time of the month, but there was no way she was going to tell this stranger the truth.

Did Marco think an expensive dinner at Harry's Bar entitled him to taking the dessert course in bed? And it had been expensive. Emma had roughly totalled up the bill in her head. She could do mental arithmetic.

Suddenly she heard Marco's voice booming up the stairs. 'Would you like a hot water bottle?' Then he paused. 'I know sometimes it helps.'

Emma could not believe what she was hearing. He was offering her a hot water bottle, like a kindly aunt, fussing over her. How did he know, anyway? Had it been the wife or the mistress, demanding this attention on occasion?

Perhaps the girls who worked in his vineyard were allowed the odd hour off or did they soldier on? Maybe there was even a first-aid/nurse-type person on his staff. Emma realized how little she knew about him.

She leaned over the balustrade of the grand staircase and peered into the brightly lit hall. Marco was standing at the foot of the stairs, as he had before, not so many hours ago, jacket slung over his shoulder. He did not look dismayed at her refusal. He looked interested, almost as if pleased to discover that she was a fertile female.

The colour flooded into her face. Why would Marco want to know if she was fertile? This was her overactive imagination again. She had never had that much of an imagination before. It must be the Italian air.

'No, thank you,' she said primly.

'I could rub your back,' he offered.

'No, thank you.'

'Goodnight, then, my young accountant, worn out with saying no, thank you.' She knew he was grinning. She could hear it in his voice.

Emma shut the door of her bedroom thankfully. She'd had enough of his charm and masculinity for one evening. She wanted what was left of the night to herself. To calm down and get her thoughts straight. She took off the black fringed dress and hung it in her almost empty wardrobe. She wondered if she would ever wear it again.

She took a quick shower to shake off the day's cobwebs and put on some warmer pyjamas. At least they were maroon silk, her one luxury these days. She loved the feel against her skin. She never wanted to feel a man against her skin, against her body. This soft material was her solace.

Although she was tired from the day's crowded activities, there was still time for one last look at the figures. There was a light tap on her door. For a moment, she thought it was Maria and got into bed.

But it was Marco, carrying a tray.

'Scusi,' he said. 'I bring you some warm milk and in a glass some good 12-year-old brandy. To mix them might be ver' medicinal.'

Her pyjama jacket had fallen open and she was suddenly aware that the rise and fall of her breasts was not conducive to work. Marco's glance went to the soft curve of her swelling bosom and the deep cleavage, shadowed and sweet smelling. He felt his senses quicken and his skin tighten. He wanted to sweep her into his arms and smother that enticing valley with kisses.

He put down the tray quickly in case he dropped it. If he was not careful he would spill the whole lot. He sensed that Emma was a shy, damaged creature.

'Thank you,' said Emma, pulling up the quilt, inch by inch. 'That was very thoughtful.'

'Do not cover yourself,' he said. 'You are beautiful. Such skin, such gorgeous curves are made for a man to admire. Will you not let me admire them?'

'No, I don't think so,' said Emma, wondering how she was going to get him out of her room. She had had too much to drink. All that champagne and a Bellini. Now he was offering a *good old brandy* which might be 100% proof. It would knock her out completely. 'It's very late.'

'It's never too late, *cara*,' he said. 'And I will prove it to you.'

He sat on the side of the bed and leaned towards her. He felt waves of desire as he took the sheets of figures from her hands and tossed them on the floor. They fell like confetti. Then his hands cupped her breasts, his thumbs brushing her nipples. It was the lightest of touches but it sent an electric shock through her body.

She threw back her head and Marco bent to kiss her throat. His mouth was soft and warm. Again, only the lightest of kisses but it felt as if her whole body was set on fire.

'Please …' she gasped.

'Please more or please stop?' he said.

She had to laugh. Emma did not know what she wanted. No one had ever made her feel like this before. No man had ever got this close. She had never allowed it. She had built a wall around herself and topped it with barbed wire.

'I don't know,' she faltered.

'Well, sadly I do,' he said, getting up with a sigh. 'This is not the time. You should drink some of this brandy and get some sleep. But *cara*, now you know that it could be so good. It could be ver' good. Some other time, perhaps.'

She did not know if it was a threat or a promise.

He left the room and closed the door swiftly. Emma was left staring into space. If only she could take those ecstatic moments into a dream with her. It would be a perfect dream. Not like the nightmare dream when she was locked into a letter-box.

Maria woke her with a tray of tea, as before, and pulled open the curtains. A stream of wintry sunshine reflected on the fallen papers. Maria bent to pick them up.

'Signor dell'Orto has already gone to work. He sent his excuses. You will be escorted to the office as yesterday. Breakfast is on the balcony when you are ready.'

'Thank you, that's very kind,' said Emma, glad that she would not be seeing Marco at breakfast. Had he felt the same rising desire last night? Or had he already forgotten her?

The routine was well organized. Breakfast in the spacious, glassed-in balcony. She took her coffee to the window to watch the busy water traffic below. Then the launch came for her and a car was waiting at the end of the Grand Canal. She liked the freedom of travelling by herself. She must ask Marco for a few hours off so that she could explore Venice on her own, with a guidebook and sunglasses perched on the top of her head looking very touristy.

She smiled to herself. She was beginning to feel like a tourist. Perhaps she would come back one day, by herself, and really explore Venice. Its magic was endless. Yet everyone said it was a decaying city, that its days were numbered, that it was sinking, millimetre by millimetre each year, into the sea.

The staff greeted her like an old friend. Coffee and snacks were brought immediately even though she had just had breakfast. They seemed to know that she was on their side and did not blame them for the financial crisis.

'There is a reason,' she told Signor Bragora, 'and I am determined to find it. Nothing is impossible if you dig deep enough.'

'Do not fall in the hole you dig,' he warned her, his dimmed eyes full of emotion.

She wondered what he meant. She coloured faintly, thinking of the night before, but the signor could not possibly know about that. The morning passed quickly with work and more work, till her eyes ached and her fingers were cramped.

Luka and Rocco made her stop for midday lunch. They insisted that she go with them to a small local café, not far away.

'It is not good to work so hard,' they said. 'Eat when pasta fresh.'

'I am here for a purpose. I've only a few weeks.'

'Signor dell'Orto cannot sack you,' they added. 'You are a special signorina from London.'

She needed to get out of the office. They were cramped rooms, too many desks and chairs and filing cabinets. Some fresh air would be welcome.

It was a typical local café: glass-topped tables and wooden chairs, paper napkins stacked in a wooden rack. Amazing smells came from behind the counter where great bowls of different pastas were served with the topping of your choice. The cheerful hot-faced cook beamed at Emma as if she was an old friend.

They wanted Emma to try some of the local fish sauces but she stayed with cheese and tomato. 'Small, small, please,' she pleaded, when she saw the size of the bowls. 'Piccolo?'

'Ah, piccolo,' said the cook, giving her a half-portion.

It was a happy lunch with tumblers of rough red wine that only cost eighty cents and much talk, most of which she did not understand. Emma wondered if she would be able to do an afternoon's work. She felt more like going to sleep. And she ought to learn some more Italian.

'What did you say about this computer expert who came in to fix the new computer system?' she asked.

'He was ver' expensive. Charge much money. Smart blue suit and Rolex wristwatch.' They shook their heads. 'Classy.'

'And did he fix the system?'

'No. It was still all wrong and so slow. We lost many things. It was bad time. Signor dell'Orto had many hot words with him. The man said we had to get in new terminals.'

Emma did not like the sound of *hot words*. It didn't help to antagonize people in business. But she was not here as a counsellor, she was here to sort out the accounts. She had to keep reminding herself, not having grounded herself from the previous night's emotion and tenderness.

'Back to work,' she said, rising, wondering if she could stand steadily after the rough wine. But she was fine. Her digestion was getting used to it.

Marco was waiting in the office, arms akimbo, face like thunder. 'This is your London working?' he stormed. 'An expensive long lunch hour? Drinking? Don't deny it. I can smell it on your breath.'

So these were his *hot words*? Emma flushed. It was not a fair accusation. She put her bag down with deliberate slowness, slipped off her grey jacket. Her grey suit was warmer than her black one.

'It was a normal lunch hour,' she said calmly. 'Cheap pasta and a glass of red at a local café. Nothing excessive. Perhaps you'd like to join us tomorrow? It's how the workers take a break.'

He was breathing heavily. Her heart was hammering like mad.

It was a confrontation in front of his staff, something he did not like. Emma felt sorry for him. She had never been so drawn to a man and her expression hid her longing. She felt bold, wanton and beautiful, yet she knew she was none of these things.

'Signor dell'Orto, let me show you what I have unearthed this morning,' she said, switching on her laptop and connecting it to their system. 'You will be interested, I'm sure.'

He stood behind her. It didn't help. She had to pretend that she felt nothing but she could not deny that slow, soft yearning for him. His dark looks were devastating and that deep voice. It was a sickness of love.

'This group of customer files, each with the name of a customer,' she began.

'I know these names. You don't need to show me.'

'But when I bring up a file, there is nothing in it. Look.'

'That is ridiculous. Of course there are many transactions. They are regular customers for my wine. A shipment every month. My wine goes all over Europe.'

'Your wine may travel over Europe, but the money isn't travelling back to Venice.'

Emma's mobile phone rang and she picked it up. 'Hello, Mr Stone? Yes, it's Emma. I sound different? I'm no different. I'm the same, working hard as usual.'

But she was different. She felt more alive than she had been in years. She seemed more acutely aware of everything. The smells, sights, colours, feelings, atmosphere of Venice. The world was sharply in focus, not blurred at the edges.

'Yes, there is some progress. I'm getting somewhere.' But Emma was not sure where. It was too early to say. Marco was listening to every word she said. 'I'll send you a progress report at the end of the week.'

'If you have time from lunch,' Marco growled.

'"Scusi, if I have time,' she repeated. She saw a flash of amusement in his dark eyes. It was if they connected, momentarily. It was like wine. A glass of his sparkling Prosecco with the bubbles bursting in the roof of her mouth.

Marco had restored communion between them. Emma turned back to her work, knowing that she needed to contact each of the customers with empty files. But her minimal Italian made this impossible.

'Print out a list of these customers,' he said. 'I will telephone them from Signor Bragora's office. *Pronto.*'

'*Pronto, per favore,*' Emma murmured.

He shot her a quick look but made no sign he had heard. Tea arrived soon, brought from a local café with a dish of sweetmeats. There was no such thing as an office kettle in sight.

Emma accepted the tea but shook her head at the cakes. She could not eat another thing.

'But you are wasting away, signorina.'

'Hardly,' said Emma. 'I am bursting with food.'

Soon the afternoon light was fading and the staff beginning to shut down their computers for the night. Marco was still in Signor Bragora's office. She could not leave before Marco. She needed that lift. She felt helpless, not able to get about on her own. London was different. She knew every street and short cut and often directed a lost visitor to the right bus stop or Underground station. A wave of homesickness hit her. She wanted to go home.

'Signorina, this so melancholy?' It was Marco. 'You are sad. Why?'

'I'm missing London and my home. Strange really, when I love it here.'

'Then tonight we will go party, to cheer sad lady up. I have an invitation to the gallery of modern art. A special showing of a new painter. It will be fun.'

A gallery of modern art, even in Venice, did not sound all that fun, but it might be interesting.

'No food, please,' said Emma. 'I don't want to eat.'

'No food,' he promised. 'Only the food of the gods.'

Emma was longing to ask Marco what he had discovered from all the phone calls, but he seemed lost in thought. Perhaps he also needed the distraction of some modern art. Back at the palazzo, he handed her the key to the locked bedroom.

'We shall take a vaporetto,' he said. 'Find something elegant but warm to wear.' Emma nodded. She wanted to look around the locked bedroom again.

'We shall not be in for supper,' he told Maria, who was waiting in the hall. 'We are going out.'

'*Si*, signor.'

Emma wondered if anyone ever went into the room; certainly not Maria, for she would have dusted away the traces of face powder on the dressing table and hung up discarded clothes. It was as if the owner had only gone out and left everything. Perhaps that is what had happened. Perhaps the woman had walked out on Marco.

She wandered in, taking in the atmosphere of the locked bedroom. It felt a strangely happy place, nothing menacing about it.

She looked at the photographs of the beautiful young woman again and at Marco, often in the background, attentive and admiring. But none of the photographs held a clue. Most of them were taken at parties.

What did one wear to an art gallery in Venice? Warm and elegant, said Marco. She decided to wear her own black trousers if they were travelling on a vaporetto, solving the prospect of skirts blowing up as she stepped aboard. She found a slender tunic top of creamy lace, lined with silk. It was beautiful, with long sleeves that fell to a point.

The answer to keeping warm was a black three-quarter-length cashmere wrap-over coat with a cowl collar. The buttons were embossed silver. Emma cut off the price tags without looking at them. She did not want to know that she was walking round wearing a fortune. Her own flat shoes would do perfectly well tonight.

On impulse she tucked in the red and gold scarf that Marco had bought her. He did not seem to notice the scarf. He looked at her, up and down. She wished she had done something different with her hair.

'Always the black,' he said, as he opened the front door, his dark eyes glinting. 'What are you in mourning for?'

If only he knew, thought Emma. It was her own dilemma. Perhaps love would change everything.

A man was standing on the steps, not very tall, but lean and muscular. He had very short dark hair, as if it had been shorn recently. His chin was dark with stubble. He looked hungry and tired.

'*Buono sera*, Marco,' he said. 'This is not convenient? So, tomorrow?'

'No, Claudio, please come in. Emma, this is Commissario di Polizia, Claudio Morelli. Emma Chandler, my accountant.'

'Signorina,' said Claudio Morelli, bowing over her hand. 'I have pleasure in meeting you. Forgive if my English is not good.'

'It's very good,' Emma assured him.

Claudio had a sealed, clear plastic bag under his arm. 'Please, signorina, if it will not upset you. Can you identify this raincoat? It is needed for forensics still, so I cannot take it from the bag.'

'Yes, that looks like my raincoat,' said Emma. 'I'm pretty sure it's mine. It looks like mine but of course they must have sold hundreds.'

Claudio took another smaller packet from his pocket and handed it to her. 'We have dried them carefully but might you recognize these bus tickets and a receipt for a sandwich?'

Emma was trembling as she took them. 'I can't vouch for the bus tickets. They could be anyone's but yes, the sandwich receipt is mine. Look at the date and the time, when I left the office two days ago. Where did you find the raincoat?'

'It was on the body of a young girl found drowned in the canal yesterday morning. We do not know who she was, maybe one of the many homeless or street girls.'

'How awful. But I lost my raincoat at the airport.'

'That is possible,' said Claudio Morelli. 'Many things are lost at the airport. It is a losing place.'

'I'm sorry about the girl. She could have kept the raincoat. I wouldn't have minded if she needed it more than me.'

'She did not have much choice. You see, signorina, the girl was murdered.'

Emma swallowed hard. Murdered?

six

Emma was totally unprepared for the glorious sight ahead of her. Although she had travelled by launch up the Grand Canal several times now, taking in the Byzantine, Gothic, Renaissance and Baroque wonders of the Venetian palazzos, this Ca' Pesaro was magnificent.

The building was classical but the ornamentation was a riot of garlands, swags, cherubs, masks and rosettes. Massive blocks of stone, diamond-pointed, gave strength to the lower walls, those at the water's blackened edge. The two upper floors had tall, recessed windows behind columns with semicircular heads. Light shone from every window with a shimmering reflection, dancing in the water.

'Is this where we are going?' she asked. 'It's amazing.'

'This is the Ca' Pesaro, the Gallery of Modern Art.'

'All of it?'

'All of it.'

'It's fantastic. It's so big.'

'It is three houses, made into one. The palazzo was donated to the city in 1907 by the family.'

'We shall be here all night to see everything.'

'I hope not,' said Marco drily.

When they left the vaporetto, they walked along a path close to an inner canal and over a red-bricked bridge to the back of the palazzo. The entrance was a huge doorway with high, wrought-iron doors which dwarfed every visitor, even Marco. The great doors opened out onto a courtyard with an ornate stone well dominating the centre, surrounded by slabs of black and white marble paving.

'I can't stop saying wow!' said Emma.

The lobby stretched forever, with busts of past doges high on the walls, stone benches for the weary to sit on and a flooring of beige and white marble. In the centre was a famous piece of contemporary statuary to remind everyone that this was the Gallery of Modern Art.

'I believe it is on loan,' Marco murmured. 'Big insurance.'

It was as grand and ornate upstairs. They went up a sweeping stairway to the first floor where tonight's showing was taking place. A new artist was making his debut into the art scene of Venice and he was easy to spot, pacing the floor nervously, pretending not to look at people's faces and their reactions.

A waiter offered a tray of champagne. Emma politely took a flute. It was freshly poured and still bubbling.

'You need not drink it,' said Marco. 'Just sip.' He sniffed the aroma. 'Not my Prosecco,' he added. 'Inferior.'

Emma drew her breath in sharply as Marco escorted her into the first-floor room. It looked indeed like the inside of a palace with high ornate ceilings, gilded cornices, tall windows framed with white brocade curtains and gold sashes. The polished parquet flooring was a herringbone pattern. There was not one but several translucent chandeliers hanging from the ceiling, light sparkling from the crystal teardrops, illuminating the scene below.

'Take your time,' said Marco. 'We have all evening. This must have been the main reception salon, now perfect for an art exhibition. You will be warm,' he added, taking her woollen coat and handing it to a waiter.

It disappeared somewhere. Emma hoped she would get it back. The cream lace tunic and black trousers were perfect, casual and comfortable, but elegant. Many of the women were overdressed, wearing sleek couture dresses and coats, dripping with jewels. Some of the younger women had not bothered at all and were still in their daytime jeans and T-shirts. But they still had that effortless, smooth cosmopolitan Venetian look.

Marco looked magnificent, so tall and powerful. He stood out among the crowd and many of the women slid sly glances at him, wondering if he was available. Emma made no move to look possessive but she noticed that Marco kept closely to her side.

'Promise to protect me from the pack of female wolves if they approach,' he said in an aside. 'I am not in the market.'

'I'm sure you might meet a very pleasant lady here,' said Emma. 'Someone who shares your interest in art. A nice dinner companion.'

'My only interest is seeing the paintings through your eyes,' he said enigmatically.

The artist's big paintings meant nothing at all to her. They were vast canvases with some splodges of paint, or stripes or dots. More like samples of modern wallpaper. Emma made no comment but moved on to a collection of smaller watercolours which were displayed down the centre of the room. They were exquisite. Fragments of an old Venice, a shadow, a courtyard, a bridge, an old woman selling flowers. Most of them were A4 size, as if the artist had bought a bargain pad of 140 gram drawing paper from a shop and wandered round Venice with it tucked under his arm and a palette of paints in his pocket.

'This is his minimalistic mood,' she murmured.

'You like these?'

'Very much.'

She was sipping the champagne. Marco had barely touched his. She could imagine him pouring it into a pot plant, like in an American film. She smiled at the thought. He caught the smile.

'You like it here?'

'Very much,' she said again. 'It's lovely.'

'I'm glad. I want you to enjoy Venice, to think of it as part a holiday, not all that work, work, work as in your smoky London office. It cannot be good for you, all that close work. I see you wear glasses.'

'For close work, yes. But you also work very hard. It's the same.'

Marco shook his head. 'But I love my work. I love my vineyards, the smell of the grape and making the good Prosecco. I bring much happiness to many people. Does your work make people happy?'

Emma had to admit that her work did not make people happy. 'I bring order to their lives. Maybe that gives them a form of contentment.'

'Clever answer. Now, signorina of the orderly life, what do you think of this disorder?' They were standing in front of a huge canvas covered in scattered stripes of red and yellow, put on thickly with a big brush. It did not look like anything, maybe a seaside deckchair for a giant.

'It is called *Sunset*. Does it look like a sunset to you?'

'The colours are right for a sunset,' she admitted.

'So the artist is nearly there,' said Marco with a straight face.

Now they were sharing an amusement and the feeling was almost as good as when his arms were round her and he was taking possession of her mouth. She felt his hand slide over hers, fingers long and cool, clasping hers lightly.

'I see another she-wolf approaching,' he whispered urgently. 'Protect me, please.'

A woman was walking towards them purposefully. She was wearing a slinky, emerald-green silk trouser suit and strapped heels so high, it was a wonder she could walk. Her blonde hair was piled into a smooth roll on the top of her head and held there with emerald clips. Her make-up was flawless.

'Marco,' she said, her brilliant blue eyes flashing. 'You have not been to see me for ages and ages. My life is empty without you. I have missed you.'

'Emma, may I introduce the Countess Raquel Benedetti? Her family history goes way back. This is Signorina Emma Chandler, my English accountant.'

Emma noticed the way Marco rolled the Countess's name as if he was chewing it and then spitting it out.

'Accountant? Is that what they call it these days?' Her scarlet bowed lips curled in derision. Her eyes swept up and down, pricing Emma's clothes, with a sort of velvet languor.

'It is a responsible job,' said Emma coolly. 'Do you work?'

'Work? What is this odd word? No, my family would never allow me to work. It is so degrading. Besides, I have my own fortune.'

'You are fortune-ate,' said Emma, finishing the conversation with a neat play on the same word.

'I am having a small dinner party tomorrow night. Only the best people in Venice. You will come, yes?' Raquel turned her back, was talking to Marco. It was more of a command than an invitation. Her eyes moved to Emma. 'You could bring your little friend.'

'How very kind of you, Raquel,' said Marco smoothly. 'But I am afraid we have other plans for tomorrow night. Plans that cannot be changed, even for you.'

It was the first Emma had heard of any plans.

'What a pity. Then I will telephone you and make another time when you do not have other plans.' She reached up and planted a kiss on Marco's cheek. It left a smudge of lipstick.

'*Ciao*,' she said and sailed across the room towards a different man.

Marco steered Emma into a different salon. Here were sculptures, some large and imposing and some so small that Emma wished she had brought her glasses. Marco was staring up at a thin and beautiful angel whose wings seemed so fragile it was difficult to believe that they were carved from stone.

'Dreadful woman,' he said, wiping away the lipstick with a tissue.

'She seemed to know you.'

'She wishes she knew me. But no luck for her. I have no time for these predatory women with nothing to do but find new men for their amusement. I am not fudder for her appetite.'

'Fodder,' corrected Emma.

Marco grinned and wrapped his arm round her waist. 'So has my young friend had enough of culture? I think it is time to begin the amusement of the evening. Will you be my fodder?'

Emma broke into a giggle, then hushed herself as people turned and looked at them. They would not complain. Marco was too authoritative and powerful-looking for anyone to dare cross him. And too handsome, thought Emma. He was the best-looking man in the salon. Even with a lot of competition from the sophisticated clientele at the art gallery.

'What do you suggest?' she asked.

'I would like to take you for an evening stroll round Venice and we will eat snacks and drink a glass of wine at a little café and behave like the other tourists.'

'I would like that,' said Emma, glad that she had put on her own shoes for walking round Venice.

'There is a ladies' room over there, not so old as the palazzo. Venice does not have many in the streets. I will meet you downstairs in the entrance courtyard.'

Then he was gone, striding away without a backward glance. Emma sipped some more of her champagne before she returned her glass to a convenient counter. The ladies' room was updated twenty-first century, nothing medieval or draughty.

Marco was waiting downstairs with her long woollen coat over his arm, which he had retrieved from somewhere. He helped her into it.

'Ready to go?'

She nodded, not letting him know how much the familiar gesture affected her. For a moment he was close, his hand guiding the coat over her shoulders, her arms into the sleeves, momentarily brushing her skin. His breath fanned her cheek, his eyes concentrating on each movement.

Marco wondered at his own self-control. He was so close to her, the sweet perfume of her skin rising to him like intoxicating wine. How could he keep his hands off her? When all he wanted was to take her in his arms and kiss away all breath from her lips, crushing any protest with the passion of his embrace.

'Damn the coat,' he said for no reason.

So began an evening of more magic as they walked the bridges and streets of Venice, in and out of alleyways, up and down steps, stopping now and then to look in some brightly lit shop window at very expensive goods, stopping at peddlers' street stalls to bargain over some trifle.

Emma bought a snow paperweight. It was a crude plastic replica of a palazzo that was hidden in snow on shaking. It would sit on her desk in London, to remind her of this starry evening. The sky was as black as pitch, yet the stars were brighter than diamonds.

'You paid him too much,' said Marco.

'I wanted it, as a souvenir.'

'Always start at half their price.'

'I am not used to bargaining.'

'You are not used to living, signorina.'

Emma knew that was true. She was not used to living like this, walking through a magical city built on the sea, with the most handsome man in Venice walking by her side, taking her hand if it was a high step or an abrupt corner.

She knew she was lost, not only in this maze of streets, but in the maze of her own emotions.

But some of the back streets were reeking of decay, dark and crumbling, stacked with uncollected refuse. Some of the canals smelt of refuse. Emma would hate to be lost in them, long shadows like ghosts of the past. She moved closer to Marco.

'I took this short cut on purpose to show you,' said Marco. 'Venice is not all grand buildings. It is sinking into the sea, a millimetre or so a year. And we are overwhelmed with the smell of rotting stuff. I long all the time to escape to the countryside, to my beautiful vineyards.'

'It's hard to get used to the smell.' And it seemed everyone wore perfume, even the men. Marco did not but there was always a freshness about his skin that was the result of expensive bath products. She could breathe it into her lungs without shame.

'I shall take you to my vineyards for the fresh air. You will breathe the real Italian air. I have a family house there, an old farmhouse. You will stay.'

Marco did not ask. He just said you will come, you will stay. No argument, no discussion. He was used to getting his own way.

They wandered along the waterway fronts, ate a snack from a counter here, drank a glass of wine from a counter there. It was so different from the formal meal of the evening before. Marco knew his city well and it was not always dry history, or wet history. He described the great flood of 1966, when there was so much destruction.

'People saw their belongings floating away on the water. And many valuable manuscripts and books were lost. It was sad.'

Emma did not ask about his parents. They did not seem to be around. Perhaps they were long gone or were divorced and he did not mention it.

They stopped at a small café and strains of music were coming from inside.

'Would you like to dance, small orderly accountant?' he asked, taking her arm. 'It would be the perfect end to a perfect evening.'

Emma was tired. Her feet hurt from all the walking. But a dance in Marco's arms was too much of a temptation. The music was soft and melodic, some old tune from the fifties. He took her inside, paid for drinks to be delivered to a table, took her straight to the minuscule dance floor.

His arms went round her immediately. She could feel the hardness of his body. She cleaved to his shape. His hand was firm in the small of her back. Their feet moved to the old romantic melody. It was a time warp.

Emma closed her eyes, wondering how she could survive this onslaught on her emotions. She wanted to be with Marco. She wanted to be part of his life. But her independent spirit said no. Cut loose. Be yourself, girl. This was not the time to fall in love with a man, however handsome, however wealthy and powerful.

But his tall, rangy body so near her own was hard to dismiss. It was as if he had planned some gigantic plot to seduce her. She entered into another world, where she did not want to move, did not want to change a moment.

The music, the lyrics, were so soothing, it was if the streaming stars were spiralling. How could music betray the way she felt? It was not fair. She had to stay here and work, not let his seeking hands absorb her into his bed.

He bent his head so that his cheek was close to her hair. She could feel the soft, late-evening stubble growing on his firm chin. His fingers threaded themselves in her hair and he tipped her head back. His eyes were glinting in the darkness, but with a warmth that was disconcerting.

'I shall have to kiss you,' he said. It was a stolen kiss. He tasted her mouth hungrily. Emma moaned in soft surrender, but her response shocked him. It was a fire stoked by years of restraint and unfulfilled yearnings. She responded with a passion that set his blood alight.

When they parted, they were both shaking, unable to dance another step. They left the little café and walked through the silent darkness, their pulses hammering, like flickering flames, till the night air cooled their ardour.

But Marco did not take her to bed. When they reached his palazzo, he left her at the bottom of the stairs, said goodnight briefly, and went to his study for a brandy. He knew he would not be able to sleep when his physical longing for Emma was so compelling. The confusion was hopeless.

'*Buono notte*, Emma,' he said.

'*Buono notte*, Marco,' she said. 'And thank you for a lovely evening.'

 Sometimes she seemed to be seeking his touch, but then she withdraw, back into her pearly shell, was cool, efficient and distant again. The remote English miss. He wondered when he would discover the real Emma.

Emma went back outside onto the coolness of the front steps. Black water was lapping over the lower steps. Lights from the other side of the Lagoon hung in the darkness. She needed air and a few moments of solitude before she went to bed.

Her emotions were in turmoil. She was here in Venice to work, to solve Marco's problems, not to fall in love with him. It would be a disaster. She would go home in shreds.

There was a sudden, hard thump in the middle of her back. She flung open her arms, hoping to find one of the pillars to steady her balance. But there was another hard thrust and Emma found herself staggering down the steps towards the black water.

'Marco,' she screamed. 'Marco.'

She fell into the cold lapping water, struggling to find the steps, to get back onto the landing stage. But everywhere was so slippery. She found herself sinking away into the wash of a passing vaporetto. Emma could swim. She made herself strike out despite the heavy weight of the woollen coat. She tore off the clammy wool and struck out for the nearest solid-looking place.

Hands were pulling her ashore. The voices were all Italian. She did not understand what they were saying. She was being wrapped in a blanket. She was surrounded by spectators, late-night revellers, interested onlookers.

'*Chiamante un medico.*'

'*Un ambulanza.*'

'Signorina? Are you all right?' The man was speaking in English. He was leaning over her with a kindly face. He was waving away the onlookers with an air of authority. 'Do not try to speak. Nod for me, *si*. A drink is coming from a café.'

Emma nodded. She had seen him before, somewhere. But her shocked mind could not place him.

'I am Commissario Claudio Morelli. Do not be afraid of me. I am an old friend of Marco dell'Orto. But this is bad. Someone has tried to drown you. The Lagoon in Venice is beautiful but not for the drowning of young ladies.'

'Marco?' she spluttered.

'Marco is coming. I have telephoned him. He is coming. You are safe now.'

seven

Emma awoke to the sound of bells ringing. Every church bell in Venice seemed to be ringing, including the big brass affair beside the front door of the palazzo. She stumbled over to the window and peered down into the Lagoon.

She was able to look at the canal now. She had recovered from the nightmare of the dark when someone pushed her into the water. Marco had come for her and carried her back to the palazzo. Maria had taken off her sodden clothes and washed her, wrapped her in warmth and fed her sips of a warm drink.

Emma tried to forget why someone would want to drown her. Marco pretended it was some drunken reveller but she did not believe him. Nor did Commissario Morelli.

'She is too clever,' he told Marco. 'They do not want someone too clever around your accounts. She will find out who is responsible and someone will not like that.'

A vaporetto was disgorging a dozen or more children onto the stone steps and the tallest child was ringing the bell. Its clang was discordant. No one ever rang the bell so vigorously.

She heard Maria opening the door and the children clamouring and laughing as they came into the hall. Was this Marco's family? So many children? Was she going to learn something at last about this enigmatic man?

She threw on some blue jeans and a fleece jersey and hurried downstairs. Maria had produced trays of fruit drinks and sweet cakes, even at this time of the morning. The children clustered around Emma, chattering away in Italian, which she didn't have a chance of understanding. But she smiled and nodded and pretended to be part of whatever occasion it was. It was obviously a special occasion.

Marco came through from his study, his arms full of small parcels wrapped in coloured paper and tied with ribbons. He was grinning, a natural welcome on his lips. He also was speaking rapidly in Italian. Emma was quite lost in the noise.

'*Buongiorno, buongiorno,*' he said, then reverted to English. 'This is the feast day of St Nicolo, the patron saint of sailors and children. He is ver' generous to children. We all have a holiday. No work today. That is good, *si*?'

'But I have to work,' said Emma. 'I've a lot to do.'

'The office will be closed. There is no one there.'

'You could let me in.'

'But I am not going there,' said Marco, handing out the gifts to the children. They clamoured round for the biggest and brightest of the parcels. 'I have to take gifts to the children of my workers at the vineyard. They expect it. You will come with me.'

There was no arguing with him. He was always obeyed. What he said was the law. Maria was happily clearing up the mess as the children left to call on some other hospitable household. The hall was strewn with torn paper and ribbons. Emma went on her knees to help gather up the rubbish.

The quality of the paper and the ribbon betrayed that the gifts had been professionally wrapped. She could not imagine Marco wrapping all the gifts in his study late at night.

'A bit like Christmas?' she said.

'It's an early Christmas. The children never let anyone forget that St Nicolo is their patron saint. Half of his bones are in a church on the Lido.'

'Only half?'

'The other half are somewhere else. No one knows where.'

Maria was tut-tutting and trying to stop Emma from helping, but Maria wasn't successful. Maria and Emma continued collecting bits off the marble floor.

'Quite the little domestic,' said Marco, amused. 'Can you also cook if the good Maria is taken ill?'

'I can do soup,' said Emma.

'Then we shall have to live on soup. I could manage to live on soup for about a month so no problem there.'

He was making fun of her again. He enjoyed teasing her.

'We should take turns if Maria is taken ill,' said Emma. 'That's democratic. What can you cook?'

'Everything,' said Marco expansively. 'All Italian men are good cooks. It is born in us. The gourmet genes.'

She did not believe him but at least the arrival of the children had removed any awkwardness from their first meeting this morning. She could hardly forget her wanton response to his kiss when they danced those nights ago. It was enough to make her cheeks burn at the thought. Even her limbs felt weak at the memory.

'Ah yes, the gourmet genius,' said Emma meekly, keeping her eyes down. But she saw that Maria was smiling broadly. Perhaps Marco's talent for cooking was limited to toast. But she had not seen toast at all in Venice.

'*Grazie*,' said Maria, taking the rubbish from Emma and piling it on the trays.

She carried the first tray out to the back kitchen. Emma went to carry the second, but Marco stopped her.

'Come into my study,' he said. 'Bring your laptop.'

So it was not going to be all holiday, thought Emma. While Maria was preparing breakfast, Emma was shut in Marco's study, going through all the figures that she had unearthed. Column by column, while Marco followed closely.

Since the water incident, Marco had provided an escort for Emma to and from his office. He was not going to risk any more accidents. Claudio was right. Emma was getting too close to answers.

'So you are saying that the money paid to the company for consignments of wine has been disappearing for two years? My customers have paid their bills to my accounts but now there is no trace of it? We do not know where it has gone?'

'I think a cyber-hacker has got in. Somehow your whole system has been infiltrated and the money diverted elsewhere, to another account. Their account. Maybe it is abroad somewhere. And heaven knows what other funds have been diverted. Every one of your bank accounts has to be investigated and backed up with paper evidence. We need a paper trail.'

'This is very serious,' he said.

'It is serious,' she agreed.

Emma realized now why this conversation was taking place in his study and not in the office. Although he trusted all his staff, there was always the suspicion that someone close might be cheating him. Perhaps a relative of his staff. Someone who had problems or a grievance. Maybe someone who had been sacked.

'Could one of my staff have done this hacking?' He didn't want to know but he had to ask. He knew them all so well. Many of them had worked for him all their working lives.

Emma shook her head. 'No, I don't think so. It is far too complicated for any ordinary computer user to do. Hackers are computer boy wonders. They can get into anything. They understand the most complex of programs, know how to break in. They create new programs for themselves that are solid and untraceable. And they can break complex passwords and system codes.'

'So do I need to ask Commissario Morelli to take it as a criminal case? Do I report it to the Questara?'

'Not yet, that would alert the hackers and they'll cover their tracks in minutes and disappear with all your money. We should pretend to be puzzled, completely at a loss, making no headway. Perhaps deposit some money in an account and watch what happens.'

'I have some money in a small bank on Lake Garda. I can draw on that. It is there if I need holiday money.'

'Good. We'll set a trap. There are security operation managers in London, used to unravelling the most complicated hacking. It would be best to consult one of these experts.'

'So we have to go back to London?'

'Sometime. But not yet. I must get all the evidence. Then I'll contact Irving Stone.'

Marco nodded, switched off his computer. 'Enough of work, Emma. The rest of the day is for St Nicolo. Breakfast first and then we will leave. It is a long drive. Wear something warm. I sometimes put the hood down.'

He was telling her what to wear again. Emma wanted to answer back but Marco looked drawn. The news had come as a shock to him. It was something one read about in the newspapers but never thought could happen here.

But now he had a whole day in Emma's company and even though she had been the instrument of the bad news, he could not help remembering, with a tingle in his limbs, her ardent response to his last kiss. Perhaps the clean air of his vineyards would help soften her hard shell.

After a balcony breakfast, his launch took them out of the Lagoon and along the coast to a quayside where a car was waiting. No chauffeur today. Marco was driving a different car. It was a well-polished pale-green convertible with a grey hood but Emma had no idea of the make. She could just about recognize a Mini. Inside were deep leather seats and the dashboard was a mass of knobs and dials. It looked like the cockpit of an aircraft.

Emma had brought along the long woollen cardigan, remembering its warmth, and a cashmere scarf. Maybe one day she would find out who had bought it, owned it, but never worn it. Seeing him with those children this morning had made her wonder if he had a family. He had been so easy with the children, answering their chatter, making them laugh. They didn't care about his power and authority, even less about his disturbingly masculine good looks.

Marco was wearing a leather jacket against the cold. He drove through the industrial area outside Venice. Stacks of chimneys belched grey smoke. It was much colder than Venice and the further out into the Veneto countryside they drove, the colder it got. In the distance Emma could see a range of mountains, topped with snow. The snow was glistening. Marco switched on the heater, adjusting the angle of heat so that Emma's feet felt the benefit.

'*Grazie*,' she said, wishing she had put on her boots.

'Nearly there,' he said.

It was beautiful countryside, rolling hills and fields, crops and trees, isolated villages where people gazed with interest at Marco's car passing through. Or perhaps they knew it and recognized him. Some of them waved. There could not be so many vineyard owners. They drew closer to the mountains and Emma was reluctant to let him know that she had no idea of their name. Were they the Alps? She realized how ignorant she was, about almost everything except keeping books and figures.

'Nearly there,' he said again, his face losing the tension. He always felt like this when he was nearing the home where he grew up as a child. 'This is the Trevisco province of Veneto.'

Marco was slowing down, giving her time to look out of the window. On either side were miles and miles of luxuriant vines, in tidy rows, stretching into the distance, up and over the hills.

'These are my vineyards,' he said, unable to keep the pride out of his voice. 'The dell'Orto vines.'

They seemed to drive forever and they were still his vines. Marco relaxed at the wheel, at peace now at the home where he belonged, no unpleasant fraudulent hacking to investigate. He was going to show Emma his family inheritance, what he was fighting for.

They came at last to an unsigned wrought-iron gate and it swung open at the touch of a button in the car. They drove along a straight lane, lined with cypress trees, vines now almost within touching distance. Far away, tucked into the curve of a hill, Emma could see a stone building, almost growing out of the hill itself. The front was two-storied built of red brick and stone, with a slate roof, and creeper growing over its walls, almost swallowing the house.

But as they turned into a courtyard, Emma saw there was a further house, three stories high, behind the smaller front building. An outside staircase led up to the first floor and then to the floor above. Everywhere were flowering bushes and on every step pots of geraniums and herbs.

'My home, my farmhouse,' said Marco. 'Very rural. Outside privy.'

But Emma knew now from the tone of his dark voice that he was teasing her.

She turned to him quickly, in time to catch the smile on his face.

'Oh good, an outdoor privy, my favourite kind,' she said.

Marco swung the car around in the gravel courtyard and from nowhere the children appeared. They had been waiting for him. They clamoured round Marco, shaking his hand, stroking the car, beaming at Emma.

She got out, stretching, back and legs stiff from the long drive, and they immediately turned their attention to her. It was not for the presents, she realized, but simply because they were pleased to see a new person, especially someone who had come with Marco.

His authority here was different. Not the man of immense

money and power and luxury possessions. Here he was, the owner of the earth, the vines, the giver of everyday necessities, the man who made work for their families, who settled disputes, who made sure they went to school. It was almost feudal.

Marco opened the boot of his big car and there was a shout of excitement from the children. It was full of more brightly wrapped gifts. He must have bought the entire toyshop.

Emma stood back as Marco gave out the presents. The children swarmed over him. He was made to be a father. He had forgotten all about the hacking. Emma felt a stirring far within her body. She was falling in love with him and it was the last thing she wanted to do.

A woman came out of a door, smiling and beaming, drying her hands on her apron. 'Welcome, Signor Marco,' she said in Italian. 'We knew you would come. We knew you would not forget the children.'

Emma took a quick second look. Surely it was Maria? Same build, same height, same round face and greying hair pinned back in a bun. Perhaps a little plumper and wearing her own clothes, with an ample apron.

Marco returned the greeting, but had seen Emma's puzzled look. 'This is Paola, Maria's sister. She looks after the farmhouse and me, when I have time to stay here. Let me introduce you.'

Paola seemed pleased that Marco had brought a guest and was reassured that Emma was no fancy fashion-plate signorina, in her normal jeans and jersey. 'Will you be staying, signor?'

'*Si*, we will stay tonight and return to Venice sometime tomorrow.'

'Then I shall prepare your room.' Paola hesitated for a moment. 'One room or two rooms, signor?'

Emma understood enough to say quickly. '*Due camere, per favore.*' She had learned her numbers.

'Lunch will be ready in half an hour, signor,' said Paola, now shooing the children into picking the up the torn paper and ribbons, and clearing the courtyard. Emma saw that the girls were saving bits of ribbon for their hair. They all looked fresh faced, tanned by the sun and well fed. The Veneto air was good for children, unlike the polluted fumes of Venice.

Marco led Emma up the outside staircase to the first floor and opened the door. It led straight into a large room with windows on all four sides. It was filled with comfortable sofas and armchairs, stacked bookcases and valuable antique pieces of furniture. So unlike the salon in the palazzo, which was ultra-modern. A wood fire burned in an open grate, throwing out a good heat.

Marco was smiling at her, watching her reaction. He knew she felt safe here.

Emma went straight to the fire, holding out her hands. 'Oh, a real fire.' She turned and twisted in front of the heat.

'You will be warm here,' Marco promised.

Emma went from window to window, exclaiming in delight. Every view was of vines in straight rows. 'It's like a green carpet,' she said.

'And before the harvest it is like a purple carpet. Such a sight. Every vine laden heavy with the grape.' Marco went to a drinks cabinet and of course, a bottle of Prosecco was waiting there, cooling in ice. He poured out two glasses in crystal-cut flutes, glasses so old it seemed sacrilege to use them. They were from another century and fragile. He handed one to Emma.

'Welcome to my home, Emma, to you on the feast day of St Nicolo.'

She took the champagne and returned the toast, taking a sip. 'To your next harvest, Marco,' she said. 'The feast day of St Nicolo. I shan't forget this next year, when I am back in smoky, rainy London.' Then she added impishly, 'Do I get a present, too, signor, from St Nicolo?'

Emma regretted her words instantly. Marco was standing far too close. She could smell the freshness of his skin and the good leather of his coat. Any moment now he would put down his glass and crush her in his arms and she would be lost, unable to resist him.

He put down his glass. Emma held her breath. But he did not move towards her.

Instead, he turned and went to his briefcase, which Emma had not noticed before. He opened it and took out a flat rectangular parcel, wrapped in more bright paper and tied with coloured ribbon.

'Of course I would not forget you. St Nicolo brought this specially for you.'

Emma's hands were trembling as she took the parcel from him. It was heavier than she had first thought. She did not tear at the paper as the children had, but untied the ribbon carefully and unfolded the paper wrapping.

She could not believe what she held in her hands. It was the watercolour painting of the old woman selling flowers at the foot of a bridge in Venice, the sunlight caught on her flowers, making them alive and vibrant. They were more alive than the old woman, whose face was in the shadows. The painting had been on show at the art gallery.

'It's beautiful,' she breathed. 'I love the painting. But I can't accept it, of course, Marco. It's far too valuable to give me as a gift. But thank you, for a wonderful and generous kind thought. Thank you so much. You must hang it in your palazzo. Perhaps in your study, to remind you of that wonderful evening at the art gallery.'

As she looked up at him, her eyes filled with tears. No one had ever given her such a gift. She knew it was easy for him to write a cheque, but he had known she liked the small paintings and arranged to give her one.

'But it is to remind you of that evening,' he said softly. And she knew what he meant. He was reminding her of that searing kiss when they were dancing in the little café. When every fibre of her body longed for him to crush her even closer. When they had lost all sense of where they were and who they were. When nothing mattered but their closeness.

Would she ever be able to forget this man, this tempting man? A man who could have any woman he wanted. Who had only to click his fingers and a woman would rush to his side, ready to fall into his bed.

No, she would never be able to forget him, even when she was as old as the flower seller. His deep and resonant voice that could make her toes curl. Those hands that could bring her skin alive with the briefest touch. Those dark eyes that could see into her very soul. These things mattered more than his good looks, his tallness and his muscular body. It was his voice, his touch, his eyes.

Marco took the painting from her and propped it on a small

side table. Then he linked his arms loosely round her waist. 'And when do I get my present?' he asked with a wicked gleam.

Emma did not know what to say. 'That's a secret,' she said.

'You are making me wait for my present?'

'Of course.'

'It will be worth waiting for,' he said, taking a tendril of her hair and curling it round his finger. 'I am a patient man.'

eight

Paola shattered the moment by calling up the stairs that their lunch was ready. It was too cold to eat outside so she had laid it in the dining room.

Marco eased himself away from Emma with regret, his fingers trailing over her waist.

'Damn the lunch,' he said. 'Shall we forget it?'

'That wouldn't be fair to Paola,' said Emma. 'She probably looks forward to when you come home so she can cook for you.'

'You are right. Always the good English manners.' He led her to the stairs. 'The dining room is below, the soul of the house. You see, this is an interesting home. And the heat rises upwards.'

The dining room was on the ground floor, another wooden-floored room with a fire burning and a heavy oak table, big enough for a party. An old sideboard was creaking with lidded dishes and boats of sauce, bowls of fresh vegetables and salad.

'Paola always cooks for the five thousand,' he said, cheering up at the good smell. 'But she can really cook. Her mother used to cook for my grandfather.'

'Your grandfather? You haven't told me about him.'

Marco was taking off the lids, steam rising in his face. 'Three different sorts of pasta. I must teach you all the names. There are over fifty different kinds. I shall take you to the pasta shop in Venice which stocks them all. The English only know spaghetti and macaroni.'

'We know cannelloni,' said Emma, defending the entire race.

Marco was looking at the dishes, trying not to feast his eyes on every inch of her. It was not easy when she looked so luscious and tasty.

'There is cannelloni here,' he said. 'Stuffed with our home-grown spinach and cream cheese. This you would like?' He was serving her before she could answer. He brought the plate over to the table with the salad bowl. 'You like the salad, yes?'

He chose her clothes, now he was choosing her food. He was impossible. But it was exactly what she wanted to eat.

'In the summer we always eat outside on the patio. When it is harvest time we eat with the workers in the yard. Maybe twenty or thirty of us at long trestle tables. All cooked by Paola.'

Emma could imagine it. Marco sitting with his sleeves rolled up, the wealthy city entrepreneur forgotten and left behind in Venice. He would enjoy it. Back to his roots.

'You were going to tell me about your grandfather.' The cannelloni was delicious but almost too hot to eat. She forked some salad to cool her mouth.

'Antonio dell'Orto, my grandfather's name. He began the vineyard with a smallholding. He worked every day of his life. Never took a day off, not even when his wife, my beloved grandmother, died. He was back working, only hours after her funeral.'

Marco stopped ladling food onto his plate, his Italian temperament showing deep emotion for a moment. He paused, gaining control again.

'They were good people. They brought me up when both my parents died in a car accident, taking a mountain curve too fast in a poor car. They gave me a good education, taught me how to run the vineyard. Grandfather bought up more acres when neighbours went bankrupt in the recession.'

'But he is no longer with us?' Emma found she couldn't say the death word, not when the man sounded so alive.

'He died out in the vineyard, among his beloved vines. It was a heart attack, they said. He was still working in his eighties. And he is buried where he died with vines as his headstone. It was his wish.'

Emma could image the fire and the passion of his grandfather, which Marco had inherited. 'Do you have a photo of him?' she asked.

'No, there is no portrait. He would not have a photograph taken. But they say that I look much like him, when he was younger.'

'He sounds a wonderful man,' said Emma.

'Meaning I am not that wonderful?'

Emma didn't know how to answer. She stumbled over the words. 'Not the same as your grandfather. You are amazing in that you have built the Prosecco champagne into a global enterprise. This took vision and hard work, I know that. I can see the growth in your records.'

She sounded like a computer. Somehow she had to bring the conversation down to a less emotional level.

'So I have vision and I work hard, but I am not wonderful?' He was teasing her again between mouthfuls of Paola's good cooking. He had another vision but this was not the time to tell Emma. 'I am wonderful-less?'

He floored her with his quick wit. But Emma rallied her good sense.

'Wonderful takes a long time to prove,' she said.

He laughed. It was a good sound. It was the first time she had heard him really laugh for days. He had been shocked by her narrow escape from the water. He needed this respite from Venice, from the disturbing turmoil of the accounts office. If she could give him these few hours of enjoyment, then she had done more than sift through hundreds of pages of figures.

Dessert was fresh peaches, so sweet and ripe the juice ran down between her fingers. He watched her lick her fingers, wanting to taste that sweet taste, wanting to taste every inch of her skin.

'After lunch we will walk through the vines, unless of course you would prefer a siesta?'

'A walk would be lovely,' she said quickly. 'I want to see your land.' A siesta would be dangerous. Marco might decide to join her.

A cool wind was blowing off the mountains and Emma was glad of the woollen coat and scarf. Marco took her hand as easily as if they had been going out together for years.

'The ground is rough,' he said. 'You might fall.'

They walked along the straight rows of vines, up and down slopes, stopping occasionally if Marco spotted a late grape and fed it to her lips. They were still sweet and delicious.

'We are not walking over your grandfather, are we?' Emma asked anxiously, looking at the trodden ground.

'No, I would not do that,' said Marco. 'One day I will show you where he is buried, but not today. It is marked. Today is for the living. For love and enjoyment.'

Emma was not sure about the love and enjoyment, but it was certainly turning into a wonderful day. She could understand why Marco cared so much about his vines and the ancient farmhouse. But he had to live in Venice, to be near the airport and the railway station. He travelled so much, promoting Prosecco around the world, attending conventions and trade fairs. The sexy champagne would not sell itself even though it was delicious.

But she sensed he was lonely in his palazzo, despite the many available women and whoever had once lived in the bedroom of unworn clothes. She would ask him before she went back to London. But not today. She did not want to spoil today. It was too perfect.

They reached the top of a hill and Marco stopped, his arms held wide. 'This is all dell'Orto vines, as far as you can see in every direction. One day it will all belong to my son, Marco II. This is his inheritance.'

It was a shock. His son? Did Marco have a son? He had never mentioned a son, but then why should he? This was the first time they had talked about his family. Perhaps he did have a wife, was now divorced, his son away at some expensive boarding school, learning three international languages, being groomed for his inheritance.

Emma shivered, despair quaking through her. She was already dreading the thought of leaving him, but she had to get him out of her thoughts, out of her heart. She had her own life to live in London, her own career, her own pathway. She knew she would never again meet anyone like Marco. A man who made her body yearn for him in every way, whose kisses could beguile her into a surrender she was not prepared to give.

She gave a long, shuddering sigh.

'You are cold, *cara*. We will return to the farmhouse, to the fire and some hot coffee. Paola makes the best coffee in Italy, better than all these big expensive coffee shops you have in London.'

The caressing warmth of his hand was telling her something quite different. She could feel the urgency in his body, of his growing need.

'I would like to make love to you now, here out among the vines,' he said. 'It would be perfect, the smell of the grapes, the clear sky above.'

'Much too cold,' said Emma briskly. 'And the ground is much too hard.'

'I would bring rugs and cushions,' said Marco as if she had not said a word. 'I would keep you warm with my body and my kisses. You would not feel the cold. It would be like summer. I will bring you here in the summer and we will make love, feeding you the grapes between kisses, champagne kisses.'

'I shan't be here in the summer,' said Emma. 'I am going home to London soon.'

'So? Perhaps I will not let you go.'

His voice suddenly hardened.

This was not the time to have an argument. Emma had no idea of which direction to take. They had walked up and down so many rows of vines. She could not even see the farmhouse tucked away in the curve of the hill.

'Coffee sounds perfect,' she said, smiling up at him.

The kiss was sudden and caught her off balance. She fell against him and he swept her into his arms with a ruthless kiss that went on and on. The hot insistence of his mouth fired feelings she never dreamed she possessed. She clung to him as if she was sinking in a vast sea of grapes.

'This is more perfect,' he said at last, his voice dark with emotion. 'But we must get back before the light fades. Even I could get lost in the night. The lines of vines are all alike.'

The lights were on in the farmhouse, warm and comforting, guiding them back to the lane and the cypress trees. Paola was waiting for them with a tray of hot coffee and sweet apple cakes in front of the fire.

'There have been three phone calls for you, signor,' she said. 'But I told them you were busy.'

'Yes, I was very busy,' he said.

'I wrote the names for you.'

'Thank you, Paola. You are more efficient than any secretary.'

Paola looked pleased and bustled away down the outside stairs.

She obviously enjoyed having Marco at home, looking after him. The stairs were now lit with small lights on every step and lamps on the landings.

'Paola and her husband live in the front part of the house,' said Marco. 'It is private for them. I do not go there unless by invitation or necessity.'

'I'm sure they appreciate your consideration.'

'You use such long words for a little person,' said Marco, pouring the coffee into old shallow cups. The aroma rose to her nose like perfume.

'You keep saying I am small or little,' said Emma. 'But I am not. I am quite a normal height for a woman.'

'It is because I am so tall,' he said. 'So you look ver' small to me. And you do not wobble on those stupid high heels like other women, heels that distort the feet.'

Emma thought of the stilettos she had seen in the wardrobe of the unworn-clothes bedroom. She longed to ask him who they belonged to but still did not dare. Nor did she want to spoil the warmth of the evening together. She curled up on the sofa, watching Marco sip his coffee. He looked rested, the tautness gone from his face, the chiselled features outlined by the light from the fire.

This was another evening to remember when she was an old, old lady. She thought of her cold London flat, which never seemed to get warm despite the cranky central heating that ate up her cash.

'We are burning old vines,' he said. 'They burn well. We are never short of wood. It is ver' cold in Venice in the worst of a winter. Next month is the worst. The palazzo was built to keep cool in the heat, so much marble and stone and high rooms. We put down carpets in the winter for warmth, roll them up in the summer. The summer is so hot, you cannot breathe. The heat hangs like a blanket.'

'So you come here, to the vineyard, in the summer?'

'I come whenever I can. And I help with the harvest, as often as I can. But I am always flying everywhere. Soon I am going to Japan to meet customers. Perhaps this week. There is a growing market for champagne as the Japanese become more westernized.'

'That seems strange, one can't imagine it.'

'It is the perfect drink, for any time, any occasion. We shall have some this evening. What would you like Paola to prepare for our supper?'

'Not a meal,' said Emma. 'I couldn't eat anything more. Lunch was delicious and I am completely full.'

'Then we shall have delicious snacks on a tray in here, and you will find again your appetite. No one can resist Paola's small eats.'

Marco disappeared down the stairs to talk to Paola. Emma went to look again at her watercolour picture which was still propped up on the side table. It would look perfect in her sitting room, bringing a dull wall to life, reminding her of Venice, reminding her of Marco. If she could bear to think of him.

She hoped she would never have to tell him why no man could come into her bed. There were two bedrooms upstairs and prob-ably a shared bathroom. It was after all, an old farmhouse, built before the days of en suite. She closed her eyes, trying to blank out his face. This was going to be difficult.

When Marco returned, he had changed into casual jeans and an open-necked, long-sleeved shirt. The room was warm and Emma was regretting her fleecy jersey. She wanted to pull it off, free her neck from the restriction, wear something loosely cool and floppy. Perhaps his wife had left behind some clothes in her bedroom upstairs.

'Did your wife like living here?' Emma asked. 'Or did she prefer the sophistication of Venice, all the shopping and cafés?'

'My who?' Marco looked startled. He put down his coffee cup. 'I do not understand. Please explain.'

'Your wife,' Emma faltered. 'I was asking if she liked it here, in the country, away from everywhere except miles and miles of vines. Or did she prefer living in Venice?'

'Did I say I had a wife?'

'Well, not exactly.' Now Emma groped for words. 'You didn't say you had a wife, but you said you had a son, Marco II, and usually that means that he has a mother and she is your wife. Though, here, of course, in Italy …' She began floundering. 'It might be quite different.'

Marco went down on his knees beside the sofa and took her hands, loving the feel of her skin. 'You are a ninny. Is that the word? A ninny-poop? I have no wife, though many women would like to be my wife. And I have no Marco II. *Mi dispiace.* But one day I shall have a son and he will inherit. It is written in the stars. So I know it must be so.'

Emma felt a rush of happiness. No wife. But no son, yet. One day there would be Marco II and the boy would be as strong and handsome as his father.

'Nincompoop,' said Emma. 'That's the word you want.'

'I want more than words,' he said.

There was a knock on the door and Paola arrived with a tray of her little eats. Over her arm hung some folds of gaudy cotton material, a riot of red poppies and blue cornflowers. Marco got up, took the material from Paola and shook it out. It was a simple blouse top, straight sides, scooped neckline, long sleeves.

'Paola has made this for you on her sewing machine. She is so quick at the sewing, up and down and round and it is done. I have seen her make dozens of these tops for the children when they go swimming in the pond and have brought nothing else to wear.'

Emma took the top, delighted and surprised, not quite sure what to say. It was not exactly haute couture. 'Thank you, thank you, Paola. I am getting so hot in front of this fire. *Grazie, grazie.*'

'I think Paola must have bought a roll of this material at a market stall. A bargain, perhaps. All the girls wear these poppies.'

It was not something Emma would ever dream of buying or owning, but it would be far cooler than this fleecy jersey which was now making her itch. She could not wait to get into it but wondered where she was going to change.

'I shall not look,' said Marco, amused by her embarrassment. He turned away.

Emma pulled the fleece over her head and straightened her white lacy bra before slipping into the bright top. She did not know that Marco could see her reflection in a mirror and that the sight of her rounded breasts set him aflame. He longed to plunge himself into that shadowed valley, longed to catch her taut nipples between his teeth, to tease that soft flesh into submission.

'That's better,' said Emma, her tousled head emerging from the field of red poppies.

'Beautiful,' said Marco but he was not referring to the poppies.

*

Commissario Morelli closed his computer for the day. The drowned girl in the raincoat had been identified. She was a street girl called Pia who worked the airport. She had obviously seen her opportunity and lifted Emma's raincoat.

But the rest of the story was hazy. Maybe she had been brought to Venice by car. There was no record of her boarding a bus. There was a bad fracture on the back of her head caused by a heavy blow. She had been unconscious before she was tipped into the water.

She had no relatives. No one wanted to bury her. It would have to be a pauper's funeral. He had viewed the body and felt sad that someone so young had lived a short life that ended in death. She was about the same height and build as the female accountant from London. Someone did not want this Emma to continue her work on the missing Prosecco fortune.

He picked up his phone. He must warn Marco. He must warn Emma.

nine

Emma hung the poppy top on a hanger in an empty wardrobe in the second bedroom on the top floor of the farmhouse. It was not a big room, but was dominated by a double bed with a white cotton quilt, as large and puffy as a feather pillow.

She had the bathroom to herself as Marco stayed downstairs, on his phone, unable to leave work behind for a whole day. The bathroom had a huge bath on clawed feet that would bathe several small children, all at once. And Marco could lie flat in it, without having to bend his knees. How she would love to wash the corded muscles of his lean back and his shoulders. Or those long legs.

A shiver of feeling made her tremble. How she wanted to feel him sink inside her but it was not possible. It would never be possible.

She wondered if he would come upstairs to her. It would be so painful to have to disappoint him yet again. But he did not come.

Emma crawled into bed in her bra and pants, to find that Paola had put a hot water bottle at the foot of the sheets. Her toes curled into the warmth and she fell asleep almost immediately, trying to remember the right words in Italian, so that she could thank Paola in the morning.

Marco was up long before Emma. He was already helping himself to breakfast and coffee downstairs in the dining room. It was the usual simple breakfast.

'I have to return to Venice straight away,' he said. 'No more holiday.'

'Never mind,' said Emma. 'We all have work to do.'

'I am flying to Japan, sooner than I thought.'

'And I have to talk to Irving Stone. I have to tell him everything.'

'Buy a new phone. Do not use the ones in the office, nor your own mobile. Claudio says they may be tapped.'

'Yes, I'd thought of that,' said Emma. 'We can't be too careful.'

'The girl in your raincoat has been identified. She is a street girl called Pia, who worked the airports. They think she was abducted and driven to Venice. Claudio believes that the abductors thought she was you.'

'You have spoken to Commissario Morelli?'

'He thinks you are in danger.'

'Nonsense. I am an accountant, not a detective.'

'That does not mean that you don't already know too much. I will make sure that Enrico, my driver, is with you all the time. He is a reliable young man.'

'I don't want someone tagging me everywhere.'

'You will do as you are told,' said Marco sternly.

Paola was sorry to see them go. She packed some of her sweet apple cakes for them to eat on the journey. There was much exuberant talking in Italian and extravagant farewells. Emma could tell that Paola had really enjoyed their visit.

'I have told Paola that we will come again soon,' said Marco as he held open the door of his car. Again, he was arranging her life. No asking her or suggesting another visit. 'Very soon.'

'*Grazie*, Paola,' said Emma, miming the poppy top and hoping her smile conveyed her gratitude. 'It was so kind of you. *Bene grande.*' Paola seemed to understand and her face beamed with pleasure.

'You have made a friend,' said Marco, as he switched on the engine of the powerful car. 'Paola will now make you a dozen more cotton tops in different colours. It is her hobby.'

Emma laughed. 'And I shall have to wear them.'

'Of course, you will wear them, at least once,' said Marco smoothly. 'I should not like you to offend such a kind lady.'

Emma swallowed her annoyance. She was the one who should be offended. He seemed to think that he had to tell her everything, as if she had no manners.

'I have better manners than some people I know,' she said.

They were driving along the lane with the shady cypress trees. She wondered if she would ever see them again. She was only passing through Marco's life. And now he was off to Japan. No more galleries or dinners out. But she could get by, shadowed by Enrico. There was nothing to stop her.

'You will not go out at night by yourself while I am gone,' he said, reading her thoughts, giving her more orders. 'Although Venice is not as dangerous as your London streets, it is easy to get lost in the dark and you are at risk.'

Emma didn't answer. She was not going to spoil the drive back. She wanted to enjoy seeing the countryside, the little towns, the snowy mountains. She remembered the stone bridges they had driven over, where the river water was clean and blue, not the murky colour of the canals.

They stopped for coffee at a small village café, where they sat outside in the cold sunlight. The welcome was effusive as if the owner did not see many expensive convertibles in the winter. Or perhaps it was the generous tip that Marco gave her.

'Are you always so generous?' Emma asked as she got back into the car.

'Si, always. I have so much and they have so little.'

'But you work for it.'

'And so do they. Long hours. We get paid at different rates. Life is not always fair.'

They went straight to the accounts office. The staff looked surprised to see them, as if they expected the feast day to last longer. Marco went into Signor Bragora's office to arrange his flight to Japan. He was flying to Tokyo. He had already withdrawn all warmth from her. Suddenly Emma was homesick for England, the London office and her cold little flat. But she would soon be home. A few more weeks was not forever. She would make the most of this time in Venice before it sank into the sea.

Marco did not join the staff for afternoon coffee and cakes. It was as if he had completely forgotten her existence. Perhaps it was just as well. If he could forget her so easily, then she could forget him.

When it was time to leave the office, she found the car had gone, taking Marco to the airport. She had to find her own way but was not dismayed. It was not a long walk to the station where the vaporetto stopped. There was a machine for buying tickets. She stood in a queue with the rest of the homeward workers, hoping she would get on the right waterbus.

'Palazzo dell'Orto?' Passengers nodded and smiled. Once they were moving down the Grand Canal, Emma felt more confident. She could get off anywhere and walk the rest of the way.

But she would have found herself a long way down the Lido if the other passengers had not urged her to get off. They pointed and gesticulated in a direction, although she could not see the palazzo. The vaporetto did not stop at the front steps as Marco's launch had taken her, but somewhere close by. She could not remember what the back of the building looked like. There was a back door for deliveries. But it had been dark when Marco had walked her there.

She stood on the waterfront, among the tourists, wondering which way to go. She was completely lost.

It was lucky that she caught sight of Maria, walking through the crowds with a basket of fresh produce. She called out to her.

'Maria! Maria! Wait for me, *per favore.*'

The woman turned and searched through the people for the voice. Emma hurried, not wanting to lose sight of the one person who could help her. Then Maria saw Emma's vibrant hair, stopped and waved. Emma caught her up.

'I am so glad to find you. I had no idea where I was going.'

'The palazzos are so ornate in the front but ordinary at the back. You will get used to it. I will tell you the number of the vaporetto stop to get off at. You have come too far down the canal.'

Emma took the basket from the older woman. Maria was not used to this but did not argue. Perhaps she had walked a long way from the market. They went over several bridges and then along a pathway to a yard where a line of washing hung, drying in the breeze.

'You must remember this. It is the door with the brass knocker of a lion's head,' said Maria, producing a key. 'Signor Marco has already gone. The chauffeur has taken him to the airport. He has left instructions. You are not to be left alone. This is your supper. He said that you like salad.'

It was not the first time that Emma had been in the kitchen, but it looked different. It was another high-ceilinged room with rows of polished brass saucepans hanging on the walls, a large chopping table in the middle. But all the equipment was modern and gleaming white. Marco had not stinted when it came to modernizing Maria's workplace.

'This is a lovely kitchen,' said Emma, looking around. 'So much space.'

'Twenty years ago it was dreadful, signorina. An old range, smoking and spilling out ash like a volcano. And two brown earthenware sinks, side by side. A refrigerator that leaked onto the floor. I came here as a maid to the former cook. I had to scrub the floor every day.'

The floor was now black and white tiles. Easy to mop over. Emma smiled at Maria. 'Please don't go to any trouble for my supper. A sandwich will do.'

Maria looked horrified. 'Guests of Signor Marco do not have a sandwich. Supper will be ready in half an hour. Would you like it on the balcony as you are eating alone?'

Emma nodded. 'Yes, that would be perfect. Then I can look at the view and watch the lights come on.'

'Would you like some wine first?'

'No, thank you. I have drunk a lot of wine in the last few days. More than I usually do. Just water will do.'

This seemed to please Maria and she bustled away with her shopping. Judging from the whiff of the sea as she unpacked her purchases, it would be a fish salad.

So Marco had gone. Emma had the whole palace to herself, would be able to pretend that she owned it. She observed now how and where the rooms had been winterized with thick carpets and heavier curtains. But the long corridors were still chilly.

It had been a busy day, up early, then the long drive, and catching up at the office. Marco had not even said goodbye to her. Perhaps he did not say goodbye to people. Tomorrow she would buy a new mobile phone. But first a wash and a change into something warm and comfortable.

She wondered if she dared use Marco's computer in his study. There were so many things she wanted to look up on the internet, which was not appropriate to do in Signor Bragora's office. Maybe he kept his study locked. More secrets. Like the bedroom with unworn clothes.

Emma wanted to find out what she could about hacking before she spoke to Irving Stone. She knew it was a severe internet crime and carried a ten-year prison sentence. Someone must have monitored the accounts for weeks even to expose the vulnerability of the security system.

Luka and Rocco said the computer system had been playing up, became very slow. But no one had noticed the drive light blinking when no one was using the machines, a sure sign that they were being hacked. Somehow the hackers had discovered the system's digital fingerprint, the digital ports and the software being used.

'Marco's connection on the planet,' Emma said to herself, as if she really knew what it meant.

It was a fish salad. Freshly caught and grilled anchovies and some other little fish which Emma did not recognize. There were rolls and butter on the side and a bowl of fruit for dessert. Emma took a book with her and sat on the balcony, eating, reading and watching the canal traffic. The stress of the day eased out of her as the lights came on and the golden reflections shimmered in the water, broken only by launches and gondolas ferrying people to the nightspots.

She wanted to go out and savour the atmosphere, walk with the evening life of Venice. But would she ever find the lion's head knocker in the dark? Probably not. It would be a risky venture. Better to do her exploring in the daylight.

'Goodnight, signorina. I will clear up in the morning. Please leave everything on the side. There is coffee in the sitting room in a thermos jug, if you want any.'

'Many thanks, Maria. It was a lovely supper.'

Maria hesitated in the doorway. 'The signor said I was to give you the key to the room,' she said. 'In case you are tired of your clothes. He said to choose something new every day.'

Emma could not help laughing. 'The signor seems to think my clothes are boring. But, thank you, I may find something a little ... more suitable.' Emma sensed her opportunity. Now was the time to find out about the locked bedroom.

'I am curious, Maria,' she added slowly. 'All these lovely clothes. Who did they belong to? No one has told me.'

'It is not for me to say, signorina. It is for the signor to tell you.'

'Did they belong to his wife?' Emma persisted, unable to stop. 'Such a wealthy and handsome man must have been married some time. It would have been natural for him to marry. Perhaps they are divorced or live apart? Or perhaps they belong to a mistress, now cast off?'

Maria seemed to stiffen and Emma was sorry if she had upset the good housekeeper. She had been tactless, probing for information.

'Forget it, Maria. Forgive me. I'm sorry I asked. I was only curious.'

Maria nodded, understanding a little. She put the key on the table. 'The signor has no wife. The clothes belonged to Francesca, his younger sister. I can tell you no more. Goodnight, signorina.'

'Goodnight, Maria.'

Emma sat still, absorbing this new information. His younger sister, Francesca, was the dark-haired beauty in the photographs. Where was she now? Why had she left all her clothes? It was still a mystery. But Marco had no wife even when so many women in Venice were tempting him with their wealth and seductive ways. How had he managed to escape their clutches?

A surge of jubilance swept through her. Not for herself, but for Marco. He was still a free man.

She did not feel so hesitant about borrowing the clothes now. Marco had left the key for her, even though he had not said goodbye. It was a thoughtful gesture. He had been thinking of her, even if only briefly.

Borrowing from his sister was different and more acceptable. She went up to the second floor and let herself into the bedroom.

'Hello, Francesca,' she said. 'I hope you don't mind me looking at your lovely clothes. Marco said I could.'

Emma would have been scared out of her wits if there had been an answer. But it seemed friendly to acknowledge who had owned the clothes. She peered at the photographs again. Yes, Francesca was a stunning beauty and she could understand why a younger Marco was gazing at her with such adoration in his eyes. He obviously loved his sister.

Emma opened a different wardrobe, not wanting fancy evening

clothes, but something more sensible to wear to work. Something that would make her look a cosmopolitan woman and less so drab English. There was a whole rail of day dresses, suits and trouser suits. Francesca must have spent a fortune on clothes, Marco's fortune.

She fingered the beautiful material. No cheap polyester here or mixed fabrics. They were all one size larger than Emma normally wore but it was getting colder and an extra layer would be sensible.

A navy trouser suit caught her eye. She loved navy. The lapels were edged with red and it had a narrow red leather belt with a silver buckle. It would look wonderful with her tawny hair. She did not look at the price ticket or the label. She also found a long-sleeved red silk blouse to keep her warm.

'Thank you, Francesca,' she said as she left the room, locking it behind her.

Marco sat back in his first-class seat on the plane to Japan. No booking the whole cabin this time. He was not sure if there was enough money to pay for it. Strange to be short of money. It had never happened before. Wages came first. He had his own personal fortune but it was tied up in the plant and land.

He hated leaving Emma so abruptly but it had to be done. She was getting under his skin and he felt deeply distraught from wanting her so entirely. Just thinking of her now made him long for her nearness. He wanted to touch her, stroke her, own every inch of her skin. She did not want him in the same way. That was clear from her cool and distant behaviour.

She had barely spoken to him in the office that afternoon, as if their time together at the vineyard had never happened.

He could not risk getting hurt again. Once he had loved a special woman to the point of an obsession. Time had built a protective wall round him and no woman would breach it. He would make sure of that.

Commissario Claudio Morelli closed down his computer. He did not like what he was seeing on his screen. Marco dell'Orto was almost bankrupt. Somehow his fortune had been siphoned off and deposited elsewhere. He knew there was a special department in

Rome that dealt with internet fraud.

But also there was the young English woman to protect. He did not want to find her floating in a canal. She did not seem to realize that she was in danger. He dialled the number for the dell'Orto palazzo.

'Hello,' said Emma, forgetting to speak Italian.

'Signorina Emma Chandler? This is Commissario Morelli.'

Emma put down her book. 'Marco isn't here. He has gone to Japan.'

'I know,' said Claudio. 'That's why I am calling. You must be aware that you are in some danger. I understand that Marco has arranged for you to have an escort everywhere.'

'Enrico, his driver. But it isn't necessary. I shall be all right.'

'A young woman hit on the head and then drowned is not all right. You were also pushed into the water. These are all serious crimes. Perhaps you would prefer that you have an escort from the polizia?'

Emma caught the touch of irritation in his normally quiet and calm voice. 'No, I'm sorry. I don't wish to take up any more of your time, Commissario. I will be careful.'

'Then tomorrow I will meet you. We shall meet at a small café. It is called Pesaro. I will email directions. We must talk. It is urgent.'

'*Grazie*,' Emma said. 'I will be there.'

ten

Maria approved. She smiled as she served breakfast on the balcony, taking note of the bright scarlet blouse and navy pants. Emma wore her own shoes. No tottering about on four-inch stilettos, getting on and off launches.

'Do you know if the launch and the car will be there to take me to the office today?' she asked.

'I'm sorry, signorina. I don't know of the arrangements.'

'Never mind, I can go on the vaporetto. I'm learning my way around Venice. I'll find the right stop.'

'It is about six euros for the ticket, no lira. Return. One price only on the waterbuses.'

Her first purchase that day would be a new mobile phone. Emma wanted to buy a mobile without being seen or watched. There were lots of different shops selling phones. She had plenty of euros on her.

It was a clear, cold morning. No low-lying mist on the Grand Canal. Tourists already out and snapping the sights. They were taking advantage of the lower pension rates in the winter. Emma wrapped the cashmere scarf round her head.

The vaporetto took her to the quayside below the main station. No problem there. No Enrico to meet her, her so-called escort. She could remember the route to the office. There were far fewer canals here and fewer bridges. It was the beginning of dry land.

She bought an ordinary new mobile, nothing fancy, barely understanding the assistant's garbled instructions. She would read the manual, printed in English, back in the office. But out in the street, surrounded by air, and people walking by, minding their own business, she dialled Irving Stone's private line in the London office.

'Hello, Irving Stone here.'

'Hello, Irving, this is Emma Chandler.'

'Hello, Emma, nice to hear from you. How are you getting on? Enjoying yourself in Venice?'

'Not exactly. I'll be brief. I have discovered that their computers are being hacked and the payments being channelled elsewhere. We need an expert out here, or perhaps it can be done in London? What do you think?'

'Hacked? That's serious. So that's where the money has gone.'

'It's very serious. Marco had no idea what has been going on. His main interest is in growing and selling. He takes little interest in the money side.'

'Have you substantial evidence?'

'Enough, I think.' She heard him speak aside to his son but could not catch what was said. Their voices were low.

'I'll arrange to send someone out. We'll find a computer expert, one that is mature enough to know what he's doing, and put him on a plane. Well done, Emma. There's a bonus on your way if this is true. Can't stop. Keep in touch.'

'But I'm in danger,' Emma added.

'Keep in touch.'

'Someone has tried to kill me.'

'Take care. Bye now.'

Not exactly reassuring but she had done all she could. She switched off the phone and put it in her bag. Now she had to find the office, if she could remember the way, tracing the route backwards. Last night she had pointed and asked for the station.

But the staff and Enrico, the chauffeur, were out looking for her. Marco had sent his car and they were worried when she did not turn up.

'The car was late,' said Enrico. He was a good-looking young man, short and well built. 'The traffic was bad.'

'I came on the vaporetto,' she said as if it was nothing. 'I didn't need the launch today. But many thanks. I am here now.'

Emma felt sure that none of the office staff could be involved. They were friendly and helpful, all devoted to Marco. Emma asked about the firm of computer experts who had been called in when the system seemed to be going slow. No one could find the contact.

Even those details seemed to have been deleted.

'We had several people in. Some seemed to know what they were doing but did not rectify the fault. Others were mere amateurs. It was beyond them. *Così complicato.*'

'Let's check their credentials. Many people set themselves up as computer experts these days without any real expertise.'

It was an exasperating morning. Now that Emma knew the system was being hacked, she was very careful what she fed in. She allowed a few minor amounts to be transferred so that the hackers were not alerted. She could do nothing more with the earlier accounts. They were out of her hands. She could go back to London tomorrow but she knew that she would not. She did not want to leave Marco.

Something strong was holding her here in Venice and she knew it was Marco. She could not leave without seeing him again, hearing that voice, smelling the freshness of his skin. He was so tall, so handsome, so compelling. She didn't care if he told her what to wear or what to eat.

Lunch was another bowl of spaghetti in the local café, topped with a fresh tomato sauce and cheese. Emma didn't worry if she drank too much of the rough red wine at eighty cents a glass. There was no one to tell her off, to demand her attention, to tell her what to do. Marco was already on the other side of the world.

'Be careful,' said Signor Bragora, as she left the office that evening. 'The Countess is out for your blood.'

'The Countess? I don't understand what you mean.'

'The Countess Raquel Benedetti or whatever she calls herself these days. She has been making inquiries and now is spreading rumours about you, signorina. She is not a good person.'

'Oh, Raquel?' Emma remembered the woman in a green silk trouser suit at the art gallery. 'The woman with the claws? She can do nothing to me.'

'Beware, her claws are very sharp.'

'Thank you, Signor Bragora. But I'll never see her. And I never go out.'

'Still, she will find a way.'

'Well, thank you for the warning.'

Emma wondered if the Countess had paid someone to push her

into the water. It was a possibility. But surely not the street girl, Pia, as well? Perhaps she should mention this to the Commissario.

Emma remembered those words as she sat alone in the sitting room, reading and sipping coffee, that evening. Maria had produced another delightful salad supper of goat's cheese and roasted tomatoes.

She heard a visitor arrive and momentarily her heart jumped, hoping Marco had returned early. But of course he would not ring his own bell and it was far too soon to have travelled back from Japan.

Maria came to the tall doorway of the sitting room, looking apprehensive.

'It is the Countess Benedetti, signorina,' she said. 'I have told her that you are working and are not to be disturbed. But she insists.'

Emma stifled a sigh. She had no wish to see the Countess but it would be better to get it over with. 'All right, I'll see her, but please interrupt me in about ten minutes and say I am wanted on the telephone.'

'*Si*, signorina.'

Emma heard the stabbing sound of stiletto heels coming up the stairs, each one sounding like the thrust of a knife.

'So this is what the English call working,' said Raquel, her eyes sweeping over the coffee and the book. 'We have another word for it.'

She walked round the room, looking at the modern paintings on the wall, glancing at the flower arrangements.

Emma stood up but did not shake hands. Raquel was dressed to the nines in a white trouser suit with a gold belt, masses of gold necklaces, rings and bracelets. She threw off a cream mohair wrap.

'Good evening,' said Emma. 'Marco is not here.'

'I know he is not here,' said Raquel archly. She paused for effect. 'That is why I am here. He asked me to look after you personally. To keep an eye on you, he said. Now I know why.'

Emma didn't believe a word. This was totally out of character. Marco would not ask the Countess to keep an eye on her. If he had chosen someone, it would be Maria, who was already taking good care of her. And Enrico, her escort to and from the office.

'We have been on the phone constantly,' Raquel went on. 'Marco is concerned that you will get into trouble.'

'I am perfectly all right,' said Emma coolly. 'It was so very kind of you to call. I'm sure you have far more pressing personal engagements for this evening. Maria will show you out.'

Raquel flounced onto a sofa, arranging her legs so that Emma had full view of her celebrity gold and white sandals. It was obvious she never walked on the waterfront. They reeked money. The heels were studded with brilliant stones and the straps were woven strands of gold.

'Nice shoes,' said Emma, giving them their due.

'They cost more than you earn in a month.'

'Money well spent,' said Emma drily.

'I think you should know something that Marco has obviously not told you. But why should he tell you his private business? You are only his little London accountant. He will never see you again. Accountants are nobodies, two a lira.'

Raquel looked at the silver coffee pot on the side table. 'Are you not going to offer me a cup of coffee? It would be polite.'

'It's gone cold.'

'Then order some more.'

'I do not give Maria orders.'

Raquel laughed, showing her perfect white teeth, the product of expensive dentistry. It was not a pleasant sound. 'I'm glad you know your place. Even if you are too inefficient to deal with Marco's fortune. I have my own sources and it is not good what I hear.'

'So what do you hear? I was unaware that rats could speak.'

Raquel lit a cigarette and put it in a long ivory holder.

'I hear that money has disappeared from Marco's bank and the little accountant is the only person who knows where it has gone. Signor Bragora was very helpful. Such a nice old man. Pity about his eyesight. Perhaps he does not see you as everyone else can see you.'

'That's not true.'

'Much more, I know. It is not pleasant. All Venice is talking about you. Perhaps it is time that you went back to England, to your damp and dusty office in some nasty London skyscraper. You are not wanted here in Venice.'

'I have work to do here.'

'Maria will help you to pack tonight. There are plenty of flights back to London. Don't take anything that doesn't belong to you.'

'I've heard quite enough of this nonsense,' said Emma firmly. 'You are being deliberately rude and insulting. I suggest you go now and take your insinuating lies with you.'

'I have one more thing to tell you,' said Raquel, drawing on her cigarette and letting the ash drop anywhere on the floor. She was talking through the smoke.

'I have no wish to hear anything more,' said Emma. 'I'm not interested.'

'You see, Marco and I are secretly engaged. We have been so for months. We do not show affection if we meet accidentally in public, as we did at the art gallery. We pretend we do not know each other. It is so amusing, really. There is much gossip in Venice. We both enjoy fooling everyone.'

'Congratulations,' said Emma, expressionless. There was nothing else she could say.

'I thought you should know so that you don't get big ideas above your station. Marco is spoken for, betrothed. We shall be married in the spring in Santa Maria della Salute, which is the magnificent church on the other side of the Grand Canal. It will be a beautiful wedding, all the gondolas decked out in white and gold. A Venetian wedding is so beautiful. And my wedding dress ...'

'Your dress will cost more than I earn in a year,' said Emma.

'More than you earn in five years.' Raquel laughed again, clearly enjoying herself. 'So sad that you will not be here to see it.'

'I'm very glad I shall not be here to see it. But be careful as you leave. You might fall into the canal in those unsuitable shoes.'

There was a discreet knock on the door but Emma was up in an instant. It was Maria in the doorway, uncertain in her role of rescuer. 'There is a phone call for you, signorina.'

'Thank you, Maria. I will take it now. Please show the Countess out. I'm sure her launch is waiting to take her elsewhere.'

Raquel rose, shedding ash, picking up her wrap. 'Remember what I have told you, signorina. I am your friend. People are watching you.'

'That's very reassuring,' said Emma. 'I feel I need protection from friends like you.'

'I see you are helping yourself to new clothes.' It was a final thrust but Emma did not answer. 'Always the something for nothing is your way.'

Raquel swept out, following Maria down the stairs. Emma waited, drawing deep breaths to steady herself. She did not know what to believe. It could be true. She hardly knew Marco. A secret engagement might suit him.

Maria returned. 'There really is a phone call for you in the study, signorina. It is Signor Marco.'

Emma tried not to rush, but a phone call from halfway across the world would be expensive. She slowed her feet but her heart was racing.

The door to the study was open and the landline receiver off the hook. She picked it up, longing to hear his voice again.

'Marco? It's Emma.'

'You took your time.'

Not exactly, hello, darling, how are you? But he did not sound angry, more impatient that he had to wait.

'I had a visitor. I ran down the stairs.'

'Anyone I know?'

Emma wondered if she should say *your fiancée*, but decided this was not the time. 'Someone from the art gallery,' she parried.

'Are you all right? Are you safe and warm? Is Maria looking after you? And Enrico? I worry all the time.'

'Everything is fine,' she said with relief. 'We are all working hard. Irving Stone is going to send the best computer expert over from London from a security company. I bought a new mobile, an ordinary one, and phoned from the street.'

'You cannot be too careful, now that we know our system is unsafe.' He paused. 'I'm sorry I did not get to say goodbye to you before I left for Japan. There is the possibility of setting up a plant here and the negotiations are *complicato*.'

He did not tell her the whole truth. That he could not bear to be in her company for a minute more, without taking her to his bed and making love to her. The urge was too strong and he couldn't fight it. But he knew if he forced her, then it would be the end. She would turn her back on him forever and he didn't want that.

The only answer was to put half the world between them.

'Prosecco does not travel well long distances in bottles. It also goes stale quickly, three years at the most,' he went on. 'We are thinking about sending the grapes instead in big containers. The secondary fermentation is in stainless steel containers. It could be done anywhere in Japan.'

'That's ambitious,' said Emma. 'And complicated. To set up a new plant.'

'It may not happen. But I am glad to talk to you. I will tell you more when I am home. Are you sure you are all right?'

Missing you, she wanted to tell him. Missing you, like mad. Thinking of you all the time, watching for you in crowds, longing to hear your voice.

'Are you … coming home soon?'

He caught the catch in her voice and the tiny inflexion gave him hope. 'Ver' soon, *mia cara*. Sleep well.' Then he added, 'Perhaps you will dream of me.'

She wanted to say something, to make him stay talking, but it was too late.

He had gone and his voice echoed in the empty hall of air. Emma stood, holding the receiver, willing him back. But the miles unravelled instantly and she was alone again.

Maria stood at the door, holding a tray with a glass on it.

'I think perhaps a small brandy after the visit of the Countess,' she suggested. 'For the courage.'

'What a good idea,' said Emma. 'Thank you.' She heard another bell ringing. 'Surely the Countess has not come back?'

'That is the back doorbell, signorina. Someone who does not wish to be seen.'

'Please be careful before you open it,' said Emma quickly.

'I shall not open the door without a proper identity,' said Maria. 'We have many children who play silly games with the doorbells after dark.'

Emma nodded and took the brandy into the sitting room. The coffee was cold now. But she heard voices and steps coming up the main staircase. Surely not another visitor? And she knew no one in Venice who might call.

It was Commissario Claudio Morelli. Maria was taking his

damp overcoat. He looked cold and tired. Emma wondered if he had recently been ill. There were shadows on his face and a map of fine lines.

'Please sit down,' said Emma, indicating a seat near the fire.

'Shall I bring fresh coffee?' Maria offered.

'*Grazie,*' said Emma. 'That would be good.'

'That is welcome,' Claudio said, holding out his hands to the glowing electric bars. 'We get many power cuts in Venice, but not tonight, we hope.'

'It's very kind of you to come and see me,' said Emma, giving him time to warm up. 'I really appreciate your concern. Enrico is escorting me everywhere.'

'You should take different routes to work each day,' said Claudio. 'You are being watched. Sometimes go out of the back door, not the front porch. Not always use the signor's launch. Hire a taxi. Make many changes.'

'You really think I am in danger?'

'I know you are in danger. We have found the weapon used on poor young Pia. It is a piece of iron pipe. It was found in some rubbish.' He did not add that it still had hair and blood on it and that the evidence matched Pia's blood group and hair.

'How awful. That poor girl. I feel so sorry for her.'

'We have tried to trace a family but there is no one. She shared rooms with other girls but they know nothing about her. It is a sad story.'

'What will happen to her?'

'We cannot release the body yet. She is a guest of the hospitality of the doctor's cold refrigerator.'

Emma shivered as if she was also sharing that hospitality. Maria came in with a tray of fresh coffee. She had added a plate of little cakes and almond biscuits.

'Ah, home baking,' said Claudio with appreciation, as if he had not tasted home baking for years. He did not look as if anyone was looking after him. His shirt was a non-iron, drip-dry garment bought from a chain store. His tie was not chosen with any thought. His closely cut hair was merely a convenience.

'*Grazie,* Maria,' said Emma. Maria went out, beaming.

Emma poured out the coffee and offered cream and sugar.

Claudio refused the cream but added a spoonful of sugar. He took a small cake.

'*Perfecto*,' he said. 'I cook very little. I eat out a lot. It is not good for me but there is so little time. Always so much work.'

'Perhaps you would like to join me for supper one evening? Maria is a very good cook. I don't know when Marco will be back,' Emma heard herself saying.

'*Mille grazie*, signorina. I would like that but do not be surprised if I don't come. Something always happens when an arrangement is made.'

'That's no problem,' said Emma, smiling. 'We will make another day and time. I should enjoy your company.'

Claudio Morelli smiled back. It was the first time she had seen him smile. 'Now I know why the dell'Orto office likes their new accountant from London. Word gets around, signorina. Venice is like a small town. All gossip.'

Emma was glad that the detective stayed a while, keeping her company. He had demolished most of the cakes when his phone rang. He took it out of his pocket and spoke in rapid Italian, his face grim. He switched off and stood up.

'A launch is drifting down the Grand Canal, on fire. The fire boats are on their way to put out the blaze before it causes damage or spreads to the land. I need to be there before the firemen destroy all the evidence.'

'I'm sorry you have to go,' said Emma, getting up. 'At least your coat will be dry now. Maria has it for you downstairs.'

'*Buona notte*, signorina,' he said, his eyes full of warmth and concern.

'*Buona notte*, Commissario.'

Claudio Morelli hurried down the stairs to where Maria was waiting with his coat. He had not told Emma that it was Marco's private launch that was on fire. That it had been identified by the family crest on the bows.

Emma went to bed, relaxed and warm. Claudio Morelli was a good man. Perhaps she would dream of Marco tonight. And perhaps she would not be so afraid and her fears fade into nothingness. It was time she began to live again but someone had to help her.

eleven

Marco had not said when he would be returning. It could be days, weeks even. Emma knew that she must learn to carry on without him. She might have returned to London before his Japanese trip was over. They would never learn to know each other when life was so complicated. *Cosi complicato.*

Now that she knew who had once owned, but never worn, all the beautiful clothes in the locked bedroom, she did not hesitate to find another trouser suit for the next day. She chose a conservative grey pinstripe but it was a far cry from anything a sober city gent might have worn. The lining of the jacket was a gaudy blue, pink and turquoise stripe, and one lapel was edged with a fine line of the same silk. There was even a flowing silk scarf to match.

Emma had never worn anything so glamorous to work before. She cut off the price tag without even looking at it, then tousled her bright hair and added more than her usual touch of mascara.

Her boots were perfect with the slim trousers. Maria nodded her own approval. She said something in Italian that Emma roughly translated to mean that all the gondoliers would be queuing to take her in their gondolas.

'No, thank you,' said Emma. 'Not in the mood for operatic singing, first thing in the morning.'

'You will need a raincoat, signorina. It is raining. Signor Marco has several raincoats. This one may fit you.'

'*Grazie*, Maria.'

She went out, wearing one of Marco's raincoats. It was a short black one, belted. Big on the shoulders but she was not complaining. It was a wet morning.

She took the vaporetto, joining the commuting crowd, merging with the other travellers, and the car was waiting for her alongside the station. Marco had phoned Enrico again, to make sure she was being met. She was glad to get in out of the rain. The office staff crowded round her when she arrived. They had takeaway beakers of coffee ready.

'We have discovered more of this hacking person,' Rocco said. 'Look what we have found.'

It was not important but it was a clue. Someone had used the office computer to book flights, using Marco's American Express card to pay for them. But they had left the receipt evidence on the computer. Careless hacker.

'Brilliant,' said Emma. 'We'll find out something from this.'

There was not much that Emma could do. She felt surplus to requirements. She emailed the airline, trying to find a name, but the hacker had used Marco's name. She could not discover how they had come by his card, unless he had lost it and they used it before a replacement arrived.

'But it was not Marco,' said Signor Bragora. 'He was here, all the time. He did not go to the States. We do not sell Prosecco to America. Not yet. And the takeover offer is of no interest. I will report this to the fraud squad.'

'But this hacking person as you call him must have a contact in America and had to fly there,' said Emma. 'This is really valuable information. Thank you, all of you. I will let London know immediately.'

She went out into the street and found a small empty square with a fountain in the centre. It was a cloudy day and still raining, so the sound of water falling would drown anything she had to say. She phoned Irving Stone's private line from the shelter of a doorway and gave him the information. He sounded pleased.

'Well done, Emma. A Security Operations Manager is flying over this evening,' he said. 'Perhaps someone could meet him at Venice airport? The plane from London gets in at seven o'clock.'

'I'll arrange that. What's his name?'

'Professor Gilbert Windsor. He's quite elderly, grey beard, walks with a limp. I've also informed the e-crime squad at Scotland Yard. They have special officers trained for this sort of work now. Don't worry. The hackers will be caught.'

Emma decided she would meet the professor herself. They

would have a chance to talk in the car on the drive back.

'I suggest booking him into a local hotel so there is no need to put him up at Marco's palace, though I suppose this palace probably has about ninety rooms, all en-suite?' Irving Stone suddenly sounded resentful.

'No, not at all. It's a tall, narrow palazzo, quite small compared to many of the others on the Grand Canal, but it's very beautiful with delicate tracery and a balcony built along the front. It was built in the space between two other very fine palaces. A sort of afterthought.'

'Don't get ideas,' said Irving. He sounded like the Countess. 'We need you back here, pronto. Some new accounts have come in, right up your street. We're keeping your job open. No one is using your desk. The one with a window.'

'Thank you, that's very reassuring. I like my window. I look forward to seeing you all again. Is it raining in London?'

'It's raining.'

But how would she feel in her tiny one-bedroom flat, those cold rooms, after living in a palace for several weeks? She would have to get used to London again, travelling on the Underground, straphanging in the rush hour. Shopping for food in her lunchhour. No one cooking her delicious meals. It wouldn't be easy.

Emma forgot to switch off her phone, put it in her pocket, turning her face to the rain. Brixton was a million miles away.

It would be difficult to leave Marco, knowing that as soon as she had gone, a bevy of Italian beauties would be after him, their pearly white teeth flashing. One day he would be ensnared and that would be the end of her hopes and dreams.

'Emma? Emma? Are you still there?' It was Irving Stone again. 'There's another line you could look into. Do you know who installed their new computer system and who did they buy it from? The system might have been infected with malware before it was delivered, in spite of being new and factory-sealed.'

'That's a possibility. You mean the system might have already been bugged before it arrived and was installed?'

'Apparently that's the latest in the cyber-criminal world.'

'Don't worry. I'll look into it straight away.'

At least a new avenue to search would help her take her mind off Marco. If a computer system could be bugged before it even reached its destination, then nothing was safe. Perhaps Irving Stone should look into his own office system.

Luka and Rocco kept her supplied with black coffee. It was a productive day. The company which supplied the new system had also sent the so-called computer expert when they first reported difficulties. It was a firm called Craxio Inc., which was a definite link.

Rocco had looked into the airline booking. He was keen to help.

'The signor has no interest in this American offer. They would only spoil the great heritage of Prosecco. They would call it Prosy Secco or something equally stupid, put it into a fancy coloured bottle, just to capture a younger market. To take to these rave parties, some teenagers or trendy twenties.'

'So Signor Marco didn't go to the States on this plane reservation?'

'No way. He was here at that time. We all saw him. He came in several days. We remember. Someone had a birthday and he was here.'

Emma wondered if there was a link between the bugged system siphoning off money and the American takeover offer. If the dell'Orto company was in financial trouble, then the offer would be lowered and Marco might accept it.

Emma took the vaporetto back to the palazzo. Enrico came with her, not talking. It was raining and she was glad she had the borrowed raincoat. A dense mist loomed over the Lagoon, disguising the buildings. She could hardly see lights or palaces. Where had the magic gone?

She got off at the stop on the quayside nearest the dell'Orto palazzo. Maria had given her the number. Enrico waved goodbye. He had a date. He was courting a girl who worked in a local hotel.

'Be careful, signorina,' the driver called out, in Italian. 'There is going to be a very high tide this evening. Acqua....'

Emma had heard all about the tides. She recognized that word. Venice had more tides than anywhere else along the Mediterranean. She stepped carefully ashore. She knew her way to the back door of the palazzo and Maria had lent her a torch. It was beginning to rain quite hard. She could see drops sleeting in the beam from the torch. If only Marco could be there to meet her.

Everything would be perfect.

She was met by a panicking Maria. She was scurrying about with mops and buckets, distraught, her hair coming out of its tidy bun.

'The water is coming in,' she exclaimed. 'Today, the high tide and more rain. Together they are no good. Look, signorina, already the hall. It is awash.'

Emma hurried through the kitchen and found herself ankle deep in the hallway, water coming in under the main door that led from the quayside steps for the launch. It was dirty and grey.

'Sandbags,' said Emma. 'This must have happened before. Where did the signor keep the sandbags? He knows about these emergencies.'

'I forget. Yes, sandbags. We have sandbags. But I don't know where.'

Emma went into immediate search mode. Marco would not have neglected this simple precaution. She found several sandbags in an outer house on the pathway behind the palazzo. She and Maria managed to drag each bag in, one at a time. Each bag was heavy with sand and now with moisture from the rain.

They piled them against the front door which at least stopped the high tide from coming in. The water was reduced to a trickle. Emma helped, on her hands and knees, to scoop and bucket the water, then to store the buckets outside. No point in simply pouring the water back into the canal.

It was filthy work. Emma took off her good boots and put them high up on the stairs. The hem of the posh trousers was already wet and soaking up more moisture. She rolled them up to her knees.

'We need more buckets,' said Emma, sinking back on her haunches. There was nowhere to put the water. Marco ought to have a proper reserve supply. She would tell him. Buy buckets.

'I will find more, from my friends,' said Maria, belting herself into an old raincoat with a hood. Maria went out into the now heavy and relentless rain, which was slanting diagonally in the sea wind. She was scrounging buckets from her friends. When she returned, she was drenched, but with more buckets slung from each arm.

Emma took one look at the bedraggled Maria and decided that she came first before the flooding of the precious palazzo, which had survived many such disasters for centuries.

'You get dry, Maria,' said Emma, taking the buckets. 'I'll make coffee. Change and put on dry clothes and then sit here, have a drink and get warm.'

They could hear the rain pounding the walls, the roof, the windows. They felt surrounded by water.

'But, signorina …' Maria was white-faced and exhausted. She sank onto a kitchen chair, breathing heavily. She was showing her age. 'All the mud on the floor. I must clean it.'

Emma shook her head. 'Not yet. No arguing. Please get yourself dry first. The signor would not want you to become ill. He relies on you to run his home.'

The uneven floor of the hallway and smaller side rooms still had an inch deep of water when Maria returned, some colour coming back in her cheeks. But they set to, mopping and scooping, any furniture of value already sitting on bricks. The naked statue at the foot of the stairs had a rim of dirty water round her feet. Emma had never seen these smaller rooms before, but they seemed to hold nothing but relics and files, sports gear from ancient years.

It was hard work. Emma was not used to such hard labour. Her back ached and her knees hurt. The trousers were ruined. Maria regained some of her energy, now in dry clothes and fuelled with coffee and sweet cakes. It was Emma who was flagging, wiping sweat off her face. Her make-up had long ago run away.

'No need to cook any supper tonight,' said Emma, sitting back on her heels, exhausted. They could hardly send out for a take-away. 'Open a tin of soup and we'll eat together in the kitchen.'

'Open a tin?' Maria was shocked at the suggestion. 'I do not open tins. I have home-made soup in the freezer. I always make too much and it comes back from the dining room. I never throw it away, put in freezer. I remember too well, as a child, many days of hunger.'

'Sounds perfect,' said Emma. 'And I'll eat in the kitchen with you.'

'Signor would not like that. I will serve you as usual, upstairs.'

'I think you have done quite enough work for today, Maria.

Please,' said Emma. 'It's warmer in your kitchen and I'm really cold.'

Emma looked frozen. Maria waved her upstairs to a hot bath. Soup would be ready in twenty minutes, she said.

The bath was bliss. Emma eased her tired limbs in the geranium-scented water, ducking her head under, letting the water run down her face. She had come to Venice to fix figures, not mop up flood water. But how could Maria have coped on her own? Not very well, that was obvious.

Emma wrapped herself in the biggest bath towel and wished Marco was here with her. He would have dried her so carefully and so lovingly, inch by inch. Maybe they would never have left the steamy bathroom, but lain on the floor, legs entwined, until sleep overtook them.

She shook herself awake. She had almost dozed off in the basket chair. Maria's soup would be ready soon and Emma was hungry. She threw on some warm London fleece and raced downstairs, moving gingerly in the hallway as the tiled floor was slippery. The naked statue still needed a wash. Tomorrow would do.

Maria had laid the kitchen table with mats and napkins, glasses and cutlery. A basket of fresh rolls stood in the middle with a slab of farm butter on a dish. She was serving up the soup in big farm-house bowls.

'That smells delicious,' said Emma, wrinkling her nose.

'Vegetable soup, all fresh vegetables from the market. And local red wine to drink. Not the signor's good wine. This is a bottle that I bought. Drink, signorina. It will warm you.'

What a housekeeper! She did not drink her employer's wine but bought her own. Maria was a star.

The soup was hot, creamy and floating with grated vegetables. There was Parmesan cheese to sprinkle on the top. It warmed them both, their bodies and their spirits. Even the rolls were warm and the butter slid off them. Emma could not waste the melted butter but mopped it up with bread.

Maria talked a lot but Emma did not always understand what she was saying. She was relapsing more into Italian, thinking that Emma understood. Now she was talking about Francesca.

'Francesca was eight years younger than Marco. *Benissimo.*

Bellino. Bello, bello. She got in with a bad lot, boys and girls, drinking, dancing, parties. *Bibita, bibita.'* Maria mimed drinking with her glass. 'The signor, he ver' angry. They had many hot words. But she could, what you say? Curl him round her small finger?'

'Twist him round her little finger.'

'Like she was a little girl again, a *fanciulla.'*

And Marco had loved his sister, Emma knew that from the photographs. He had doted on her. But where was she now? When would someone tell her? She opened her mouth to ask Maria when the phone rang.

Maria took the call on the phone which hung on the kitchen wall. *'Si,* signor.'

There was a spate of rapid Italian. She turned to Emma, her face beaming. 'The call is for you, signorina, in the study.'

Emma walked carefully on the wet floor to Marco's study. It could only be Marco. He was phoning her again. He had not forgotten her. Her heart was racing as she picked up the phone and Maria transferred the call.

'Marco,' she said, breathlessly.

'You have been running?' said the voice she loved so much.

'No, I was downstairs.'

'I like it when a woman comes running.'

'I was downstairs in the kitchen, otherwise I would not have come running.'

'What were you doing in my kitchen?' he asked, bemused.

'I was having supper with Maria.'

She could hear the shock at the other end of the line. 'This is unheard of. My guest does not eat in the kitchen with my housekeeper.' Marco sounded stern and forbidding. 'That is a rule. It is unbroken.'

'And is it an unbroken rule when you allow your palazzo to be flooded and waterlogged because a guest is not allowed to help one elderly housekeeper stop the flood coming in and soaking everything?' Emma rattled on, quite annoyed at his reaction. 'And because both elderly housekeeper and guest were dead tired, wet and exhausted and had no energy left for a dining-room meal?'

'What flood? Tell me.'

So Emma told him, all about the high tide and the heavy rain, about dragging the heavy sandbags into the hall, about borrowing buckets, about endlessly mopping up the mud. She described the tide washing in grey wavelets, the statue with her wet feet, the sandbags.

'I've ruined my trousers. And they were really nice ones that I borrowed.' She hesitated on the word. 'They came from the locked bedroom. They are ruined. Designer label, too.'

There was a long pause as Marco imagined the chaos on the ground floor. 'I will buy you a hundred pairs of trousers with a designer label,' he said. 'What is your size?'

Emma was exasperated. 'I don't want a hundred pairs of trousers. I want you to come home and be where you are supposed to be, running your vineyard and stopping floods and looking after everyone. And you need to buy more buckets before the next flood.'

'I am coming home. I fly tomorrow. I have had enough of this raw fish and rice and saki. I want a good bowl of pasta with rich tomato sauce and plenty of Parmesan. Tell Maria.'

'We had Parmesan on our soup in the kitchen,' said Emma, trying to hide the relief in her voice. 'Are you really coming home?'

'Do you miss me?'

She couldn't tell him, could she? She missed him so much, her bones ached. 'I don't miss you telling me what to do.'

'I miss your sweet lips, *caro*. I cannot wait to kiss you. Please be there to meet me. We shall never be parted again.'

This was one romantic Italian man speaking. That voice spoke to her very soul. He had forgotten she was going home in two weeks' time. She was going home to dreary Brixton. Venice was only a dream. Marco was a knight in armour but he was not real. She had to go back to London, step back on the career ladder, and make a solid future for herself.

'That's wonderful, Marco,' she said, playing the same game. 'Together again. See you very soon, then?'

'*Mia caro*, we will celebrate. We shall have much to talk about. You and I together. Till then, *ciao*.'

When Marco rang off, Emma realized that she had not told him anything about the new discoveries concerning his computer system. Her common sense had gone out of the window, into the relentless rain, into the receding tide, into the canal. But then, nor had he thanked her for mopping up his hall and dragging sand-bags in from nowhere.

Was she beginning to think like an Italian? It was a delightful thought. Being so English was rather dull.

twelve

Enrico drove Emma over the Porte della Liberta to the Marco Polo Airport. It was a two-lane bridge which ran alongside the railway line. It seemed strange to be driving over the Lagoon, all that deep blue water washing beneath them. She had got so used to water travel that land travel seemed almost alien.

She was meeting Professor Gilbert Windsor, the computer expert from the security response company in London. She hoped he knew what he was doing. It was easy enough these days to label yourself an expert at anything. He had a string of qualifications after his name.

'I'm an expert at ruining a perfectly wonderful love affair,' she said to herself. Marco would not wait for ever. She could not forget that hurt and withdrawn expression on his face when she had refused to let him make love to her. He did not brush it off and go find another woman. He looked genuinely hurt, his dark eyes clouded with disappointment.

'I will never force anyone against their will,' he had said. 'I am sorry, Emma … I thought you liked me but I was mistaken.'

'But I do like you,' she had said. 'Perhaps I like you too much.'

It was a futile explanation. He didn't understand. She knew that. She had to make it up to him somehow.

When he returned from Japan, she would do her best to explain and she knew it wouldn't be simple. A man might find it difficult to understand. Yet the fiery Italian was all emotion, brimming with passion, sometimes anger, full of compassion. Marco, of all people, ought to be understanding. But the truth might also turn him against her. He might not want her any more when he knew the whole story.

Marco Polo Airport was a modern three-storey building, with

plenty of parking space. Emma asked Enrico to park somewhere and wait for her outside the exit while she went into the Arrivals lounge on the ground floor. The plane from London had arrived and passengers were being ferried by bus to Immigration while their luggage was unloaded.

Beard and a limp. It ought not to be difficult to identify the professor. She spotted him almost immediately by the grey beard and the limp. He was wearing baggy cord trousers and an old tweed jacket, trilby hat pulled down over his eyes. It came as quite a shock. Emma had got used to seeing Italian men, smartly dressed, at any time of day, any place. Marco was always immaculate. This was a typical English professor, although typical was an unfair description. She had met many well-dressed academics in her time.

'Professor Windsor?' Emma went forward to greet him. 'I'm Emma Chandler from Irving Stone Accountants. It's good of you to come at such short notice.'

'Absolutely no problem at all, young lady,' said the professor in a far from academic voice. 'I always enjoy sorting out other people's problems. So who are you? A secretary?'

This was a common mistake. 'I wish I was a secretary,' she said. 'I would have fewer headaches and more time off. I'm a junior partner in the firm, an accountant.'

'Phew! An accountant? Accountants get younger every day, like policemen.'

'I've a car waiting outside,' she went on. 'Have you collected your luggage?'

He had a rather shabby backpack hunched over his shoulder. He gave it a tug. It was bulging at the seams. 'I always travel light.'

Emma wondered if he was going to stay in the same clothes for all of his stay in Venice. Maybe he had only brought one spare shirt.

'We've booked a hotel for you. It's small but very good. I hope you'll be comfortable.'

Emma was glad now that they had not booked him into one of the big, luxury hotels. They had picked a middle-of-the-road hotel, recommended by Signor Bragora. His relatives always stayed there when visiting Venice. It was in a quiet square but not far from the Grand Canal and the busy bars and cafés.

Enrico had been watching for Emma to appear at the exit doors and brought the car round smartly.

'Some car,' said the professor, admiring the well-polished black limousine. 'Plenty of money around, is there?' He got in, not opening the door for Emma. Enrico went to open it for her, his face expressionless. He had inherited good manners.

Emma noticed that the professor had a laptop with him in a well-worn case. He opened it immediately without asking if she minded.

'I couldn't use it on the plane. Damned nuisance. Thought it was allowed these days.'

'Maybe there was some hitch in their communications system.' Emma had no idea what she was talking about. Marco had used his laptop during their flight in first class.

'Damn it. The battery is low. Have you got a charger in the car?'

'I've no idea,' said Emma faintly.

'I'll ask the driver bloke.' The professor leaned forward to tap Enrico on the shoulder, even though he was driving in heavy traffic. 'Have you got a charger in the car? My battery's nearly flat.'

'No, signor,' said Enrico. 'There will be one in the hotel.'

The professor sat back in the seat. 'Damned nuisance,' he said again. 'I can't stand it when my laptop won't work. It might have a bit of life left in it. I'll give it another try.' He began tapping on keys.

Emma's heart fell. This was not a good start.

'There should be a charger in a fancy car like this, you know. It's all the thing these days.'

There was just enough life left in the battery for a red warning sign to suddenly flash onto the laptop screen. 'What am I being warned about?' the professor muttered to himself, touching keys, but the flashing still continued. She noticed that his hands were flying over the keys, no arthritis or knobbly joints. His nails were badly cut, chewed.

Emma was not interested. She had already had quite enough of the professor and was thankful that it was only a short journey to Venice. Signor Bragora was going to escort him to the hotel as he had made the booking. Emma would be free of the tiresome man soon enough.

'Whose car is this?' he said, looking up at Emma. 'Is it a hired car?'

'No, of course not,' said Emma. 'It belongs to Signor dell'Orto. It's his personal property.' She did not mention the pale-green convertible.

'Well, the damned thing is bugged. I'm getting a warning bug sign coming on. Where the hell is the damned thing?' He began searching around the inside of the car, down the sides of the seats, under the mats, round the seat-belt fixtures. Emma shrank back. She didn't want him searching round her seat belt, touching her, coming anywhere near her. She would panic. She would have to stop the car and get out.

'Are you sure? It seems very unlikely,' Emma began.

'My laptop doesn't lie. It knows when there's something alien in the vicinity. It's not daft. I need a screwdriver. It's probably tucked inside something.'

'Please don't start unscrewing things in the car,' said Emma firmly. 'It's not your car. We'll take it to a garage and have it properly searched if you really think it's bugged.'

'Of course it's definitely bugged. The computer hacking in your office could be linked to this, and if your boss uses his laptop in this car. It's all clever stuff these days. It could be collecting transmitted information, his private information through some sort of link-up.'

Professor Windsor did not seem to know exactly what he was talking about but then neither did Emma. It might be true. The bug might be a link.

It was not an easy drive. Twice, a big 4x4 seemed to crush them against the barriers but Enrico was a good driver and escaped the collisions.

Emma was thankful when the car crossed the bridge and they arrived at the main car park. Signor Bargora was waiting for them with a hired launch at the quayside.

Professor Windsor got out of the car and limped over to the launch.

'Done half the work for you already,' he said. 'That car's bugged.'

'The car needs to be searched at a reliable garage,' said Emma. 'Taken to pieces if necessary.'

'No stone unturned,' said the professor.

'I will arrange it,' said Signor Bragora. Then he turned to Emma.

'Can we give you a lift, Emma?' said Signor Bragora kindly. 'We can go your way and drop you at the palazzo first.'

'No, thank you,' said Emma. She didn't want the professor seeing Marco's elegant palazzo and deciding he would rather stay there with her. 'I've got a return ticket for the vaporetto. I'll see you in the office tomorrow.'

'Goodnight, Emma. See you tomorrow.'

Emma escaped. Enrico would take the black limousine to their regular garage and have it properly searched. It might well be the key to the hacking. If so, the tiresome professor had already earned his considerable fee.

The vaporetto was crowded with tourists. They jostled her. She was already nervous, hoping no one was going to push her into the water.

It was late but there was a light supper waiting for her in the dining room. It was too cold to eat on the balcony. Emma had a few mouthfuls of the soup and some salad so as not to disappoint Maria, changed into some warmer casual clothes and decided that a quick walk along the quayside would blow away the day's cobwebs. She would not venture into the labyrinth of side streets but keep to the open waterfront.

She borrowed an old raincoat that was hanging by the back door and tied a scarf over her hair. She wanted to look local and anonymous.

It was still bright and noisy along the quayside, street lamps reflected in the water, cafés and bars open, plenty of trade. The tourists loved strolling Venice at night and so did the inhabitants. This was the time they came out, well wrapped up, to meet friends for a drink and a chat.

She strolled through Piazza San Marco, passed the Café Florian where she and Marco had sat together, listening to music. It seemed years rather than days ago since that night. So much had happened since then that had changed her life. She felt like a new person, ready to meet any challenges. Except the most important one, her longing to love Marco. That was going nowhere because she could not let it.

She wondered if her new mobile would work in the Piazza. She dialled Marco's private mobile number but it didn't register. She kept getting an unobtainable signal. Perhaps it was interference from the friendly but greedy pigeons who thought she had stopped to feed them and were swooping around her. She didn't want to eat or drink but kept walking through the crowds of tourists. She understood Marco's apprehension. Tourists were taking over Venice.

There was a lot of raucous laughter coming from one of the open-air cafés, seats and tables out in the cool evening air for the hardy. A bunch of young men were clustered round a table that already had a forest of empty beer bottles.

Noisy disco music was coming from inside the café. It was very popular with the younger, lively clientele.

A voice stood out from the noise, almost shouting. Where had she heard that voice before? It rang more than one bell but she could not place it.

'Tell me about your sinking Venice. All water and very wet. Where are the best bars while there's still time?'

Then it hit her. The London accent. The rawness. The lack of rounded vowels. It was Professor Gilbert Windsor. He had obviously abandoned his sedate hotel, decided to sample the nightlife and had joined this crowd of noisy youngsters on the front.

Standing well back in the shadows, Emma tried to spot Gilbert Windsor. But she couldn't see him although she was sure it was his voice.

'Damned charger. Even the hotel hasn't got one with the right connection.' She heard the voice again. She peered into the open. A young man was astride one of the chairs, sitting facing the back, a beer bottle raised to his lips. She recognized the tweed jacket and baggy cords. They were the same. But the beard had gone and so had the hat. His hair was blond, short and spiky with gel. He looked in his late twenties. No walking stick either, as far as she could see. The limp was miraculously cured.

He was giving his admiring new friends a step-by-step account of his recent arrival in Venice. They were listening and drinking, waving over new orders of beer.

'Got my own private launch to go where I like,' he was saying.

'The driver will take me anywhere I say. There's plenty of money around in this enterprise. Wanna come with me tomorrow? This hacking problem can wait a day or two. A few more days won't hurt. I can soon fix it. I'm a pro.'

Oh no, you won't, buster, thought Emma. I'll see you don't take your friends off for a jaunt in Marco's hired launch. This was no grey-haired, bearded professor with a limp. And he shouldn't be talking in public about the hacking. He was a fake, she felt sure. She would check with Irving Stone first thing in the morning. This young man might know a lot about computers but he was certainly not the professional they expected.

'We could find a beach and take a couple of crates of beer,' he went on, importantly. 'Do you know a couple of nice girls?'

Emma retraced her steps and took the badly lit back street that led to the back door of the palazzo. It was unnerving, so many shadows in every doorway. Anyone might be lurking there, waiting to jump out on her. Her mouth went dry with fear. She thought she heard footsteps and quickened her pace.

The back door of the palazzo was about twenty metres ahead. She broke into a run, almost slipping on the wet stones.

Then she heard a young girl giggling and the deeper voice of a youth. It was a courting couple, looking for a dark doorway. There were plenty of those around.

She fumbled for her key, only breathing freely when she had bolted the kitchen door behind her. Maria had gone to bed but there were still plenty of lights on in the downstairs rooms. Emma went round, turning them off and making sure all doors were locked. It was as if she was the mistress of the palazzo. But of course, she was not. She was a paid employee like everyone else.

She turned on the lights to her bedroom and immediately spotted the white envelope on her pillow. And she recognized that bold handwriting. It was Marco's thick-penned script. He did not like a thin nib.

She took the envelope over to the chair by the window. He had never written to her before. It was a special moment. He must have left it with Maria and asked her to give it to Emma sometime as a surprise. And this evening was perfect timing. If only he was here beside her.

She opened it carefully, not wanting to tear the heavy vellum envelope. Inside was a small, tissue-wrapped packet, slim and whispery, tied with ribbon, like one of the children's presents.

She opened out the sheet of vellum.

My angelo, Emma. I am not with you, so many thousand of miles and abandoned without you. You have captured my heart and thrown away the key, and my work is going up the river. Distraught that you are not here, to calm my weariness. Please wear this for me until I am back in Venice and can put it round your neck with my own hands. Till that day. Marco.

His written English was not as good as his spoken.

She unwrapped the tissue paper carefully. There was the finest of gold chains inside, resting on a bed of velvet, with a tiny cluster of creamy pearls hanging from a single strand. It was utterly beautiful and delicate.

She fastened the chain round her neck and settled the cluster of pearls on her throat. It was as if Marco was touching her. She would wear it forever.

'We've lost her again,' the man said angrily in Italian on his mobile. 'We nearly got her then.'

'Are you sure it was her? She looked different.'

'Old raincoat, scarf over her hair. Not her usual posh gear. Don't forget I've seen her before. It was her all right. Better luck next time.'

'Do we really have to do this? She looks rather nice.'

'Maybe she is nice but there are more important things at stake. Euros, for a start. It's what we are being paid for. And we need lots of money, don't we? So stop acting stupid and get on with it.'

Emma was almost asleep when her phone rang. She always kept it beside her bed. She took the call, the earpiece pressed against her ear and against the soft linen pillow.

'Signorina Chandler? Are you all right? It's Commissario Morelli.'

'I'm fine,' she said sleepily. 'Why are you calling me so late?'

'You were followed when you went out this evening. I cannot protect you if you go out alone. Please not to do it.'

'I thought everything was all right now. Nothing has happened. I only went for a short walk. How did you know?'

'After the incident the other night, we put CCTV cameras trained on the front and the back of the palazzo. Marco agreed. We have been following your movements. It is necessary if we are to keep you safe.'

'That is very kind of you, Commissario, to take so much trouble. But I can look after myself. Venice is such a lovely place. Nothing bad could happen to me here.'

'You seem to forget that one young woman has been murdered, wearing your distinctive London raincoat. You were pushed violently into the canal. Someone set fire to Marco's launch. We found traces of petrol splashed over it. You call this nothing bad happening?'

Emma swallowed her guilt. 'I'm really sorry. You are quite right. I must be more careful. I promise. No more going out, unless I have a police escort.'

She heard a faint chuckle. 'There are many of us who would do overtime for that pleasure,' she heard Claudio say. '*Ciao.*' Then he switched off.

thirteen

Emma flew into his arms. It was a rapturous moment after the recent dark days. The gloom and rain of the morning lifted as Marco wrapped his arms round her and held her close. He looked and smelled so good, even after the long flight.

'*Caro*,' he murmured against her hair. 'It has been a long time, such a long way. Have you missed me?'

'Every minute of the day.'

'*Si, molto minuto*, I have thought about you. You are inside my mind. I cannot think straight because of you.'

Emma laughed. 'I don't believe you for a moment, Signor Marco dell'Orto. Italian men do exaggerate so. You wouldn't let anything or anybody get in the way of your business talks.'

Marco pretended to look forlorn but failed completely. 'Perhaps every other minute of the day. Do you believe that?'

He saw that Emma was wearing the gold chain necklace and the cluster of pearls lay glistening on her skin. He wanted to touch them but he dared not.

He did not kiss her. It was a public place and despite the milling crowds, someone would be watching them. Marco's height and dark good looks made him a focal point of interest. People took photos of him on their mobile phones in case he was a film star or a television celebrity.

He guided Emma through the crowds, a hand lightly on her arm. He carried only a briefcase which held his papers and laptop. He noticed she was wearing an elegant navy and red trouser suit with the scarf he had given her tied at her throat.

'Where's your luggage?' Emma asked.

'I don't travel with luggage.'

Of course not. He would buy everything new wherever he

landed. Send out for pyjamas from his hotel, if he wore them. Perhaps order suits and shirts on his laptop to be delivered in advance.

'Was it a long flight?' Emma asked. It was casual conversation to hide her delight at being with him again, to be walking by his side, their thighs almost touching. 'From Venice to Japan?'

'It's not long from Venice to Rome, but the flight from Japan to Rome is twelve hours. Long enough for a sleep but nowhere to put my legs. My legs were not comfortable. They are not made for flying.'

'Tonight you'll be able to sleep in your own bed.'

He raised his dark eyebrows and looked down at her intently. 'I was hoping I would sleep in your bed.'

Emma was thrown by his directness. 'There is a lot I have to tell you,' she said hurriedly. 'About myself. And about things that have happened.'

'Soon, I think you must tell me,' he said. 'I cannot wait forever. You know that, Emma. Where is the car?'

'Waiting outside,' said Emma. 'But that is the first thing I have to tell you. There is a new chauffeur, Bruno. He is a nephew of Signor Bragora but he's only temporary. You may want to employ someone else of your own choice. If you don't like the look of him we can always get the scheduled bus to Venice.'

'Quite a little mine of tourist information, aren't you? So where is my normal chauffeur, Enrico?'

Marco looked down at her, wondering how he could have kept away from her for so long.

'Signor Bragora has suspended him because your car was bugged and he may have been connected. Enrico was very upset. He said he was innocent. The garage searched the car and found several bugs. Did you ever use your laptop in the car?'

'Yes, all the time. I always work in the car. I never waste travel time.'

'It was picking up the signals of your laptop. It might be one of the ways they got into your accounts' computer system. We don't know yet. Somehow they got hold of your password. I hope you use a really complicated one.'

'It is not complicated at all. The password is *Prosecco,* of course.'

Emma was appalled. 'But that is the most obvious password in the world for you to use. You must change it immediately. Upper case and lower case mixed up, numbers, anything that confuses and makes it difficult to trace.'

'You will think up new and confusing password for me. It does not bother me. Any cases that you think.'

'But you shouldn't let anyone know it.'

'I do not understand,' said Marco coldly. 'Where is the computer expert from London? Is the work finished? I expect everything to be running smoothly by now.'

'Oh dear,' said Emma. 'I hoped you weren't going to ask. Professor Gilbert Windsor hasn't turn up yet. He's been delayed. One of his students, a twenty-plus-year-old mischief-maker, somehow got himself invited here using the professor's identity, but on his own passport. But we didn't know this till I checked with Irving this morning. He has no credentials. He was a fake. Commissario Morelli does not think we have grounds to charge him, but he has been warned. We cancelled the hotel booking till the real professor arrives. This may not be till next week now.'

Marco was not pleased. 'So all this happens when I am not here.'

'It's not the end of the world.'

'Did this young man come to the office, see the computer system?'

'Yes, but only for a short time. I was on the phone to London and Irving was busy at a meeting. Then I got onto the systems security company and they confirmed that the professor was unable to come to Venice until next week.'

'I hope you will meet the right person next time. Maybe ask for identity? So it is good that I have arranged for a Japanese expert to fly over, a man who is employed by their top military to make their systems safe. He is arriving tomorrow. I cannot pronounce his name. Ver' Japanese.'

Emma bit her lip. She didn't like being reprimanded by Marco. True, she had gone simply by the beard and the limp. Very inefficient. Her head lost in the clouds.

Marco spotted his limousine waiting outside and recognized the young man standing beside it. 'Ah, yes, that is Bruno. I knew him when he was a boy. That is good. Let's see how he drives.'

Bruno took them the eight-kilometre journey from Marco Polo Airport at a steady speed, over the two-lane Ponte della Libertà which spanned the Lagoon from Venice to the mainland at Mestra. It still felt strange to Emma to be driving along by the side of a train on the much older railroad bridge, even though she had done the journey several times now.

Marco took her hand in the car as they sat in the back seat. He said very little, not knowing if it was still bugged or not. But his thumb stroked the inside of her hand with the lightest touch that made her skin tingle. The night sky had clouded over and it was already dark when they reached the outskirts of Venice and the huge car park where cars had to be left.

'Thank you, Bruno,' said Marco, helping Emma out of the car. 'It's nice to see you again. What are you doing now?'

'I'm studying engineering, signor. This is vacation time. I have some weeks of studying but can drive you anywhere.'

'Of course. Thank you for helping us out.'

'It's a pleasure.'

A hired launch was waiting at the quayside, bobbing up and down, below the steps of the station. Marco looked at it apprehensively.

'Where is my launch? Is my launch also bugged?' he asked angrily as they walked across to it. 'What about my home, the palazzo? Shall it all be searched, the phones, the lights, the curtains?'

'There has been an accident,' Emma faltered. 'Your beautiful launch has gone. Someone poured petrol over it and set fire to it. The fire boats put the blaze out. It is in some dry dock now, for forensics, if you want to see it.'

She heard Marco swear under his breath. Then he controlled himself. 'Was anyone hurt? Was the driver aboard?'

'No one was hurt. There is a full investigation being carried out. The fire service is collecting evidence.'

'It is only a boat. I will buy a new one. If I have any money left. What about the palazzo? Is it also bugged?'

'The palazzo has been checked by the polizia and the telephone officials. Commissario Morelli arranged it. Maria was very indignant, as if they were checking for dust and cobwebs.'

Marco chuckled. 'I can imagine. The proud Maria. Everywhere is spotless despite the grime in the air. So it was only the car? Maybe the launch too?'

'Yes. We don't really know if Enrico is involved.'

'I will speak with him. He is a good chauffeur. Too good to lose. What about you? He has been escorting you, taking care of you?'

'Yes, he has been taking me everywhere.' Emma did not mention the times she had been out on her own. She didn't want to see another flare of Italian temper.

'And your office computer system probably came from the factory already rigged for leaking information. Your American Express card has been used also to buy an air ticket to New York, in your name, apparently. That's being tracked by the fraud squad in Rome.'

Marco swore again in Italian. It was not translatable. Emma did not even try. A man was allowed to swear when his American Express (Gold) was used.

'Maybe the airport CCTV cameras will trace this man travelling in my name. They have cameras everywhere these days. It is like a film set.'

Marco stifled a yawn. Jet lag was catching up on him. No private fortune could immunize a long-distance traveller from jet lag.

'Maria has made us a light supper in the dining room,' said Emma. 'It is too cold for the balcony now; besides it is beginning to rain.'

'And we shall talk?'

'There is a lot to talk about,' she agreed reluctantly.

Marco closed his eyes and sat back as the launch took them along the Grand Canal to the palazzo. He looked weary. Emma said nothing, but let him doze.

Maria was overjoyed to see the signor home and safe. She bustled about as if nothing was prepared. But it was. The long polished table in the dining room was laid with silver and sparkling glasses, napkins of the best linen, placed so that they could sit together at one end.

'And I have made your favourite fish soup, signor. You will need warming up,' said Maria. 'It will be ready to serve in five minutes.'

'I only came home for your fish soup,' said Marco, always so charming to her. 'You could patent the recipe and make a fortune.'

'I already have a fortune,' she said, looking around the hall with pride. She knew how to answer him. 'It is here.' Then she said something in Italian which also pleased him.

Emma sped upstairs to put on something warmer. The palazzo was not warm. It had to be jeans, a fleece and a borrowed cashmere shawl. She also put on a pair of socks, hardly romantic, but practical.

Marco had also showered and changed into black jeans and a black crew-necked jersey, loafers on his feet. He did not seem to feel the cold.

Maria had put a lidded tureen of fish soup on the sideboard for them to serve themselves. There was a salad and a variety of cold meat and fish and a mouth-watering flan of honey, almonds and apricots, with a jug of cream.

Marco served Emma a bowl of the aromatic soup, as if he was a waiter. He served with a flourish.

'It's good to be home,' he said. 'Always I have liked travelling, finding new markets for Prosecco. But now I only want to be here with you.'

Emma almost choked on her first mouthful. The soup was delicious. It was swimming with morsels of fish. Sometime, and that sometime would have to be now, very soon, she would have to remind him of his secret fiancée. But they must eat first. She hoped Marco would be overcome with tiredness and depart to his bed. She wouldn't be going with him.

Neither of them ate very much. It was late and both had had tiring days.

They shared light talk and warm laughter. 'So,' Marco said, breaking into the laughter. 'Now to be serious before I fall asleep. Or will it give me nightmares? Let us take our coffee into the sitting room and find a sofa for two. There are many sofas to choose from.'

Emma did not want the coffee but she took a cup with her. She sat at the far end of the sofa while Marco stretched out his long legs.

'So you are not for dessert?' he said, amused at the distance she had put between them. 'Even wearing the so fetching pink-striped socks?'

He was looking at her socks and grinning. He took her feet into his hands, and stroked them gently.

'The Countess Benedetti called to see me while you were away. She said you had asked her to keep an eye on me,' said Emma, plunging straight in at the deep end.

Marco sipped his coffee, dismissing the remark. 'The woman has a bird's nest for a brain. Did you tell her to go take a deep swim in the canal?'

'No, I didn't know what to say. I didn't know if it was true.'

'You are too trusting, my *povero* Emma. Raquel would say anything to come to my palazzo, to cause trouble between us, to make life difficult for me. Forget it. She is of no worth.'

Emma's voice went down in her throat. 'And she said that you were engaged, secretly engaged, that you had not told anyone. That there would be a big wedding in the spring. In that big white church across the Grand Canal.'

Marco threw back his head with a great laugh. 'Engaged to Raquel? *Dio Mio!* I would rather be hung and thrown into the canal for the fish to feed on. Surely you did not believe her?'

'I didn't know what to believe.'

Marco moved swiftly over the sofa and gathered her into his arms. He burrowed into her eager warmth and kissed her breathlessly. The strength of his hunger fired waves of tenderness in Emma and she cried out softly, to ease the frustration. She wanted him so much. His palm was flat against her stomach but she pushed him away.

'Why, why, my sweet Emma?' he groaned, words in scattered clusters. 'Why do you always says no, reject me? When you know that this is what we both want.' He eased back, giving her space to breathe.

The silence spread and grew into a balloon of stillness. Even the beautiful room had a forlorn, lost look. The air cooled. Emma wanted to disappear.

'You have to tell me,' he went on, his dark eyes pained. 'It is not fair. I have to know. Am I ugly? Do I smell? Why is my touch abhorrent?'

'No, no, no,' Emma rushed in to ease his hurt. 'You aren't ugly! You are the most handsome man on God's earth and you smell as sweet as mountain water. No, no, it's nothing like that.'

'Then what is it? You have to tell me, Emma. *Per favore.*'

Emma shrank back into the past, remembering a wet night in London, the pavements glistening and slippery with rain. Taxis were non-existent. Walking home through the dark was lonely. Memories swam up through the years.

'I had been to a party,' she said, her voice very low. 'But I left early because I was tired and anyway it wasn't my sort of party. A lot of cheap drink and not much food. Very loud rock music. It was making my head ache. But there was an Underground strike so I couldn't get my usual train home. I had to wait for a bus and then it dropped me quite a way from my digs. There were no taxis around.'

'So you began to walk? In the dark?'

'The rain was relentless. I could barely see where I was going though I had an umbrella. Then I bumped into someone because I couldn't see where I was going. Then … then … before I could say I was sorry …'

'He attacked you.' Marco knew instantly. He knew from her voice, from the anguish in her eyes.

Emma nodded slowly. She could not find the words. She began slowly, trembling as the memory came back.

'Yes, he d-dragged me into a doorway. I hit him with my umbrella, broke it. But he was very strong. I could smell the drink and the sweat and he had a kn-knife. He left me there. I was cut and bleeding. My clothes were torn.'

Emma began to cry, quite softly, as if she had no more tears to shed.

Marco muttered in Italian, a string of oaths, hiding his anger with difficulty.

'Somehow I tried to get myself home. I could just about walk. I tried to pull myself together, saying it could have been worse. He could have killed me.'

Emma was shivering but Marco did not touch her. She was moist, pale, frightened again. 'Some passer-by called an ambulance and I was taken to hospital. There were several cuts to my face, my neck and my arms … and my legs. I have many scars.'

Marco felt a long, thin stick of rage grow inside him. He could have killed this man, this stranger.

'The hospital and the police were wonderful but …' Emma could not say much more. The disturbing memories were too vivid. 'The nursing staff were caring and kind but the other women in the ward were cruel and heartless. They thought I was on drugs or something and had been self-harming.'

'Did they ever catch him? The police?'

'No, but I think it was someone from the party. Someone who had been there, drinking, and followed me when I left. It was a gut reaction. I had that feeling it was someone I had been introduced to, some stranger. He was never traced.'

Marco could resist her no longer. His anger embittered the air. He felt the tension in his muscles knotting. He gathered her shivering body into his own, warming her with his closeness, in a sea of sensation, awash with love. The scalding heat of his body fed her with a new emotional ease. She relaxed into his arms, the burden of telling him over. Now he knew that she was shabby goods.

'So this is why you cannot bear a man to touch you. I understand. But the feeling will go in time and I will wait for you,' he said with infinite slowness. 'I will wait for you to recover from this terrible thing, even if it is forever.'

'How can you say that?' Emma trembled. 'How can you know?'

Emma could only hear the rain, beating against the windows. They were in a closed world. She had lived so long without this pleasure, without loving anyone. She did not tell him that the police had been unhelpful, that they thought she had been drinking.

'Because I am no stranger to this bad situation for women. You think sexual violence only happens in London? It happens in Italy, even in Venice. Here in this beautiful city.'

Emma said nothing. She wondered what was coming. This was Marco's story. She curled in his arms, waiting for him to begin. His face was full of emotion as if it was too painful to recall.

'I do not know how to tell you,' he began.

'Begin at the beginning,' she said.

He nodded. 'I will begin at the beginning. In February, before Lent, we have the most extravagant Carnevale of all in Venice, a ten-day festival which means farewell to meat. It is celebrated throughout Veneto. The streets are filled with revellers and party-goers. It is famous. Mostly, today, it is an excuse to wear fancy dress and cover your face with a mask, and parade around the city, drinking and eating. The masks are amazing and the costumes so extravagant.'

'I've seen photographs in magazines,' said Emma quietly.

'Grandfather left most of his fortune to my young sister, Francesca, and the vineyard and plant to me. It was fair. He had made money, saved it. For the Carnevale, Francesca always had the most sumptuous costume made by a dressmaker. That year it was a gold silk brocade dress after a painting of an eighteenth-century Empress of Italy, with a powdered wig and a golden mask of feathers and diamonds. She looked regal and magnificent. She was dark and very beautiful anyway. Francesca, my beautiful sister.'

His voice broke and Emma waited for him to go on. She did not tell him that Maria had told her a little about Francesca. He seemed to recover.

'I also went to the Carnevale, in black, cloaked, as a toreador. There were many toreadors. I meant to take care of Francesca but somehow the time went and I lost sight of her. She did not come home but I was not worried. She could have gone on to a party anywhere in Venice. She had so many friends.'

He took a few sips of his cold coffee. 'But then it became very late and I went out to look for her. She could have tripped in the crowds, was limping home. All I saw at first was the sheen of her golden dress. It looked like a heap of crumpled material. But it was Francesca, in a dark alleyway, bruised and bleeding. Her dress torn, the mask wrenched from her face, the wig thrown into the canal.'

Emma went cold with shock. She could see it all, feel it all again. 'Not more,' she whispered.

'All her jewellery had gone, rings torn from her fingers, an emerald necklace wrenched from her throat. There is more. I have to tell you everything.' Marco's face was dark and grim. 'I got her home with the help of some friends and Maria tended her. A doctor came to see her and gave her medication so that she would rest for a long time while her body and her mind healed.'

A gust of rain splattered the window like gunshot, breaking the silence. It was turning into a very wet night.

'Francesca seemed to recover her spirits slowly, but she was never the same. She took no interest in anything. She barely ate, became as thin as a scarecrow. Her lovely hair fell out. They gave her medication for the sadness. They never caught the man. How could they? Everyone had been wearing masks.'

'Poor Francesca,' said Emma. 'I know how she must have felt. I had to go back to college. I was studying for an accountancy degree. I had no choice.'

'You were stronger than Francesca. She had lived a sheltered life, a rich girl's life. She became secluded, isolated herself.'

'Perhaps she knew her attacker and was afraid.'

'We don't know. She never said. She hardly spoke. Then one day, she disappeared. She took a vaporetto to the station and caught a train to Rome, that much we have traced. We think she went to the airport but we could not discover if she had flown to some other country. I was out of my mind with worry, had detectives searching for her all over Europe.'

Marco was staring into the distance, reliving every moment. 'Then we had a letter from her, postmarked from France. But there was no address, no date, only a handwritten letter on cheap notepaper. Francesca wrote that she had had enough and that she could not bring more shame on the family. That she had a bottle of brandy and many of the doctor's pills that she had saved. That we should not look for her as there was no point and it would be too late. She even joked that it was supermarket brandy, not her beloved Prosecco.'

Emma shuddered, felt more tears brimming in her eyes. What a waste of a lovely young life. 'But surely, she hadn't brought shame on the family?'

'In those days, people were not so tolerant, especially in Italy. Francesca took the only way out she knew.'

'But you would have looked after her, Marco. She could have gone to live at the vineyard, to find peace and quiet. Paola was there to look after her. No one would know about her illness.'

'So we decide now, but it was too late to tell her. We did not know where she was.'

'I can't say how sorry I am,' said Emma. 'How dreadfully sorry for all that you have gone through, for what you have suffered.'

'Now you know why I never let my feelings run away from me. Why sometimes I am cold and distant. I cannot be hurt again.' Then a smile touched his lips, a genuine smile. 'There was a post-script to her letter. Francesca wrote: *Give all my clothes to a special lady who will love them and love you.* And now I have found you. Emma, you are my special lady and I love you. *Ti amo.*'

'And I love you,' said Emma.

Their lips met with a swooning sweetness that held the promise of so much more. The rain stopped and a watery moon peered between wisps of clouds, bringing a little light to a dark evening.

fourteen

Emma was barely awake or washed when she heard the front doorbell ringing. It was such a strident noise, it could be heard all over the house. She heard Maria open the heavy door and voices in the hall. Maria came up the stairs, hurriedly knocking on the bedroom door.

'*Scusi*, signorina. It is the Commissario di Polizia. He wishes to see you. *Urgente.*'

'Me? Can't he speak to Marco?'

'Signor Marco has already gone to the office. He said not to wake you. He said you needed your sleep.'

'Please give the detective some hot coffee and rolls and I will be down as soon as I can.'

'*Si*, signorina.'

Emma threw on some casual clothes. The only warm room in the palazzo was the kitchen and she could hardly talk to Claudio Morelli in the kitchen. No make-up, a quick brush through her hair. It would have to do.

'*Buongiorno*, Commissario,' she said as she went into the sitting room. The detective was standing by the window, drinking coffee as if he was a drowning man. No breakfast probably. He still had that gaunt look. She wondered if he had been ill.

'*Buongiorno*, signorina. *Come sta?*'

'*Buono, grazie.*'

'*C'è stato un incidente,*' he said, then translated. 'There has been an accident.'

Emma caught her breath. Blood drained from her face. 'Not Marco?'

'No, it is not the signor. It is a young man that you know. The student who acted as a professor – what is the word? I do not know it.'

'Impersonated the professor. The so-called computer expert.'

'Yes, that young man. We have found him. It is not good news, signorina. He was found hanging under one of the bridges this morning. *Morto.*'

'Oh, how dreadful. It was a harmless prank, very silly, but he didn't need to kill himself. Perhaps he had no money to get home.'

'I gave him the money to go home by train,' said Claudio Morelli.

'How kind of you.' She was beginning to think that the detective had a soft spot, a kind heart. 'Perhaps he thought he would be in disgrace in his workplace.'

'It was not a suicide. He was bound, hands and feet with wire, then hung over the bridge. If he did not die from the hanging, he would have drowned in the high tide.'

'How awful.' Emma shuddered. 'Do we know who did this?'

'Not yet, signorina. But we are treating it as murder.' He did not add that another murder was not good for the tourist trade. The Vice-Questore had made it clear to Claudio that the case must be solved, quickly and quietly.

'Is there anything that I can do? Write to the professor?'

'I need you to come to the medical room and identify the young man. There is no one else.'

'But I don't even know his name.'

'We have his name from his passport. It was Brad Phillips. He was twenty-five. Ver' young. Ver' stupid. But someone did not like him or perhaps he had discovered something. We shall have to question the people in your office.'

'Of course. Shall I tell them you are coming?'

'No, *grazie*. It is better that my visit is a surprise. Put on a warm coat, signorina. We will take a water taxi.' Claudio could order a police launch but preferred not. He used very little of his allowed expenses, preferring to walk if he had time. He could think while he was walking and often it was quicker.

'I'll ask Maria to bring you some more coffee while I get a coat,' said Emma. 'You look as if you have not had any breakfast.'

'*Grazie*. No *prima colazione*, many times. It is my failure.'

Emma spoke to Maria then hurried upstairs. Maria began

making the hungry detective a panini with a filling of cheese, wrapping it in clean paper.

It was still early and the morning air was chilled, hung with frozen dew. Commuters were already crowding onto the vaporetto. Work often started early. Emma shivered into the coat, another borrowed garment. Francesca did not buy anything really suitable for visiting a morgue. But it was dark and warm with big sleeves, the cashmere scarf wrapped round her head.

'So you thought Venice was always warm?' said Claudio, munching on his panini.

Emma nodded. '*Si*, very hot. It's the Mediterranean.'

'In the summer it is unbearable. The heat rises off the pavements. People faint in the heat, some die. You must drink *molto* water all day.'

'I shall be back in London by then.'

Claudio Morelli looked at her, without saying anything. Then he said: 'Maybe, maybe not.'

'There is no reason for me to stay longer.'

The Questura was an imposing building, bigger than Emma expected. She followed Claudio through the front door. Her bag was put through a monitor. It was cleared of guns or knives.

She followed Claudio down into the basement. It became colder as they reached the rooms of the medico. The young man lay shrouded in a refrigerator. He was slid out by a white-coated attendant. Emma had seen the scenario so many times on television, but never for real.

They took away the face covering. No grey beard, just the blond spiky hair. His face was distorted by the hanging and the drowning, hardly recognizable. Emma could not bear to look. But she had to. He must have a family who needed to be informed.

'Yes, it is the young man who came to Venice pretending to be the professor. I saw him at a café, late at night, without a beard. Then I saw him at the office the next morning.'

'Thank you, signorina. That is enough.'

Claudio escorted her through the building. There were forms to fill in. Emma signed things she did not understand but trusted the detective. He arranged for a poliziotto to escort her to the dell'Orto offices.

'You are not safe,' he said. 'You may be next on their list.'

Emma felt a shiver. '*Grazie*. I will be careful.'

'Careful is not enough. Venice is dangerous for you.'

Marco was not at the office. He had driven to the plant, where there was a problem. This came before the embezzling of his fortune. Top priority.

Emma sat uncomfortably in the office, acutely aware that she was not dressed in an immaculate suit today. But no one seemed to mind or notice. She did not mention the death of Brad Phillips nor Enrico's sudden departure. This was becoming a drama way beyond anything that ever happened in the sober offices of Irving Stone, London. She could not believe that such a sane operation as growing grapes could harbour violent feelings that resulted in the death of two young people.

'You are feeling the cold?' asked Rocco, switching on an electric fire.

Emma had the shivers but it was not merely the temperature. She was still seeing Brad Phillips in the morgue, stiff and cold, his face distorted by death. She hoped he had not slowly drowned. She hoped it had been quick. The post-mortem would reveal how he had died.

Maybe he had discovered something while he was in the office, probing about the system in his amateur way. Or maybe his killers thought he had discovered something. They were not to know that he was an impostor.

Signor Bragora did not look well. The cold was biting into his knees, aggravating his arthritis. Emma saw that he was taking painkillers with his coffee and his hands seemed to tremble as he held the mug. He stayed in the office during the lunch break, not wanting to attempt the steep stairs.

'Perhaps you should go home,' said Emma, gently. 'You should be tucked up somewhere warm and comfortable. Do you live on the mainland?'

'*Si*, I live on the mainland. I cannot afford the rents in Venice.'

'I'll ask Bruno to drive you home.'

'But there is so much work,' he began. He waved his arms over his untidy desk. 'This I must do.'

'It can all wait,' she said firmly. 'You should go home.'

As he left, Rocco said in an aside: 'Time for *il vecchio* to retire.'

But Emma heard him. 'That is for Signor Marco to decide.'

'Of course,' Rocco agreed, backing off.

Was it Rocco, Emma suddenly thought. Did he have ambition beyond his ability? But he was a pleasant young man, hard-working, nothing to suggest that he had a darker side.

She was aware of when Commissario Morelli arrived, for the atmosphere in the office changed. It was charged with alarm. They were not used to the polizia arriving on their doorstep. Even a detective so quiet and unassuming as Claudio Morelli. He spoke in Italian so Emma found it difficult to keep up with him.

'Please be seated,' he said, sitting down himself and taking out a notebook. 'I am only here to ask a few questions about your whereabouts last night. It was a ver' cold night. So perhaps you did not go out? First give me your names and addresses.'

They all looked bemused. They did not understand why they were being questioned, but they volunteered the information without hesitation. Rocco had gone dancing with his girlfriend, Luka had taken supper with his mother and stayed with her talking about family matters. The two girls, who shared a flat, had washed their hair and watched television.

'What about me?' Emma said. 'You have not asked me.'

'I know where you were last night. You met Marco dell'Orto at the airport, had fish soup for supper at the palazzo and stayed in all the evening.'

'Correct, even to the soup.'

'Maria's fish soup is famous.'

'But why do you want to know this?' asked Rocco. 'Have we done something wrong?'

'A young man was found hanging under the lowest arch of the Ponte dei Tre Archi, close to San Giobbe, early this morning. The church of the plague. It was the young man who came to work in this office yesterday morning.'

'You mean the professor?'

'He was not the professor. He was impersonating the professor. He was a fraud.'

Rocco nodded knowingly. 'I knew he knew nothing.'

'*Triste*,' said Emma quickly. 'It is so sad.'

'So what are we to do?' asked Luka.

'Nothing,' said Commissario Morelli, closing his notebook. 'But I may have to ask you more questions. Please do not leave Venice.'

He stood up. 'All of you, please be careful. Take care of Signorina Chandler. We do not want to find her under a bridge.'

That really cheered Emma, but she managed a smile.

'The young man left his laptop behind,' said Luka, going to the back of the office. 'Do you want it? It may hold information.'

'That would be most useful. We have a department that can decipher anything. There may be a clue. *Grazie.*'

Commissario Morelli made his farewells, bowed politely, went down the stairs. He had a car waiting outside, a blue and white polizia sedan. Too cold to walk today. His short hair was no protection and his ears were frozen. He must buy a hat.

Emma still looked shocked. But what could he do? He saw death every day. People were always falling into the canal.

Emma was still combing through the records when Marco returned from the plant. He had not shaved. His chin was dark. He put his arms around her for the staff had long gone home. There was no one to see.

'My little Emma. Why are you still working?'

'I am waiting for you.'

'And so it should be but now we will lock up and take a water taxi back to the palazzo, or would you like to eat out? You have not had much fun. It has been all work and the polizia.'

'You have heard about Brad Phillips, the student who came to Venice instead of the professor? You know what has happened to him?'

'The Commissario phoned me. He told me all that they know. And we agree on one thing. You should not be here. It is too dangerous. You must go back to London, tomorrow. I have booked you a plane. Bruno will take you to the airport.'

'Excuse me,' said Emma, almost exploding with indignation. 'Is no one going to ask me? I don't want to go back to London till my work is finished.'

'You are not safe in Venice, *caro*. Do you think I want to see you go? But it must be done. I do not want to be identifying you on a slab.'

Marco's face was drawn, gaunt.

'But I don't want to leave you. I want to stay here, in Venice. I will be careful.'

'They are unscrupulous people. They have no morals. You will be in the canal with stones in your pocket. No way will I allow this. We will have a life together when this is all over. So I have lost immense income from two years of grapes, but my grapes are still growing. They will be growing for my children and my grandchildren.'

'But I want to be here with you,' said Emma desperately.

'You are going home.'

'I absolutely refuse to go.'

'Then I will put you in a bag and take you to the airport myself.'

Marco's eyes were dark and passionate. He looked as if he would bundle her in a bag that very moment. Emma burst out laughing. It was such a funny thought. They clung to each other, laughing, in the growing darkness till it was time to take a water taxi back to the palazzo. Emma paid. Marco had no loose money.

'Now I am paying your fare,' said Emma.

'It is the way in Venice. The woman always pays.'

'This woman doesn't.'

'This woman need never pay for anything ever again. I will make sure of that,' said Marco, tucking her arm through his. 'It is my promise.'

fifteen

Emma and Marco heard a violent knocking on the front door and Maria went to answer it. The bell was apparently invisible this evening. Then they heard voices in the hallway, rising, one shrill and demanding. Maria was being adamant.

'The signor is not to be disturbed,' she said in Italian.

'I am not a nobody! Take me to him. I demand to see your master.'

Emma moved away from Marco. She recognized the voice and now the sharp heel steps that were coming up the stairs to the first floor. The tall door burst open.

It was the Countess Raquel Benedetti, statuesque and expensively overdressed. She stood in the doorway dramatically, her arms thrown wide open.

'I am flooded,' she howled. 'My palazzo is flooded. I am ruined, everything is ruined. I have nowhere to go.'

Unless the high tide had been worse further along the Grand Canal or the Countess lived in a bungalow-style palazzo, there was no way the damage could be as bad as she was describing. Emma said nothing. For a ruined woman, the Countess still managed to look amazingly sophisticated in a red trouser suit, a full-length mink coat thrown over her shoulders, her boots red leather with golden heels, a Louis Vuitton case at her feet. The colours begged not to be overlooked.

She turned round and dragged in another suitcase. 'I have brought my things. I am staying here, Marco, with you. Find me a room.'

Marco stood up, always courteous and polite. 'I am so sorry to hear of your unfortunate circumstances, Countess. So the flood reached the first floor, did it? How very alarming and distressing for you. Please sit down and I will ask Maria to bring us some fresh coffee.'

'I will stay here tonight,' said Raquel, shrugging off her mink coat. It fell onto the floor in a heap, abandoned. 'Ask Maria to prepare a room for me.'

'I am sorry but you cannot stay here tonight. There is no room and it is not convenient. This is quite a small palazzo, small but beautiful. '

'I will sleep in the English accountant's bedroom. Move her things to the servants' quarters where she belongs. New linen sheets, of course. Everything new. Make sure the room is disinfected. I am allergic to anything cheap.'

Emma bit on her tongue. She would not respond to this rudeness with her own brand of sarcasm. It was up to Marco to deal with her.

'That is not possible,' said Marco coldly. 'Miss Chandler is far too exhausted from her day's work to be moved anywhere, and she is certainly not a servant. She is a valued and efficient member of my staff. Please remember that or I shall have to ask you to leave.'

He said nothing about Emma returning to London. He said nothing about his embezzled fortune. The Countess was a small irritation compared to these problems.

The Countess began to cry, her eyes filled with tears, but she was being careful not to smudge her heavy black mascara. She took out a lace handkerchief and began to dab at her eyes.

'Marco, Marco, how can you speak to me so, after all we have been to each other? All these many years of caring for each other. We have been so close, so intimate, such amazing lovers. Do you not remember all our times, all those intimate times together?'

Marco's face went even darker and colder. It was as if glass formed over his face. If icicles could have appeared, they would have. His eyes glinted with ice.

'There have been no such times together, no intimacy, never lovers. It is all in your imagination, Raquel. What intimate moments? Only in your imagination. Perhaps you should see a doctor? You are obviously a very sick woman. You need medication. It is a mental problem.'

Raquel broke into fresh howls and hurled herself across the sofa, spilling Marco's coffee. The brown liquid dripped over the sofa and onto the white carpet in a pool. It spread like dark blood.

Emma swiftly picked up the cup and saucer before there was more damage. She put them on a side table and sat on another sofa, well away from the drama and out of Raquel's reach.

'Oh, Marco, *un grand'uomo*, how could you speak to me so?' Raquel went on, her voice at a dramatic pitch. 'I am distraught. You would not be so unkind and act this way if that little English miss was not sitting here like a rabbit. We would be together, in a loving embrace, celebrating our united love.'

Emma had never heard herself described as a rabbit before. It was a new one.

'This is ridiculous,' Marco said. 'I am asking you to leave now. You are making a fool of yourself.' He was lapsing into Italian so Emma did not understand all that he said.

Ye gods, thought Emma, it was like something out of an operetta, an amateur production.

Raquel made to throw herself into his arms, but Marco was faster than she and he stood up abruptly. He went over to the other side of the room, to find his jacket. He took out his mobile phone and turned away. He began speaking rapidly in Italian. He nodded several times. *'Prendo questa. Grazie, grazie.'*

He switched off, a polite but icy smile on his face. 'I have arranged for you to have a deluxe room at the Hotel Gritti Palace. Only the best for you, of course, Countess. You will be very comfortable. I have arranged for the account to be sent to me so you will not be inconvenienced. You may stay there until your palazzo is dry and redecorated.'

He emphasized the last three words as if to make sure she did not think she could stay there forever. The five-star Hotel Gritti-Pisani Palace was one of the three most expensive hotels in Venice. Emma had seen it from the outside. It was on the final stretch of the Grand Canal, a two-storey historic fifteenth-century palazzo of pink and white marble with a long canopied terrace and waterfront for launches and gondolas.

'I have also arranged for a water taxi to take you there. Now you will be able to sleep dry and warm, something which your bones will appreciate, as we all appreciate warmth and comfort as we grow older.'

Emma thought Raquel's face would crack. She would not admit to any age. She was ageless. The tears dried immediately but she knew when she was beaten. Besides, the Hotel Gritti-Pisani had many other attractions. It was where the rich and famous stayed. Ernest Hemingway had stayed there and so had John Ruskin. She might meet someone richer and more gullible than Marco dell'Orto. A new and available millionaire, waiting to be snared. It might be the open door to a new life. She was always optimistic.

'Since it is obvious that I am not wanted in this little love nest, I will leave you,' she said smoothly. 'Please send your servant for my suitcases.'

'Maria does not carry cases,' said Marco. 'The driver will carry them down for you when he arrives. He will be here immediately.' He did not point out that she had managed to carry them up by herself.

Raquel swept out of the room, trailing her mink coat like a Hollywood star.

She did not look at Marco. She did not want to see the expression on his face.

'This is not the end,' she flung at Emma. 'You will not snatch this man from me. He is mine. He has always been mine.'

Marco waited a few moments, listening to her footsteps retreating downstairs on the marble, and then let out a sigh of relief.

'Are you all right?' he asked, coming over to Emma.

'I'm fine,' said Emma.

'I thought she might turn on you, but she had more sense.'

'She took it out on your sofa.'

'I shall have to buy a new one,' he said. 'And a new carpet.'

'Maria and I will get the stain out of the carpet,' said Emma. 'Then you can stand the new sofa over the spot if we are not a hundred per cent successful.'

Marco laughed and linked his arms loosely round her body. 'Ah, says my thrifty little accountant. She's always looking after my money. And always talking in percentages.'

'You've been quite generous enough, paying for the Countess at that expensive hotel. If you have any money left to meet the bill.'

Marco laughed again. 'I was not that generous, *caro*. I did not book her into a Heritage Suite. It is well worth a few thousand euros to get rid of the woman. A *buon prezzo* at the price. She will soon find herself another millionaire. I will take you there one day, to the Gritti Palazzo, to eat a fine meal, the two of us alone. The restaurant is perfection. Or if it is sunny, we could eat on the terrace. You would like that?'

'You are still a very generous man.'

'And to you, I will be even more generous. I will give you my heart, my soul, my body. Everything I own will be yours, yours and mine together. We will share my wealth and my life.'

Emma fingered the gold chain that lay around her neck. 'But I have nothing to give you. I have only a small flat in Brixton and even that has a horrendous mortgage.'

'You will give me yourself, when you are ready. And your love. That is all that I want. You and your love.'

She moved against him in almost total surrender. She was lost in her need for him. It was a tide of emotion that refused to be stemmed, like a dark Venetian flood surging at the door. She knew that life with Marco would be unlike anything she had ever dreamed.

Their love would be a pleasure too intense to be denied. She could feel his heart hammering against her and knew that he wanted her too. It was almost too intoxicating to bear. She slid her fingers up his arms with butterfly probing. She longed to give him everything possible, but there was still that frightening reserve in her.

'Soon,' she promised. 'It will be very soon.'

'I will wait.'

Emma left him. He was sending her back to London the following morning. London was so cold and bleak at this time of year. She did not know how she would survive the separation.

Marco worked late in his study, anything to take his mind off the coming separation.

The house was asleep. His sweet Emma was asleep. One day, soon, she would learn to trust him and invite him to her bed. It would be worth waiting for.

He heard a noise. Someone was outside. At this time of night? He sensed it even though no one had knocked on the great door or rung the bell. He went to open the door carefully, an old sword in his hand.

But something hit him straight in the face. A heavy piece of masonry. He did not know that it was a fallen piece from the Santa Maria Gloriosa dei Frari. The first church that was built by Franciscan friars in 1250. Then the larger building which was completed in the mid-fifteenth century. Titian's spectacular masterpieces adorned the walls, Canova's tomb was planned as a marble pyramid. But this piece of masonry came from the restoration work.

Marco stood in the hallway, blood pouring from the wound in his head. He managed to slam the door shut before staggering into the kitchen. He grabbed a kitchen towel to staunch the bleeding, blood dripping between his fingers.

Maria's phone was in its usual place, on the wall. Marco took down the receiver and dialled the emergency number.

'Polizia. Ferito gravemente. Qualcosa e successo. Fretta. Un'ambulanza.'

He dared not speak loudly. He did not want to wake the whole house. Emma must not know of this incident. She might not come back. And that would shatter his heart.

sixteen

London was like an alien city. Emma kept looking for water taxis and vaporetti and all she saw were red, double-decker buses trundling along and black cabs. The streets were as crowded as Venice but not as good-natured. People shoved and pushed without a word of apology. She began to think she was invisible as she was again forced to walk in the gutter or was bashed by a lumpy backpack.

The winter weather was as cold and damp, but it did not have that sharpness of a Venetian winter. It was depressing and bleak, like someone dying, all alone and on a trolley, forgotten in a corridor in A&E.

Emma arrived early at the Irving Stone offices. She was dressed warmly, a big winter coat over the navy and red trouser suit, her head wrapped in a red pashmina. Her little flat in Brixton had looked lost and forlorn when she first arrived, but she had soon warmed it up with late-night shopping at a supermarket: fruit and flowers and a bottle of red. She had slept well.

Marco had not seen her off from Venice. He had gone to work early, Maria said. No other explanation. Bruno had driven her to the airport. She could not find out what had happened to Enrico.

'Enrico is, what you say, hung up,' said Bruno.

'You mean suspended?'

'Still being paid but not working.'

'I understand. I'm sure it will be sorted out. I cannot believe that he is to blame in any way.'

'*Grazie*, signorina. He will be pleased to know that.'

Irving Stone wanted to see her straightaway. He took in the tailored navy and red trouser suit, her hair combed back into a chignon, the boots. She had gained a certain sophistication.

'So, Emma, why are you back in London? Have you solved the mystery of the missing millions?'

He looked suave, so cosy and safe in his office. Even his hair parting had been devised on a drawing board. He did not offer a coffee. Italians immediately offered coffee. They were born with hospitality fizzing in their blood.

'No, I haven't solved it but I have tracked the source. I have returned to London because there have been two attempts on my life and Signor dell'Orto did not think I was safe in Venice.'

'What nonsense,' said Irving. 'Two attempts on your life. Why ever? What an exaggeration. You are of no use to anyone.'

Emma bristled. No use to anyone? 'One young woman, Pia, was drowned, wearing my raincoat.'

'So, she had your raincoat. What does that prove?'

'She was hit on the head with an iron bar.'

'This does not mean that she had anything to do with the dell'Orto fortune embezzlement. She could know nothing about computers.'

'But I do,' said Emma, feeling she was banging her head against a brick wall. 'They thought she was me.'

'I don't believe it. You have been reading too many books. Too much television. All those crime programmes.'

'Then someone tried to push me into the canal.'

'That is unfortunate, of course, but it was probably an accident. It is very slippery everywhere in Venice, I understand. All that water washing about.'

Emma could see she was getting nowhere with Irving Stone. 'I think I've tracked the source of the initial hacking back to the firm who supplied the computer set-up. Would you like me to write up a report?'

'That would be very useful, thank you, Emma. Venice obviously suits you. Have you been well wined and dined? You are looking amazingly well, very Venetian if that is the word.' He did not seem pleased or impressed.

'Thank you, Irving.'

He was already turning his attention to another file. Emma felt dismissed. She made her way to the office kettle jug and switched it on. The jar of instant coffee was stale. Her desk, by a window, was covered in unopened mail and dust. There was an empty sandwich package on her desk. Someone had been eating at her desk. Colleagues greeted her as if she had never been away, some with warm greetings. They had not particularly missed her.

Rain was sleeting down her window, so no different from Venice. But Mediterranean rain had a different consistency from Atlantic rain. It was less depressing, less destructive and obliterating. London rain was debilitating, like cold fingers of death.

Her computer was on the blink so Emma wrote her report in long-hand on a lined pad. It felt almost archaic. It would have to be typed up later but at least she was getting it down while everything was still fresh in her mind. She wrote a step-by-step logic of her recent discoveries.

It had not registered to her before that it was almost Christmas. She would be alone again. The younger staff were planning a Christmas meal out. Their numbers were too small for a party. Emma put her name down, slightly amused that the booking was for a well-known Italian restaurant. At least she could pretend that Marco was sitting next to her, translating the menu.

'Es ver' good,' he would have whispered. 'You order.'

'Es ver' 'ot?' she would whisper back, mimicking his accent. Then he would start laughing at her and they would eat whatever was put in front of them, eyes only for each other. If only he could be with her.

When it was time to close the office, Emma discovered that there was a wildcat Underground strike on. They chose their time, she thought. The streets were crowded with elbow-to-elbow people lining up for buses. It would be a very long wait till she boarded a bus going as far as Brixton. She decided to start walking, with the hope that she could get on a bus further along the route, when the vehicle might have emptied out.

She was taking a short cut down a residential street of old houses, when the name registered and she realized she was near where Professor Gilbert lived. It was a tall, four-storey town house with an imposing flight of steps going up to the front door and a dull copper push bell. It would be polite to make a social call. When she heard the dull bell echoing through the house, the place sounded empty.

But then she heard footsteps coming down and eventually, after what seemed ages, the door opened. An elderly gentleman with a grey beard peered into the darkness.

'Sorry to keep you waiting,' he said, slightly out of breath. 'It's such a damned long way down.'

'Hello, Professor Gilbert. So you have got a beard,' said Emma, smiling. 'Have you also got a limp?'

'Only when I want to impress people,' he said. 'And who are you, young lady, standing on my doorstep? I hope you're not one of those damned carol singers.'

'Not a carol in sight,' said Emma. 'I'm Emma Chandler from Irving Stone Partners. I was going to meet you in Venice.'

The professor immediately thawed, became all bustling hospitality. Perhaps he did not get many young lady visitors. It was a narrow hallway with an umbrella stand and some coat hooks, and ahead of her Emma saw narrow stairs rising up to nowhere. It was dark and not well lit.

'These old town houses have only two rooms on each floor,' he said. 'So my sitting room is on the first floor and my study on the second floor. Still, I suppose it keeps me fit. Can you manage these stairs? Hold onto the banister. I'll put on the lights.'

Emma followed the professor up the stairs. At least his house was warm and she was glad to shed her coat and scarf when they reached the first floor. The two rooms had been knocked into one, so it was a good-sized room with windows at either end with London views. The bachelor professor had filled the room with floor-to-ceiling books and pictures and deep, well-worn and comfy armchairs.

'I have heard the sad news about Brad,' said the professor, going straight to the point. 'If that's what you've come to tell me. Signor dell'Orto telephoned me. It's very sad but so like that boy. An excellent student and one day he would have been a brilliant computer expert.'

'But how did he know about your travel arrangements to Venice?'

'He had a key to this house so he could let himself in. I let him come and go as he pleased. Those damned stairs. And as you can see, I am very untidy. I probably left the emailed documents on my desk and he printed out the air ticket. I suppose he thought it was a lark to impersonate me.'

'It was not a good impersonation,' said Emma, not letting on that she had seen Brad drinking beer at the café. 'He was not so distinguished.'

The professor grinned. 'I have been perfecting the distinguished look for years. But the poor young man was murdered, hung from a bridge? That doesn't seem possible and for no reason. Why?'

'The hacking of Marco's computer system is part of cyber-criminal activity. They have siphoned off the income from his vineyards for the last two years. His bank accounts have been emptied.'

The professor nodded. 'So maybe Brad found out something that would lead to them. These hackers modify computer hardware to accomplish a target outside the computer's original purpose; in this case, the flow of deposited funds. They find flaws in the computer's system that they can violate.'

'The polizia have Brad's laptop,' said Emma. 'There might be something on it. We'll get it back so that you can look at it.'

'Good. These black-hat hackers destroy data or make the network unusable. They open ports that do respond and allow access where they can do their unscrupulous work. It's simply stealing. They channel money into their own accounts.'

'It's a foreign language. All beyond me,' said Emma helplessly. 'I'm a simple accountant.'

'We have our different strengths. I cannot even add up my weekly shopping bill.'

'But how did it all start?'

'Information gathering helps them get access to the system. It's called social engineering. Did the office call in people because the system was slow or kept breaking down?'

'Yes, they did. They had a lot of trouble with a new system.'

'That's when it began. But don't worry. When I come to Venice, I will set a honeypot.' Seeing Emma's bemused expression, he went on: 'A honeypot is a trap set by computer security personnel. We'll catch them. We'll find out who set this up and where the money has gone.'

'That sounds great, thank you. I must go,' said Emma. 'Thank you for your time, professor. I'll see myself out.'

The professor opened a cupboard door in the sitting room. It was equipped with coffee-making equipment, an electric kettle, mugs, coffee. It saved him going down to the kitchen. 'Would you like some coffee? You look cold. I make excellent coffee.'

'Yes, that would be nice. Thank you,' said Emma, suddenly feeling very much at home in the professor's ramshackle house. 'I would love some coffee. You are very well organized.'

'It's those damned stairs,' he said again. 'It's a long trek to the kitchen.'

An hour later, Emma felt as if she had known the professor for years. He insisted that he rang for a taxi to take her the rest of the way home.

'Brixton is a jungle,' he said. 'A young lady is not safe on the streets.'

'But that's only parts of Brixton. Some of it is very pleasant. I was not safe in Venice.' He had been appalled when she had told him about the death of the young woman wearing her raincoat, and then when someone tried to push her into the water of the Lagoon.

'Danger is everywhere,' said the professor. 'Even among beauty. Venice is the most beautiful city in the world. I look forward to seeing it again.'

'So do I,' said Emma, suppressing a sigh.

'And seeing again perhaps this wine-growing Signor Marco? He asked me to take care of you but I did not know how because I didn't know you. But I am glad that I know you now.'

'Marco is an amazing man,' said Emma, unable to stop the words spilling out of her mouth. She did not mention that he was also handsome and sexy. 'Hard-working, kind, caring. And he is lonely. The man at the top is often lonely.'

She remembered that unforgettable day at the vineyards, giving gifts to all the excited children, and the painting he had given her. She had hung it in her small sitting room, where it reminded her so vividly of Venice.

'I know,' said the professor. 'The man at the top only has a few friends. What are you doing for Christmas, Emma? This is almost the festive season. Would you like to have Christmas lunch with me? Not exactly home cooking but all the trimmings, I promise you. Do you play Scrabble?'

'My favourite game if I am allowed to use a dictionary.'

'What a sensible woman.'

seventeen

It turned into an enjoyable Christmas after all, especially for Emma. Marco phoned early in the morning to wish her a happy *Natale*, full of remorse that they were not together. His voice warmed her heart.

'This will never happen again,' he promised. 'Next year everything will be perfect. We will be together.'

'I am being treated to a slap-up Christmas lunch by an elderly admirer,' said Emma wickedly.

Marco groaned. 'They are the worst, the elderly admirers. They believe it is their last chance.'

'The professor is a perfect gentleman. It's our professor, the computer expert, who is coming to Venice. He was on his own for Christmas and so was I, so instead of watching old films on the television, we decided to enjoy a meal together and then play chess or Scrabble.'

'That sounds even worse,' said Marco, only pretending to groan this time. 'Chess is a wicked game. Mind he does not take your queen or your king.'

Emma nearly said *but you are my king* but thought it was over the top, even for an Italian.

'Are you going to your farmhouse and vineyard?' she asked instead.

'Yes, ver' soon. Paola is preparing a huge meal, enough for many giants. She is asking everybody around to eat with us. We shall drink much Prosecco and be ver' merry, but I shall only be thinking of you.'

'And I shall be thinking of you.' And Emma meant it. She would not be able to get Marco out of her mind.

*

The professor had said not to bring anything but Emma could not arrive at his house empty-handed. She had a bottle of good claret and a box of Belgian chocolates. She had discovered that the professor had a sweet tooth. His kitchen bin was full of chocolate wrappers.

The bank-holiday bus service was down to a minimum so she walked part of the way. She wore a red velvet skirt, black jersey and boots, a white coat and red and white knitted bobble hat. Very Christmassy.

'Happy Christmas, my dear,' the professor said, opening the door. 'You look like a Christmas parcel. Where is your label? Or are you reserved for the kind and caring Marco?'

'He might like to think so, but I'm a single, independent woman and intend to stay that way.'

'Quite right, too. The days of goods and chattels are gone. Come along in, out of the cold. You don't mind eating in the kitchen, do you? My dining room has no furniture. I use it for storing equipment too heavy to take upstairs.'

He had laid the big kitchen table with a red tablecloth and there were red candles and sprigs of holly. He had made it look very festive. And Emma could smell good cooking.

'It's all from M&S,' he confessed. 'I'm a poor cook. But they know how to do it properly, all the trimmings. All I have had to do is light the gas.'

Emma took off her coat and hung it over the banisters.

'Would you like me to see how it's all coming along?'

'Would you, Emma? And I'll open this lovely bottle of claret that you have brought and let it breathe.'

As the professor had promised, there were all the trimmings. A boned and rolled turkey was cooking to perfection, the skin golden and crispy. He had followed the directions. Ready-roast potatoes were about to go in the oven, with Brussels sprouts, carrots and courgettes. He had defrosted the chestnut and sage stuffing. Even the gravy was ready to heat and serve. She only had to open the carton.

'This all looks wonderful,' she said. 'I would probably have had a turkey sandwich and a bowl of soup.'

He poured out the claret into beautiful glasses which did not match. She noticed that the plates did not match either and the cutlery was a mixture of silver. He was a typical academic. His mind on higher things.

'We shall not mention the lost Prosecco fortune while we are eating. It is too depressing for Christmas. But we will drink a toast to Signor Marco and his grapes as I think you would like that.'

'To Marco and his grapes,' said Emma, raising her glass.

'May his harvest be a good one.'

The professor might not know how to cook but he knew how to carve. The meal, thanks to a team of professional chefs in some vast hygienic kitchen somewhere, was perfect. Emma cooked the Christmas pudding in the microwave and heated the brandy sauce.

They had their coffee upstairs in the sitting room. The professor made cups of good coffee from his practical cupboard store. Emma was all for not having to carry anything up the steep stairs. The walls of the stairway were covered in pictures, mostly political cartoons and framed posters. She wondered how the professor had ever managed to fix them on the walls.

He had bought her a small present. It was a CD of Delius. She was very touched that he had bothered. She had bought him a book, *The History of Chess,* and he too was moved by her thoughtfulness.

They were both pleased, not saying too much.

The deep armchair opposite him had housed a thousand students over the years but Professor Gilbert thought he had never seen anyone as pretty as Emma sitting in it. She looked relaxed and happy, the tenseness had gone from her face. When he had first met her, she was still remembering the stress of Venice.

'In the New Year, I shall be visiting Signor dell'Orto's office,' he began. 'Brad's laptop was a maze of personal stuff but he had stumbled on something in his short time in Venice. It was a jumbled password that spelt out *Plutolatry.* It is a very unusual word and means being besotted with the thought of wealth.'

Emma shook her head. 'I've never heard of it.'

'It is hardly in everyday use. However, it put me on a trail of malpractice and I need to see how far it has spread. I could do most of it from my computers in my study, but I need to be on the spot to actually rid the signor of the infestation and install a tracking device.'

'I want to come with you,' said Emma instantly.

'I was hoping you would say that. It would make my work much easier if I had your assistance. Even if it was only to reassure everyone that I mean well and that they are not about to lose their jobs.'

'I was employed by Marco to work there for a month and I didn't complete the month. And the main thing now is to find the brains behind this embezzlement of Marco's accounts. It didn't happen just by itself.'

'Exactly, there has to be someone who set it up. Do you remember, years ago, an American bank official siphoned off millions of dollars, just from his desk computer?'

'Before my time,' said Emma.

The professor sighed heavily. 'I forget how young you are, my dear. Now let's get out the Scrabble board and see who gets the best score. Far more important. I have been looking up those useful printer's words.'

Emma did not stay late. The professor was planning to get back to his beloved computers in his study. He could not bear to leave them for long. She had to admire his relentless pursuit of knowledge. She had ordered a taxi to take her home. No more buses in the dark, lumbering through the streets of Brixton.

It had been a good Christmas Day after all. Now that there was the prospect of returning to Venice with the professor in the New Year, it was even better.

Venice was still shrouded in a grey fog. The weather all over Europe was dismal and Italy had not escaped it. Emma looked out of the cabin window as they began losing height over Marco Polo Airport. She heard the landing wheels come down with their usual noisy mechanism. No first-class seat this time. They were travelling economy. Professor Windsor had slept most of the flight.

Irving Stone had not been too pleased that Emma was returning to Venice to finish out her contract.

'But you have done all you can, Emma,' he said. 'There is nothing more for you there. Besides, we need you here.'

'Marco dell'Orto is one of your most important clients. You can't afford to lose him. He wants to see this business brought to a successful conclusion and the culprit caught and tried in court. He may never recover his money but at least he'll know that justice has been done.'

'And you think you can achieve this?' Irving looked at her scathingly. 'You are an accountant, Emma, not a detective. May I remind you that you are a junior accountant and have a long way to go yet. Your loyalty is to the company that employs you, not to some handsome Italian.'

Emma tried not to bristle. It was such an uncomfortable word. 'If you say so, sir,' she said, leaving the room.

She said nothing to Marco or the professor but it seemed that telephone wires began buzzing with a passionate Italian one end and an irate middle-aged senior accountant the other. Emma was told that she could return to Venice but that the time would be deducted from her annual holiday leave.

Emma was not going to argue. Any time with Marco was definitely a holiday.

Marco was waiting impatiently at the airport. Emma immediately saw the raw scar on his forehead and the fading bruise. She stood shocked.

'You're hurt,' she said. 'What happened? Have you been attacked?'

'Emma, *caro*. Professor Gilbert Windsor. *Come sta?* I am delighted to see you both. At last, soon, this distasteful business will be over. Do not worry, my Emma. I had an argument with a piece of masonry. It was a piece from one of our oldest churches, the Santa Maria Gloriosa dei Frari, or as we simply call it, *Frati*, the brothers.'

'Did you walk into the brothers or did they walk into you?' asked the professor.

'It walked into me. Sadly, the building cannot afford to lose even a small piece of its history.'

'Does Commissario Morelli know? Did you tell him?'

'*Si.* And the piece of masonry is now in custody at the Questura, till it is returned to its rightful home. They are doing tests on it but I doubt if they will find anything except my skin and blood. But enough of this. I have my car waiting and a new launch, so no more standing in this crowded place.'

Enrico was waiting outside Arrivals with the black limousine. Emma was glad to see him.

'Do you have your job back?' she asked as he loaded her case into the boot.

'*Sì*, signorina. I was not to blame for the bugging of the car. It was a new mechanic at the garage but he is saying nothing. He will not talk. I have been cleared and Bruno has gone back to his studies.'

'I'm pleased to hear that,' she said.

The professor chose to sit beside Enrico in the front so that he had a good view of the bridge, leaving Marco and Emma the privacy of the back seat. They were overwhelmed by their delight at seeing each other again. Marco held her hand, knowing that any further intimacy would embarrass Emma. They smiled and talked, Marco forgetting half of the time that Emma's Italian was limited.

He would not tell her how he got hit by a lump of masonry. Emma knew she would get the full story from Maria. She didn't believe it had been an accident. It was part of this hacking, another warning to leave it alone.

'We are going first to the office,' said Marco. 'Professor Windsor emailed that he wanted to start work immediately. No time to waste. Do you mind?'

'No, I agree,' said Emma.

'Did you win the game of Scrabble?'

Emma smiled that he remembered. 'It was a draw.'

'We have a board at the farmhouse. I will teach you to play in Italian. I will let you use a dictionary as *non parlare* Italian.'

'I'm learning,' said Emma.

She laughed. It was all part of that heady dream that she could not believe would ever come true. Marco would tire of her once this hacking mystery was solved. He would move on to some glamorous and svelte woman from the Italian aristocracy, go back to his crazy crowded routine of work, parties, receptions and holidays at his villa at Lake Garda. And she would return to Brixton. Maybe she would get a cat. A cat would be company during lonely evenings. But it wouldn't be fair on the cat. No garden.

They were driving over the Ponte della Liberta, in a steady stream of traffic, when there was a violent thump against the rear of the limousine. Emma was thrown against Marco. He stared out of the back window. There was a black saloon close behind them.

'Imbecile. He's driving too fast. He cannot pass us.'

But there was another sharp thud and crunch as the car behind drove into the boot of the limousine. Enrico held his course. If he swerved, they might go over the bridge and into the lagoon.

Marco said something rapidly to Enrico. Emma could only guess what it was. Enrico spotted an opening and put his foot down, the faster car thundering past a dozen furious drivers, all shouting at him, till he found a safer niche between two laden white vans.

'This has happened before,' said Emma, letting out her breath slowly. 'Another car hit us as we travelled over this bridge.'

'He was trying to ram us,' said Marco. 'Do you want to go home, professor? This welcome is not kind. Not the Venetian way.'

'Certainly not,' said the professor. 'I want to find out why someone is so anxious to get rid of me. This is like a James Bond film, maybe, although I have never seen one.'

'Are you all right, Emma?' Marco asked, gently moving strands of hair from her forehead. 'You should not have come. It is not safe.'

'I want to be here, with you,' she said quietly. 'No way am I leaving you now. The professor will get to the route and root of the malpractice and Commissario Morelli will charge the malefactor. He will throw the book at him. You may even get some of your money back.'

Marco looked bemused by Emma's use of the same word twice but did not question it. He was suddenly very tired. He wrapped his arms around Emma and held her close.

'I do not care about the money,' he said. 'I only care about you. I would live in a turret with you.'

'A garret,' said Emma.

eighteen

The professor was adamant about staying on in the office and working into the night. All the staff had drifted off home. They had lives to live. He wanted to set this honeypot, a trap to track the malpractice to its source.

'Don't worry about me,' he said. 'I can sleep anywhere. I can put my head on a desk and be sound asleep in moments. This needs to be done while the violators have been lulled into a sense of security. They think that no one can trace how they moved the funds.'

But Marco would not let it rest at that. He gave the professor a mobile. It was preset to ring Enrico.

'Ring this number and Enrico will come and take you to your hotel. A room is booked for you. Turn up at any time. There is always someone on the reception desk. It is a small hotel but extremely good. One of Venice's best-kept secrets.'

'I could stay,' Emma offered. 'Make coffee, be useful.'

The professor looked up from the computer. He had made pages of calculations. He was in a different world.

'Thank you, Emma,' he said. 'But I think at this stage that I work better alone. I have to analyze the target, looking for vulnerabilities.'

'*Grazie mille*,' said Marco. 'Let's leave the professor to his scanning tools.'

Emma made sure there was plenty of coffee and some chocolate pasticceria. She knew he would not be able to resist the chocolate cakes.

The launch was waiting for them at the quayside. Emma wondered where Marco found the money to buy a new one. She knew he was broke.

'It is not mine,' he said, as he helped her climb aboard. 'I have borrowed it from a good friend who heard of the fire on my launch. He is really rich. He has several launches.'

'But who would need several launches?' said Emma, laughing, so pleased to be with Marco with the prospect of an evening ahead.

Marco shook his head in mock disbelief. 'It is someone who has several wives. A launch for each wife.'

The launch reversed smoothly from the quayside, turned in mid-canal and began a steady passage along the Grand Canal. The driver was careful not to create a wake which would rock the smaller boats.

'This is a very good driver,' said Emma.

'I think I am offering him a job,' said Marco. 'When I get my own launch.'

As they went past the beautiful and elegant palazzos, still standing after hundreds of years on wooden piles, Emma felt sad that cyber-criminals had invaded this fine city. She could not feel completely safe, even among people she trusted.

'Do you think the professor is safe in your office?'

'It's the safest place,' said Marco. 'They would not want to destroy a computer system that is at their service. But I have asked Enrico to wait outside. He will do it willingly now that I have cleared his name. Venetians are very proud of their family name.'

'How did you do it?'

'It was Commissario Morelli, not me. All the workers at the garage were checked, even temporary or part-time. It was a casual mechanic, maybe an immigrant, taken on in a rush period. He had a record of small crime and some experience in electronics. His room was searched and bugging equipment was found.'

'So who told him to bug your car? That could be a lead.'

'He said it was a phone call. Then money came in an envelope. He said he never saw anyone or heard any name.'

'Where is he now?'

'In prison. There are other charges, what you say? In the air. Do not worry, you are safe. I will not let anyone hurt you.'

'Pending. In the air.'

'*Si*, pending.'

Emma did not remind him that it had not prevented him being

hit with a piece of masonry from an old church. No one was safe until the whole gang was rounded up and put away. Pia, the poor street girl, had been murdered because of the Prosecco fortune. And her killer had never been found. He was still free to roam the city, drink beer in the cafés, steal from the tourists.

Marco saw the sadness in her expressive face and pulled her close. 'The evening is ours and we have so much to talk about. Maria will have a good supper for us and she will be so pleased to see you. She has talked of nothing else but the clever young Englishwoman who helped her mop up the flooding floor.'

'That was some flood.' Emma shivered.

'There was a worse one in 1966, November 14. The city was flooded to nearly six feet in depth. We lost many city treasures.'

'I saw a programme about it on television. It looked awful. Hundreds of old books all sodden and falling apart.'

'But no more talk of disasters,' said Marco. 'We are here. Maria has put Prosecco on ice. We are to celebrate your return.'

He turned and kissed her. 'No more going away, *per favore.*' He gathered in her sweetness, the aroma that was always Emma.

It was an evening to remember although Emma did not remember what she ate. Some delicious dishes. Maria was delighted to see her, fussed around. They drank Prosecco, of course. Marco wanted to know all about her Christmas with the professor. He felt almost jealous of the older man. He had shared a special day with Emma. She was his Emma.

'He is like a father, an uncle or a much older brother,' said Emma, trying to reassure Marco. 'I have no family. Neither has he, as far as I am able to find out. It is nothing more than that.'

'I am glad it is nothing more,' said Marco. 'I am glad that he made it a happy day for you. I went to my vineyards and Paola put on a great meal. It would have fed the five thousand. All of my workers and more. Everyone came to eat. But I thought of you all the time, wanting you to be with me.'

'And I wanted to be with you.'

'Next time, perhaps. Is it too much to hope?'

'No, it is not too much to hope. But first we have to solve this cyber-activity. I can't give up my junior partnership in Irving Stone to become a washerwoman here in Venice.'

Marco began to laugh, his dark eyes sparkling. 'A washer-woman? But why? You mean washing up the flood?'

'You will be broke. No money. You will be bankrupt. So I will have to work. And how will I get work as an accountant, here in Venice? Are there many openings for an accountant with limited Italian?'

Marco gathered her into his arms. She could feel his warmth and solidity, yet the hardness of his chest.

'No, but you will not be a washerwoman. You will be my woman. I will sell everything that I have except the vineyards and the farmhouse. I will sell the palazzo and my villa on the lake. We will live among the vines, live and work as my grandparents did. My grandfather and my grandmother had a long and happy marriage. They had a good life.'

'I should like that,' said Emma, forgetting all about her years of work at Irving Stone Accountants and her climb up the slippery career ladder.

'We will be together. We will work together. I will be in the fields, you at your clever computer. No more problems. You will make sure that the money is paid to dell'Orto and we will live well.'

'That's true. I will make sure that this cyber-hacking never happens again.'

'And I have every confidence in you. My clever Inglese accountant.'

'Not so clever yet. But I am learning.'

Commissario Claudio Morelli was scrolling through CCTV film taken at the Marco Polo Airport on the night when Emma and Marco dell'Orto arrived at Venice. He wanted to find the moment when Emma's raincoat was lifted.

He found pictures of them walking through the airport. Emma looked tired and bewildered. She was pulling a small wheelie suit-case, raincoat over her arm, carrying a briefcase in her other hand. Marco was striding ahead, only swinging a briefcase.

The raincoat was slipping from its precarious hold. A slither of fawn Jaeger fell onto the floor. Emma did not seem to notice as she was trying to keep up with Marco.

Then in a second, it had gone. Claudio scrolled back to find the exact moment that it was taken. Pia had worked like lightning. She had light fingers and fast feet.

She fled with the raincoat, feeling in the pockets for money, credit cards. But the camera caught her and put a name. She was known. She was barely eighteen.

'How many more murders?' the man asked. His face was furious. 'The wrong woman hit and then in the water. You only half drown another woman in the canal. Why burn a launch when there is no one on it? Then hang the wrong man from a bridge? He was no professor. A fake. You are imbeciles. Take your money and go. I have no time for you. Get out. I will find men with more sense.'

'We will go to the polizia.' It was an empty threat.

'If you dare. Who would believe scum like you? Get out before you are found in the canal with your throats cut.'

'We have sharper knives, signor.'

'Don't threaten me. I have eyes everywhere. You will not escape. Go back to your ratholes. I never want to see any of you again.'

The Countess Raquel was settling into her suite at the best hotel in Venice. It was perfect in every way. There were flowers and a bottle of champagne awaiting her arrival. She threw her mink coat over a chair and ordered the waiter to open the champagne. She needed the alcohol to ease the pain of Marco's refusal to take her into his palazzo. His refusal had hurt.

'I will have room service,' she said, opening the menu. 'But tomorrow I will eat downstairs. Reserve me the best table. In the centre. I will not sit at the back among the curtains.'

'*Si*, Countess. The best table. I will see to it.'

'And I want all my clothes dry-cleaned. They have been in a flood. I am in shock. But I want them back by tomorrow morning.'

'*Si*, Countess. By tomorrow morning.'

'Also send me up a guest list of everyone staying in the hotel.'

'Ah, Countess, that may not be possible. Many of our guests are incognito. I shall have to ask the general manager.'

'Then ask him, you fool. *Ti aspetto? Vattene!*'

The waiter escaped, only too glad to be leaving the demanding Countess. They were used to guests who expected to be waited on hand and foot, who asked the impossible. Yet many were pleasant and tipped generously. They knew the Countess would not tip. She had greed in her eyes and nothing in her purse.

She waited until everyone had left, then picked up the phone, dialling for an outside line. The number was written on a piece of paper. She dialled it carefully.

'Signor?' she asked. 'This is the Countess. I shall not give you my name. You want to speak with me? Is this important? I am ver' busy. I speak to no one else. Talk.'

nineteen

The professor was more than pleased with himself. He had contrived a honeypot. He had created an entirely fictitious customer called Natale Gelato Inc. They were going to produce a new ice cream flavoured with Prosecco. They had received a consignment of so many litres of the sparkling wine, not bottled, and a bill for payment of several thousand euros.

The professor had earlier circulated a series of business emails, discussing the new flavour and their plans for the future. It was like writing a story. He got quite involved and invented several leading characters.

Natale Gelato Inc. then sent by electronic transmission the entire payment to the dell'Orto account number. But the professor had tagged it with an override timeout interval.

'That means the server has to reply,' he said. 'Without a timeout interval one might have to wait forever if there is no specific period of reasonable time for the processing to complete. It could be five seconds or ten seconds, whatever you like, but the server has to reply. It's pretty standard these days.'

'I wish I understood what you were doing,' said Emma. 'It's too complicated for me but sounds a great idea. It's a trap, isn't it?'

'I should be willing to teach you,' said the professor. 'You have a good brain. It would be a piece of cake.'

Enrico had escorted her to the office the next morning. She had slept well knowing that she was back under the same roof as Marco. But he had gone straight to the plant the next morning, only having a few moments to share some coffee with her on the breakfast balcony.

'Computers are not for me,' he said, his dark hair still wet from the shower. 'I only know how to grow grapes and make wine.'

'Perhaps this has happened because you were rarely in the office.' It sounded like a reprimand but Emma couldn't stop herself. 'Whoever has been hacking your system thought you wouldn't notice.'

'I wouldn't have noticed even if I was there. Tell me what happens.'

Emma thought she understood today's computers when she could produce a spreadsheet for a customer. But now she realized her knowledge was only basic. The professor had written books about computing.

'So I have set the timeout interval for 600 seconds,' the professor went on explaining. 'Ten minutes makes more sense than having to wait ages. Meanwhile, I am going to put the rest of the financial files into a read-only mode database, so that they can't be added, deleted or edited. One more step and they won't be moved either without Marco's specific access code.'

'I'll make some coffee,' said Emma weakly. It was like watching a *Die Hard* film, with crooks rewriting sensitive data to control the detonation of a bomb or the complete blackout of New York.

'I'm also going to invent a prefix of table names, a mixture of system and user tables, so that sensitive material can be hidden or displayed.'

Rocco and Luka were equally bemused. They had both worked with their old computers for some years but only the elementary day-to-day stuff. And the two secretaries, Tina and Rosina, were competent enough to deal with the normal office mail. They thought the professor was a genius beamed down from Mars and rushed out to buy his favourite pasticceria. They bought enough for everyone.

But the honeypot didn't work. In seconds, the payment was received by dell'Orto and just as quickly it disappeared off the system.

The professor was devastated. He could not believe his eyes.

'This is unbelievable,' said the professor, tapping some keys furiously. 'This has never happened before. Someone is very clever. I shall have to start again.'

'Has the money gone?'

'Unfortunately yes. I will repay it, of course. Out of my fee.'

'Marco won't let you, I know that. He is too generous.'

'I shall insist,' said the professor grimly.

'This hacker is going to beat us, whoever he is,' said Emma, sinking back into a chair. 'He's going to steal all of Marco's money.'

'Not if I can prevent it,' said the professor. 'There is a limit to this hacking business. I'm going to build a secret developer back door which no one will be able to disable.'

Signor Bragora was not in this morning. His wife phoned that he was not well. Emma could believe it. He had not looked well for weeks. Surely he was not involved in this hacking and the sudden new activity was stressing him out? It would be beyond him. Or perhaps someone was blackmailing him to provide financial information. It was another avenue of thought, but not one which Marco would like. Signor Bragora had been the firm's chief accountant for years, maybe since Marco was a boy.

Professor Windsor managed to prevent another payment from Natale Gelato Inc. from going through. He declared the firm bankrupt and put a stop on all funds.

'No call for champagne ice cream, then?' said Emma. 'And I thought it was a brilliant idea.'

Commissario Claudio Morelli phoned, asking to speak to Emma.

'Signorina, I have to ask you some more questions. Is it all right if I come to the office? Is there a room where we can speak in private?'

'Yes, of course. Come any time. I shall be here all day.'

It was nearly the end of the day when the Commissario arrived. He looked as weary as usual. He was not that old, in his late thirties probably. But his hair was already tinged with grey and he had deep furrows between his brows.

Emma made coffee immediately and showed him into Signor Bragora's room. There were two little cakes left. Claudio sat down and opened his briefcase, taking out a big file.

'This is continuing Pia's murder inquiry. The girl who was wearing your raincoat. The girl they thought was you. There were no traces of any other DNA on her or anything that linked her to you, apart from the fact that she stole your raincoat at the airport. We have evidence of that on their internal CTTV.'

'I think I lost it as we were walking through the airport. I had it over my arm and it slipped. I was very tired and my mind was on other things.' Her mind had been on Marco, striding ahead of her, so tall and handsome.

'*Comprendo*, signorina. I have here many photographs. They are ground staff at the Marco Polo Airport and airline staff. Could you please look through them and tell me if any are familiar?'

The Commissario was happy to drink coffee and eat cakes as Emma leafed through all the photographs. He had missed his *tramezzini* lunch and breakfast had been the usual rushed coffee. He knew he was losing weight. And he was always tired. Perhaps he should see the doctor.

Face after face leafed over, every size and shape of face, every colour of skin, male and female. Emma did not recognize anyone. But who actually looked at airport staff? They were part of the faceless body of workers in similar uniforms who kept the flow of passengers going in the right direction.

Emma stopped at a photograph of a good-looking blonde girl. There was something about her but Emma could not think what it was. She did not look so dark and Italian.

'I might have noticed this young woman,' said Emma. 'But I'm not sure where. And I can't place her. Sorry not to be more helpful.'

'We are trying to find someone who noticed you. That someone who described you and your coat, who was paid to contact the thug who hit Pia and tipped her body into the canal. Did you speak to any other passengers?'

'There were no other passengers in first class,' said Emma, remembering Marco's rash generosity. 'It was empty apart from Marco and myself.'

'*Grazie*, signorina. I am sorry to have troubled you. I will leave you now to finding the missing euros.'

He got up to leave. He had finished off the cakes and emptied the cup of coffee. It was back to the office for more legwork. He did not think they would ever find Pia's killer, unless he killed again.

'Would you like to have supper with Marco and me at the palazzo this evening? He could look at the photographs. He has a good memory for faces.'

'But this would inconvenience your housekeeper?'

'Maria always makes mountains of food. There will be plenty to go round.'

'Then I accept the invitation. *Grazie*. It would be a pleasure.'

It was the first time Emma had seen Claudio smile. It was a rare sight and changed his face. It wiped away years and the stress of his work. The Commissario could almost smell Maria's good cooking. He would have time to go back to his small flat and shower and put on a clean shirt. It was the least he could do.

Emma learned some more Italian on the water taxi back to the palazzo. Marco had asked for the borrowed launch to meet him somewhere else along the Lagoon. They were taking Claudio's advice that they should vary the routes that they took. Enrico had hired a water taxi to meet them at the quayside.

'*Piove a dirotto*,' he said, waiting outside the office with a big umbrella, seeing Emma into the car. 'It is pouring.'

'Cats and dogs,' agreed Emma. He looked puzzled. What had pet animals to do with rain?

Professor Windsor went straight back to his small and secret hotel in a back calle. He took his laptop with him. He wanted to continue working.

'Don't worry about me. They have excellent room service,' he said. 'I shall order a steak sandwich.'

Emma thought that he really wanted a small and secret sleep. He was beginning to look tired. No wonder, he had been hard at the computer all day.

Marco was not late coming home. He took Emma in his arms and nuzzled her hair. She always smelled so sweet.

'These machines,' he groaned. 'It was easier when we trod the grapes with our feet.'

'But not so fast and not so hygienic,' said Emma, sinking into the warmth of his embrace. 'I have invited the Commissario to eat with us tonight. He looks half-starved and he has some photographs for you to look at.'

'You are too kind, my *piccolina*. I wanted you all to myself this evening, so that we could make plans and enjoy being together.'

'There will be time for us. I doubt if Claudio will stay late. He seems to work all hours of the day and night.'

'But I also work very hard,' said Marco.

'Then you will want to retire early to your bed,' said Emma primly.

'*Naturalmente*, if you will come with me. If you are still pre-ferring your virgin bed, *Inglese e freddo*, then I will read the newspapers and drink brandy in my lonely study.'

Marco was teasing her. His eyes were twinkling, the rain drip-ping off his hair onto her skin. He had not even stopped to take off his wet coat. They had an evening together ahead and that was magical enough.

Maria produced her famous fish soup, followed by *meloche fritte*, which Emma discovered was crab, from the Lagoon, coated with beaten egg and fried. It was delicious. There was salad and *risi e bisi*, which was rice with fresh peas. And lastly, if anyone had any room, Maria's home-made tiramisu, which was nothing like the frozen product sold in packets in supermarkets.

Claudio and Marco were so relaxed, talking, eating and drink-ing. Emma was happy to listen to their rapid Italian, even if not taking part in the conversation. They had gone to the same school and then their ways parted.

'But, *pardone*, signorina, we are forgetting you.'

'No problem,' said Emma. 'I'm quite happy to sit and listen to you. My Italian is improving. I'm glad to see you both relaxing for a few hours. Your lives are so busy.'

Claudio's mobile went off, as if prompted to interrupt. '*Si?*'

He listened for a while. 'I will be there,' he said and switched off. 'I am sorry. There has been a break-in at a garage. It is not nor-mally a crime requiring my attendance but it is the garage where your car was fitted with bugs. It may be connected.'

'Can my launch take you to the garage?'

'*Grazie*, but it would be quicker to walk.'

Commissario Morelli knew all the short cuts along the calles and over bridges. He reached the solid ground of the area beyond Venice where streets became streets and did not swim over water.

The garage had a good reputation. It was where the wealthy

Venetians took their big cars. Why should anyone want to break into a garage? What was there to steal? A few spanners, fuel?

Claudio saw the police sedans parked in front of the garage and uniformed poliziotto. He showed his identity card.

'Commissario.'

'*Quando e successo?*'

An officer shrugged his shoulders. He did not know. He didn't understand why the Commissario should be interested in this small break-in. Not much was stolen. Only a broken lock and some smashed items.

Claudio went into the repair shop. A few tools had been thrown about, nothing of any significance. But in the office, it was a different story. Every file had been torn open and the contents shredded. The computer had been wrecked, its hard drive torn out, stamped on, obliterated.

Claudio knew instantly that whoever ordered the bugging of Marco's car had returned to destroy any evidence of his existence. All the employment records had gone.

There was nothing to link the current motley of scumbags currently behind bars for the murder of young Pia, or the hanging of the young man under the bridge. But Claudio had a gut feeling they were all connected to the stealing of the Prosecco fortune.

The good supper that Maria had provided sat comfortably in his stomach. He thought of Emma at the table, her face alight with love for Marco. He would have liked to see Emma turn her face to him, alight with the same love. But he was too late to win her affection. He was doomed to being a lonely workaholic.

Marco took the file of photographs into the sitting room to look through while they drank coffee. None of the faces meant anything to him. Yet he knew every man and woman who worked for him. No face was a stranger. He knew every one of his employees.

It was a relief to know that none of them existed in Claudio's file of suspects. Some he had known since they were children, had danced at their weddings, been a godparent at christenings.

Marco closed the file. 'No, there is no one. Did you recognize anyone?'

Emma came and sat beside him. 'Only this one,' she said, opening the page to the smart, young blonde woman. 'I thought I had seen her somewhere.'

Marco shook his head. 'I don't remember her.'

'Never mind. It was a possibility that we might recognize someone.'

'I only had eyes for you on that flight,' Marco teased.

'You are such a flirt.'

'Flirt? What is this flirt? Is it some sort of insect? I deny everything.'

They were laughing when Maria came into the sitting room, carrying a tray. On it was a bottle of Moët & Chandon champagne and two flutes. She put it down on the table, then removed the coffee.

'Is this a celebration?' Emma asked.

'I don't understand. This is French champagne,' said Marco, a little annoyed.

Maria handed him an envelope. 'This was delivered by a uniformed messenger from the Hotel Gritti Palace. It is a gift for you, signor.'

The envelope was the heavy vellum of Hotel Gritti Palace's personal stationery. Inside was a single sheet of heavy cream vellum. On it was written in a bold scrawl:

'Enjoy the champagne and think of me, Raquel.'

Marco put the card aside. She had not said thank you. He wondered if Raquel ever said thank you to anyone.

'It's from Raquel,' he said. 'I suppose it's her way of saying thank you though I'm sure it's going on my bill.'

'Are we going to drink it?'

Marco shrugged his shoulders. 'It's French,' he said, as if that explained everything.

Maria was clearing the coffee cups when she saw the file of photographs open at the picture of the blonde woman.

'I know this young woman,' she said, tapping the photograph. 'She is Vikki Boccetta. She lives a few streets back. She is very smart and has a good job.'

'You know her?'

'*Si*, Vikki Boccetta. She works for the airlines. She is, you call, a hostess. She flies all over the world to places. Her mother is nice person, takes in lodgers. She lent me some buckets when we had the flooding.'

twenty

Commissario Claudio Morelli could not hide his satisfaction. Vikki Boccetta had been the hostess for the first-class cabin on the flight that brought Emma and Marco to Venice. He contacted her immediately and she insisted that she had done nothing wrong. She thought it had been a joke of some kind.

'I was asked to describe the female passenger, that's all,' she said. 'Her face, her hair, her clothes.'

'Who asked you?'

'I don't know. It was a mobile phone call.'

'And you were paid for this information?'

'Yes, but it was not a lot. I thought it was for a glossy magazine. A celebrity story, perhaps. I thought the couple were eloping.'

'How were you paid?'

'The money came in an envelope. I gave half of it to my mother.'

'Were you not suspicious of this?'

'It meant nothing to me.'

Commissario Morelli paused. He wanted Vikki to be unnerved. She seemed very much in control of her answers. He wondered if she knew a lot more. She looked like a woman with expensive tastes.

'I shall need your mobile phone, signorina. Only for a short while then you can have it back. Please bring it to the Questura immediately.'

'What have I done wrong?' There was the slightest tremor in her voice. Vikki liked her job, the perks, the glamour, flying round the world. She did not want to lose her job.

'As far as I can see, nothing wrong. Strange perhaps but not illegal.'

'*Grazie*, Commissario. I will bring the phone.'

*

Commissario Morelli gave the mobile phone to the whiz-kids downstairs and asked them to make a list of all the calls to Vikki's phone in December last year and January this year. The result was interesting. She had a lot of men-friends calling her for dates.

He scoured the list when they handed it to him. It was also confusing. But then he spotted a phone call made to her on the day that Emma flew to Venice. It was made at 4 p.m., two hours before the flight took off.

It was a London number. He looked down the list more intently.

'Trace this number, *per favore*. You are very clever with such things.'

'*Si*, Commissario. Nothing is secret nowadays. The mobile phone is an open book.'

Enrico phoned Emma. He was so sorry but he could not escort her to the office as his mother had been taken ill, and he had to go and see her in Mestra on the mainland. Emma assured him that she could manage on her own.

'Don't worry. I'm sorry your mother is ill. I'll take the vaporetto and then a taxi to the office. No one will notice me. I'll wear a scarf and glasses. I won't walk anywhere.'

'Shall I ask Rocco or Luka to escort you? They will arrive in the office soon.'

'There's no need. I can be in the office almost as soon as they arrive. I hope you will find your mother recovering. If there is anything you need, please phone and Marco and I will help you.'

'*Grazie, grazie*, signorina. You are so kind.'

Emma chose another of Francesca's elegant trouser suits. It was a navy and white pinstripe with big gold buttons. She teamed it with her own white polo-necked jersey and the trademark scarf, the one Marco bought for her. She wore it almost every day. A sort of personal talisman.

Maria helped her into her coat. 'There is a water taxi waiting outside by the front steps, signorina. Did you order one?'

'No. Perhaps Enrico ordered it to save me travelling on a crowded vaporetto. He's so thoughtful.'

Maria tucked a folded packet into her coat pocket. 'I have made some little almond biscuits for you,' she said. 'Better than ones bought in the shop.'

'*Grazie*, Maria, that's very kind.'

Emma went out onto the front step. Wavelets were washing over it and a water taxi was hovering nearby. A big man wearing a yellow, fluorescent plastic jacket jumped out of it onto the step with a rope in his hand. He twisted the rope into the ring on the wall, pulling it taut.

'Signorina Chandler? I am here to escort you to the office.'

'But I don't know who you are,' said Emma. 'Who ordered this?'

'Signor dell'Orto has account with me. He has used my service many times. Shall I help you into motorboat? There is much traffic this morning. The canal is like a freeway.'

His English was stilted but quite good. He was wearing a peaked cap to keep the mist out of his eyes. Emma was getting damp standing on the step, trying to make up her mind.

'*Si, grazie*. It's a busy morning. To the top of the Grand Canal, *per favore*. By the Statione Santa Lucia.'

'*Naturalmente.*'

The driver helped Emma into the bobbing taxi. It was a sleek, white motorboat with a lot of polished wood. He led her towards the small cabin which gave her some shelter. She shivered as a fresh wind blew in from the sea. At least she would soon be warm in the office with the heaters on full blast.

She always enjoyed any ride along the Grand Canal, taking in the magnificent palazzos, the many domed churches, going under the Rialto Bridge. She had her favourite buildings and always looked forward to passing them. It took her several minutes to take in that the view was not the usual crowded thoroughfare. It was more open, fewer boats.

'Excuse me,' she said. 'But are you going the right way?' It did not look the right way. The boat was heading towards the open sea.

'This is a short cut,' said the driver, his hand on the throttle.

Emma peered over the back of the boat. 'No, no, you are wrong. Look, you are going away from Venice. I can see the Doge's Palace and the twin columns of San Marco and San Teodoro. There's the Campanile, the bell tower. They are getting smaller. Please turn back. This is not where I want to go.'

'But it is the way I want to go, signorina. So please be quiet.'

'No, I will not,' said Emma, suddenly alarmed. She did not like the tone of his voice. There were still a few small fishing boats within hailing distance. 'Help, help,' she began shouting and waving her arms. 'This taxi is taking me the wrong way. Help me, please.'

Suddenly she found herself being smothered in rough sacking. She struggled furiously but the second man was tough and strong. He was winding rope round her arms so that they were pinned to her sides. She fell onto the hard deck of the boat, unable to move or shout.

He was wearing the strangest clothes. A high-collared black cloak and the corno-horned hat that a doge wore. She had seen such paintings in the museums. He grunted as he fastened the rope. She saw his eyes. They were mean and narrow.

'Now you will not see where you are going,' he said in a low voice. 'It will be a nice surprise.'

Emma did not move. She didn't waste her energy. She could smell salt in the air. They were heading out to sea. Thank goodness, she still had her shoulder bag which was crushed against her body but her briefcase was somewhere on the deck. Her phone was in the briefcase.

'No more screaming, signorina,' said the driver. '*Buon*. I do not like screaming women unless they are under me. *Un momento* and you will be able to scream all day and no one will hear you.'

The motorboat was slowing down. Emma felt the tug of the sea as it buffeted the boat against the waves. The bow seemed to plough forwards into a mudbank and then lurched to a stop. She was lifted up shoulder-high by both men and manhandled off the boat. She was tossed like an old parcel and landed on something that felt like sand. It might have been wet. It was not moving.

'Veneto is often called the lagoon of a thousand islands,' said the man in the black cloak. 'This is one of the thousand. *Arrivederci*, signorina.'

She heard the engine go into reverse as the motorboat lifted itself off the mudbank and back into deeper water.

Emma took several deep breaths. At least she was still alive. Those thugs had not killed her. Not like Pia or Brad.

*

The office was alarmed. Emma had not arrived. Enrico phoned through. His mother was not ill and she was annoyed at being delayed from her morning's shopping. It had been a fake call. Rocco phoned Maria. Enrico was questioned about the taxi. He had not ordered a water taxi. Maria was distraught.

'I saw her go into the water taxi. Two men. It looked all right. It was normal,' she wailed. 'How could I know?'

Professor Windsor was gaunt with worry. 'They've taken her. They think Emma knows something. But she doesn't. They will use her as a hostage. Or kill her. These people are crooks, criminals.'

Commissario Morelli felt his blood run colder than ice. He needed more information. The London number was a mobile phone but there was now no signal. Probably a mobile used once then dumped into the Thames. He needed a name.

'But I need a name,' he said.

'Shall I trace the phone number to banks? Find a link?'

'You are a genius.'

Emma rolled over on the sand. The thick rope had not been tied, only twisted round her and the end tucked in several times. The rough, Hessian sacking was tightly wrapped but she managed to wriggle out of it. She sat up, rubbing her arms and legs. Everywhere was numb. She was creased and dirty, her coat sodden.

All she could see was sea. Venice was nothing but a smudge in the distance. She could smell the sea and the faint whiff of sewage. But she was on reasonably dry land although the sand was being washed with wavelets. She crawled further back into a thick growth of gorse and saplings. At least she was still alive. But for how long? How long could she last?

She staggered to her feet. It was obvious that she was on one of the many unnamed islands that scattered the lagoon. The big ones were named and encouraged the tourist industry. But this one? It was very small, and way, way out to sea.

Emma needed to find out as much as she could about the islet before the light faded. Surely, by now, they would know that she had not arrived at the office.

She pushed her way through undergrowth, glad that she was

wearing boots. She came across some fallen masonry, stones, almost overgrown with creeper. It was a small ruin. Not a monastery or anything grand. It was more like a hovel, maybe a hermit's sanctuary or a place where they left plague victims. She hoped she wouldn't find bones or any other relics.

Emma tramped the overgrown islet several times, finding nothing. Her watch had stopped working. The islet was no bigger than an irregular netball pitch, circled with wet sand. She had played netball when at school. She was their best shooter.

She sat down on one of the ruined walls. There was a crevice full of water. It was rainwater. She cupped her hands and drank the water. She ate two of Maria's almond biscuits. They would have to last. She would ration herself.

The light was beginning to go. Dark clouds interlaced with the night. She heard the symphony of 6 p.m. bells tolling from Venice. Surely, soon, they would start looking for her? There was nothing in her shoulder bag of any use.

As the light faded and it began to get cold, Emma dragged the Hessian sacking towards the ruins and found the most sheltered spot. The sacking made some sort of bedding place. Her coat was thick and warm. She rested her head on her leather shoulder bag, tried to sleep. The night sky was no consolation. The twinkling star-scattered night was of no reassurance. She heard an early dawn chorus of birds but knew she would never be able to catch or eat one.

She ate two more biscuits and a few crumbs. She was miles from anywhere. There was no tree she could climb or wave her bra from.

Marco was out of his mind with worry. Everyone had phoned him. Rocco, Luka, Enrico, Maria and Commissario Morelli.

'We will find the signorina,' assured the Commissario. 'They haven't contacted us. It is a hostage situation, I'm sure. Their demands will come soon.'

'They may have killed her,' Marco shouted.

'No, I think she has more value alive. They do not know what she knows.'

'I am distraught. What can I do?'

'Wait until we get a demand. We are patrolling the Lagoon. Someone will have seen or heard something.'

Marco had his hands full consoling Maria. She felt guilty, responsible for putting Emma in the water taxi. She wailed into her apron.

'How could you know?' he said, his own distress now calming. 'Please make some good food for the Commissario and myself. Your best soup and hot. We shall be up all night.'

'*Si*, signor,' said Maria, wiping her eyes. 'I hope we find the young lady soon. She is like a daughter to me. I am so fond of her. Ver' special lady.'

And special to me, thought Marco. Not a daughter, but a wife, a lover, my soulmate. I want her back. Safe and secure, close in my arms.

Emma awoke at dawn, stiff and damp from the morning dew. She could barely move her neck. She drank more water from the crevice, ate two more biscuits. The rainwater ran down her arms and into her sleeves. There were only two biscuits left and a few more crumbs. She had to save them.

She must use today to be rescued. She doubted if she would survive a few more nights in this cold. What could she do? No point in screaming: as the driver said, no one would hear her. The sun rose, wintry but warm. She gazed into the sun's rays, wondering if they were her salvation.

In her shoulder bag was a small mirror. She was often checking her lipstick.

She flicked open the mirror and caught the sun's rays in its reflection. She stood on the ruined wall and sent the sharp light out into the Lagoon, towards where she thought Venice would be. It was a pinprick of light.

To be noticed, the flash had to be consistent in movement. Waving the beam all over the air would mean nothing. The only Morse she knew was the traditional SOS code, dot, dot, dot, dash, dash, dash, dot, dot, dot. Then a repeat. She did a quick north-to-south movement for the dots, then long sideways flashes for the dashes. It was pretty basic. She hoped that there were some Girl Guides or Boy Scouts on a holiday trip to Venice who did not have their noses in guidebooks or were too busy texting each other.

It was tiring. The day was wintry and the sun was soon lost in clouds. Emma was numb with cold. She couldn't start a fire. No matches or lighter. No dry wood or tinder. There was nothing in fact to draw attention to the tiny island. She was in a balloon of stillness and creeping cold. Emma was a good swimmer but the sea was icy and she knew she would not get far before the temperature claimed her.

twenty~one

The downstairs office of the Questura was busy, phones ringing, computers tapping. Several tourists had had their wallets stolen, a youth had been knifed outside a nightclub and now it was a red alert for some missing English woman. They thought she had probably gone off with an Italian lover.

'And another stolen boat,' the poliziotto groaned. 'Those damned kids. Joyriding, causing accidents. The canal has enough traffic problems.'

'We've a report of a flashing light out to sea.'

'Those damned kids,' the officer repeated. 'They are having a barbecue on a beach, lighting fires, setting off fireworks. Let them spend the night out there. Let them see if they enjoy a cold night in the open. It'll teach them a lesson.'

'Should we report the flashing light to the Commissario?'

'Don't bother. He's too busy with this missing woman. She'll turn up. Probably drinking champagne in the Cipriani Hotel on Lagoon Island.'

'He said to report anything unusual.'

'So what is unusual about kids larking about?'

Commissario Morelli stared at the information in front of him. The mobile phone number had been linked to several London banks but all the accounts had been closed and the money transferred. He tried to talk to the manager of each bank but they refused to talk to him. Customer confidentiality, they said. He was running up a big phone bill.

Morelli went into the office of the Vice-Questore, Pietro Lombardo. 'I have a problem,' he said. 'We need the help of the FBI in London. Have you a contact at Scotland Yard?'

Pietro Lombardo was nearing retirement. He did not want to rock the boat. He was looking forward to the summer, gardening at his villa in Veneto, eating his wife's good cooking, doing nothing. He was tired of police work.

'This would have to go through Milan,' said Lombardo, passing the buck.

'I will phone Milan.'

'Let me know what happens.'

'*Naturalmente*, Vice-Questore.'

'One of the fishermen has reported hearing a woman shouting for help. It was yesterday morning, out at sea where they fish. He thought it was a bit strange.'

'How did he know she was shouting for help? She could have been screaming in enjoyment.'

'*Si*. I had not thought of that.'

'Many women have a strange way of showing their enjoyment.'

'*Si*.'

'Go back to your work. There may be a hundred screaming woman in Venice this evening.'

'*Si*.'

Commissario Morelli was soon leaving his office. It had been a fruitless day. Milan did not want to know. He was no nearer finding Emma Chandler. This would be her second night wherever she was. He was beginning to feel sick.

'Commissario?' It was one of the new recruits, well-pressed uniform. Claudio did not even know his name. He was tall, had a good face, clear eyes, crew-cut hair.

'*Si*?' he said abruptly. Claudio was tired and so hungry. He wanted to go home, put his feet up, get some sleep.

'It may be nothing. But it's been reported, some flashes seen coming from an island. There was a pattern. Also, a fisherman heard a woman screaming.'

'Why did you not tell me this before?'

'I did not think it was important.'

'You are a fool.'

'*Si*.'

'But *grazie*. Take a patrol boat out to the islands. Flash the head-lamps. Call her name. *Emma Chandler.*'

'I'll go immediately. I'll take rugs and food and water.'

'On second thoughts, I'll come with you. She will only respond to someone she trusts. She knows me.'

'I will get waterproof jacket for you.'

'*Grazie.*'

All his tiredness had vanished in a moment. Claudio did not ring Marco in case it was a false alarm. He would not wish to raise his hopes for nothing.

Emma was exhausted. She had been flashing the Morse pattern every time the sun came out. She had nothing more to eat but enough rainwater to drink. She could last a few more days. She would lose some weight. She remembered all the lovely pasta she had been eating. How many days could she survive with only water to drink?

The night was coming. She wondered if she would ever see Marco again. The man that she loved so much with every fibre of her being. Maybe this was the end of her life. So many people died young. It was nothing new.

She made up her rough bed, wrapped herself in her coat. It was not looking so good now. This was her second night in the open on the islet. Darkness was looming, clouds blotting the sinking sun and no stars. She had a feeling it was going to rain. There was nowhere in the ruin that would shelter her from the rain.

She was too cold to sleep. She chanted Marco's name to herself, sending thought waves to him, hoping he would hear them. Italian men were sensitive. He might understand her message, know she was still alive.

Marco stood at the tall upper window of his palazzo, seeing the rain clouds gathering, praying that his Emma had shelter. He felt sure she was still alive. She was strong and resilient. He felt so helpless, just waiting around, doing nothing.

Suddenly he could bear it no longer. He put on big boots, a thick jersey, and took his waterproof jacket from behind the kitchen door.

'I am going out,' he said to Maria. 'I'm going to find her, even if it takes my last breath.'

'*Si*, signor. I have a flask of coffee for you and some *tramezzini*, cheese and salad. You must eat or you will not be strong enough to find the signorina.'

'*Grazi mille*, Maria. I have my phone with me so you can pass on any news.'

Marco went out the back door onto the street and over the bridge, buttoning the waterproof and pulling up the zip and the hood. It was already starting to rain, a thin cold drizzle. He was sending Emma thoughts, praying she was all right. Be strong, he thought, I will find you. I will search for you till my dying day.

He went down on the waterfront by the Doge's Palace. It was well lit in the fading darkness. A group of water taxi drivers were talking angrily, their voices raised.

'What's the matter?' Marco asked.

'Pedro. It is Pedro. He has had his motorboat stolen. The polizia say it is just kids. But still it is a crime, signor.'

'When was this?'

'Yesterday, yesterday morning. Very early. Pedro came late because his wife is sick but his boat had gone. The mooring rope sawn through. It was more than local kids. They only take small boats. The motorboat is a powerful launch.'

Marco swallowed hard. Maria had said that Emma got into a water taxi, a water taxi that she had not ordered. 'Tell Pedro to get in touch with me, Marco dell'Orto. I will help him and his sick wife. But now I wish to hire a motorboat for the whole night. I will pay well. I want a driver who knows the safe canals and the small islands.'

'That will be Giovanni. Giovanni knows the Lagoon like the back of his hand. When he is not drinking.'

'I am Giovanni. I have lived here all my life. The small islets were my playground as a boy. I fished, I swam, I had a rowing boat. Now I have the best motorboat on the lagoon.'

The other drivers laughed at his boasting but they knew he spoke the truth about his knowledge. Giovanni was old, grizzled, his beard grey but trimly cut. His motorboat looked powerful, dark and polished. It had a big headlamp.

He did not look as if he had been drinking recently.

'I want to tour all the thousand small islets, the unnamed, the unknown. Where no one goes,' said Marco. 'I want you to go slowly, with your headlamp on. Can you do this in the dark?'

'*Naturalmente*,' said Giovanni. 'I can see in the dark. I am like my cat.'

Marco climbed onto the motorboat. It was spick and span. And Giovanni had a cat. The deeply striped tabby had sealegs. He walked steadily across the deck to greet their new passenger.

'That is Capotto, called because of his beautiful coat.'

'Hello, Capotto,' said Marco.

Giovanni headed out to sea. 'There are many islands. This will take a long time. I will sweep around each island with the headlamp. Then we may see what we are looking for.' He had no idea what they were looking for. The signor was an eccentric. He had not said. Perhaps he could not sleep, liked travelling in the dark.

The polizia launch was better equipped. It had two sweeping headlamps, a loudspeaker, a stretcher, first-aid equipment, firefighting equipment, thermal bedding, instant radio connections, men trained in sea rescue.

Commissario Morelli was not trained in sea rescue but he felt that these were the first real clues. It could not all be coincidence. A woman screaming, the stolen water taxi, the flashes. Emma would do flashes. It was all she would have. A mirror from her handbag perhaps, the winter sun. So it meant she was alive and well, somewhere. What was that English phrase? Needle in a haystack? This was an island among hundreds, almost the same as a needle.

Claudio was not a religious person. Few polizia were. He prayed now to some saint. Simple words. 'Please help me find her.'

Emma thought she heard her name but she must have been dreaming. She was very cold. Her fingers and toes were like ice. She tried to remember what she knew about frostbite but it was very little. She was remembering her childhood. She had a little grey cat called Tiger that she loved dearly. But they had put her cat to sleep without telling her, without giving her a chance to say goodbye.

It was raining now, a steady drizzle that was good for the

wind-beaten bushes and saplings but not good for her.

She saw a beam of light across the sky but thought it was a meteor or a plane coming in to land at the Marco Polo Airport. The flight path must be across the sea. London seemed very far away. Yet she had once lived there. That also seemed a long time ago.

'Emma ...' Again she thought she heard her name. It sounded strangely foreign, a different language. It meant nothing. She closed her eyes, trying to sleep. It was important to sleep, to keep up her strength.

'It's no good. There is no answer,' said the new young policeman, tired and wet. 'We have been everywhere.'

'One more try, *per favore*,' said Claudio. 'These outer islets. I have a feeling she is somewhere here.'

'But she must have heard us. The loudspeaker.'

'Perhaps she is injured. Perhaps she can't walk or call out. We must circle them again, slowly. Give her time to respond. This is a young woman's life we are talking about, not some kids, drinking beer at an all-night party.'

'And if not?'

'I shall search each island myself. You will put me ashore and wait for me. This I command.'

The new recruit knew now that Commissario Claudio Morelli was very different. No ordinary poliziotto would do anything so mad or so dangerous. But he still admired the man.

'Perhaps Signorina Chandler is still in Venice.'

'No, I have a feeling. She is here somewhere.'

Giovanni was sweeping the dark water with his powerful headlamp. Capotto, the cat, had taken shelter in the cabin, curled on a cushion. The rain was becoming a downpour, drops pelting the sea like hailstones. Marco was cold. How could Emma survive such a night if she was on an island? Unprotected and alone?

It was the first time that he even thought that she might not survive. What would he do without her? He could only work, care for his workforce. Make thousands of litres of Prosecco for other people to drink. But there would be no dell'Orto children. He would not marry. He could not exist without her.

twenty~two

Emma felt some insect crawling over her face. She didn't brush it off. She might have to eat it tomorrow. It was not an encouraging thought but she had seen survival programmes that said insects were full of protein. She did not want raw protein. She wanted hot, creamy pasta sprinkled with Parmesan cheese.

She was so cold she could barely move her limbs. At this rate she would get arthritis. That is, if she lived long enough to get arthritis. She rather hoped she would live long enough to get arthritis or rheumatism. The faintest of smiles crossed her face as the pointlessness of this argument struck her as amusing.

Her thoughts went back to the day she joined Irving Stone Partners. Harry Irving, the son, had made a beeline for her, her fresh face and tawny hair a strong attraction. A luscious new conquest, he thought. He had reeled off a parade of jokes during her first coffee break. She could not remember any of them now. Laughter might keep her warm. It was supposed to be a tonic.

Harry had been a nuisance those first few months but her inborn good manners prevented her from being rude to him. He followed her everywhere, pounced on her unexpectedly, bombarded her with invitations for drinks after work. She only accepted if she knew that other colleagues were going along, too. The thought of being trapped in a corner of a bar with him gave her the creeps.

He only gave up when a long-legged blonde joined the secretarial staff. She thought the boss's only son was a catch. But Harry had no intention of being caught. He was more than footloose, although he always tied his laces.

She stumbled to her feet, dragging her wet coat round her. She couldn't try to sleep any more. Keeping warm was more important.

There was a small stretch of sand some twenty metres from the ruin. It was not flat but strewn with bits of rocks. She must be careful not to stumble and fall. A broken ankle would be a disaster.

The saplings gave her the answer. She searched among the branches in the dark, feeling for something straight and ready to break. A convenient branch broke off. She removed the bits sticking out and a few dead leaves. It was the nearest she could get to a walking stick, crooked, more like a shepherd's staff.

'My trusty stick,' she said out loud. Her voice sounded weird in the darkness, against the lashing of the sea on the shore. 'My trusty stick,' she said again, more firmly. 'Time for us to go for a walk.'

Her boots were wrecked by now but they held together. There was some leakage in the stitching on the left sole and she could feel the dampness oozing in as she walked over the sand. Her brain seemed to be working more slowly than usual. Even the most elementary things were escaping her. She could not remember her Brixton postcode. She could not remember any poetry or songs, but she could remember some nursery rhymes of her childhood. Her foster parents had no time to read to her, but they gave her a book on her birthday. It had vivid illustrations.

'And when the pie was opened,
The birds began to sing ...'

She stopped, thought she heard something, some sort of call, but it was only the wind or a bird calling to its mate. There had been a few birds on the island but they did not stay long, flying off to some bigger and more interesting larder.

'Humpty Dumpty sat on a wall.
Humpty Dumpty had a great fall.'

She heard it again. It was definitely a sound of some sort, very distant. The stick knocked against a rock and she came to a halt, tensed, listening intently. There was only the sound of waves breaking on the rocks and stones, washing back.

'Is there anybody there?' she shouted. It was useless. Of course, there was no one there in the middle of the night. A wet night in

January in the middle of the Venetian Lagoon. The rain was dripping down her face. At least her water crevasse would be filling up with fresh drinking water.

It was the faintest sound carried on the wind. It sounded like 'Emma ...'

Was someone out there? Was someone looking for her? She did not think for a moment that it was the two thugs returning to finish her off. They had left that to the weather and the total isolation of the island. If they had meant to kill her they would have crushed her head with a handy rock before leaving her.

Emma went down on her knees and found a piece of rock she could hold easily in her hand. She then stumbled across the sand to a large outcrop of rock and started banging on it with the rock she was holding. Being an accountant, it had to be a mathematical pattern. Nothing random. She hit the rock ten times, then called out ten times.

Ten hits, ten calls. Then she paused, listening for any answer. There was nothing. She tried again. Ten hits, ten calls, then a pause. She caught back a sob. What else could she do to make a noise, a noise that would be heard over the crashing waves? Her voice was hoarse. She couldn't scream. She had never been able to whistle.

The rock concert was her only chance. She heard distant bells chiming some hour in Venice. Perhaps as it grew lighter someone would come. She took off the scarf which Marco had bought for her, wrung it out and tied it to the end of her trusty stick. It was already wet and the hem was fraying. She made the knots really tight so that she would not lose it to the brisk wind.

She started waving the scarf like some revolutionary from *Les Miserables*. It was the right colours. She stood well away from the bushes and saplings. There was nothing she could climb onto, no assailable rock or wall.

A beam of light flashed over the water but it was too far away. It didn't catch her makeshift flag. But it gave her hope. Someone was out there in a boat. Maybe they were fishermen, putting down lobster pots. Perhaps they needed a lamp to guide them between the dangerous sandbanks.

Emma was tiring. She wondered how long she could keep

going. Her arms were aching from both waving and hitting the rock.

'Please, please,' she sobbed. 'Somebody see me.'

Claudio had already waded ashore on six or seven deserted islands. He was wearing borrowed rubber boots but his trousers were wet through. He had taken a loudspeaker and shouted for Emma but there was no response, only a lot of startled birds rising into the air, wings flapping and squawking.

The recruit, whose name was Barto, had keen hearing. He said he thought he heard something but he wasn't sure what it was. The wind and the rain were noisy enough. And the engine of the police launch drowned any other sounds.

'Turn off the engine,' said Claudio. 'We'll drift for a few minutes. Keep an eye open for the sandbanks. We don't want to have to be rescued ourselves. That would be too humiliating.'

'*Si*,' said the driver.

The driver switched off the engine and the sound died away into the night. Barto and Claudio stood in the bows of the rocking launch, listening intently. The waves slapped hard against the launch.

'I can hear something,' said Barto. 'A sort of knocking. But it could just be the sea against the rocks. Now it's stopped. Maybe it was my imagination. No, it's started again.'

Claudio could hear it now and a tremor of excitement ran through him. The knocking was not random. It had a definite rhythmical pattern. Emma would give it a pattern, a mathematical pattern. He began counting the knocks. Eight, nine, ten. Then it stopped, paused. Then it started again. One, two three …'

'That's Emma Chandler. It must be. *Oddio*. She is still alive. But she is here somewhere, near enough for us to hear. She's found some sound that carries in the air. Start sweeping the sea with the beam, slowly and methodically. We must find her. Sweep slowly.'

The launch was down to its lowest speed, the engine just ticking over. The powerful beam swept over the waves, seeing nothing but water. They could still hear the knocking but it seemed to be faltering.

Claudio phoned Marco on his mobile. 'We think we have heard

someone knocking. This is the location.' He gave the nautical location.

'I'm coming,' Marco said. 'I'm not far away.'

'I think I can see something,' Barto shouted, squinting hard. 'Look over there, westward, Commissario. It's moving sideways, not much, but definitely a sort of flag waving.'

Claudio grabbed some binoculars but he couldn't see a thing. Barto turned the beam of the lamp in the direction of the movement he had seen.

'Over there,' he said. 'Can you see anything?'

'Keep moving towards it,' Claudio urged the driver. 'We've caught something in the beam.'

'It's coming from that far scrap of land, barely an island at all. It would be covered by a very high tide. Yes, something is moving, Commissario. It's waving a wet rag.'

'Si. It must be Emma,' said Claudio, faint with relief. 'Move in closer, slowly, we don't want to run aground.' He hoped they were not mistaken, that it was not a lost sweater dropped from a tourist trip, caught on a branch.

The knocking had almost stopped. Even the waving seemed barely to be moving now. Once it disappeared altogether. Then they heard another sound, very weak. Barely a voice.

'Help. Help me.'

Claudio grabbed the loudspeaker. 'Emma! Emma! We're coming, Emma,' he said loudly. 'We are coming. Hold on. Show us where you are. Can you stand in the light? Stand up, Emma. So we can see you.'

Then they caught a glimpse of Emma's white face in the beam of light. She was crouched on the sand, struggling to stand on her feet, using a sort of stick to lever herself up. She barely had the strength to stand.

Claudio was over the side of the police launch the moment it reached shallow water. He waded through the waves, up onto the sand, straight to the slight figure struggling to stand.

He caught her in his arms. 'Oddio. I've got you, Emma. You're safe now. It is Commissario Claudio Morelli. Hold on. I'm taking you home.'

He couldn't carry her. Her coat was sodden and she was a dead weight. Barto jumped in the water and came over to help. The driver kept the powerful beam on the couple as they carried Emma back to the launch. She had no strength to walk but she could speak.

'*Grazie, grazie,*' she murmured. It was like a miracle.

They lifted her over the side, trying to be gentle, into the rocking launch. They took off the wet coat and wrapped her in blankets, guided her to the cabin, then held a cup of coffee to her lips. It tasted heavenly. Had she gone to heaven? But no, she recognized the Commissario, though he looked different from his usual spruce self. He was soaking wet, hair tousled, face streaming.

'Thank you,' she said again.

'Marco is coming,' Claudio said. 'I have told him where we are. He is also searching the Lagoon.'

'It was two men,' said Emma, still hoarse. 'In a water taxi. They tied me up and left me on the island to die.'

Claudio took Barto aside. 'Go back onto the island and search for items. They tied her up. There must be rope, some clues. Take a lamp. See what you can find. Bring everything.'

'*Si*, Commissario.' Barto looked dismayed at having to go back into the cold water. Young and fit as he was, he was shivering.

'This will look good on your personnel report,' Claudio reminded him. 'A good start to your career. You will end up as Vice-Questore.'

Claudio was rubbing life back into Emma's cold hands and feet. Her hands were torn and bleeding. Her boots were full of water. He towelled her face and hair. She did not seem to be injured in any way. There was not much more they could do on the launch. She needed a hot bath and Maria's good soup and a night's sleep in the safety of the palazzo.

But he needed a statement from her before she forgot vital details. A fresh memory was always more reliable.

'We have some rolls but they are from the polizia canteen, so very ordinary.'

Emma nodded. '*Per favore* ... I will eat ordinary, anything.'

She did not know what she was eating. A bread roll with a cheese filling of sorts. But it was food and not an insect. Claudio refilled the coffee cup and she sipped it gratefully, the heat, the taste, the milkiness was nectar. She could feel its warmth trickling down inside her.

'Marco?'

'Marco is coming. He is not far away now.'

The new recruit returned with his loot from the island. He had found Emma's bag, the sacking, the rope, her torn scarf tied to a branch and a linen cap. 'There's nothing more. Only a small ruin for a hermit or plague victim.'

'My trusty stick,' said Emma. She was beginning to feel very sleepy, despite the caffeine. 'My ruined scarf.'

Claudio bagged the linen cap. 'This is curious,' he said. 'Someone was wearing a linen cap. It looks quite new.'

She was drifting off into sleep, despite the hard decking. They had tucked another blanket round her and folded padded coats for her head. She was so comfortable it could have been the most expensive bed in the Hotel Gritti Palace.

She was hardly aware of a second motorboat approaching or the exchange of voices. The police launch rocked as a tall figure clambered aboard and hurried over to her. She knew it was Marco when his arms went round her and his lips were in her damp hair.

'Oh, *caro*, my darling. You're safe, Emma. We have found you. I'm so sorry that this happened. It is all my fault for leaving you.'

'Nothing matters now … you are here,' Emma murmured, her breath on his face. 'Stay with me.'

'I need a statement from the signorina,' said Claudio, not wanting to interrupt the reunion. He felt the same old stirring of envy as he watched his friend holding Emma. 'It's important.'

'You will get your statement,' said Marco, grimly. 'When I say so. In the morning. Now she must sleep.'

twenty~three

Claudio told Barto to go home and take a hot bath, get some food and sleep. 'You have done well,' he said. 'It'll not be forgotten. Come back when you feel rested. I will explain your absence.'

'*Grazie*, Commissario.'

The items from the island were bagged and labelled. Even Emma's handbag, though he felt sure it could be returned to her soon without a problem. It was not likely to have prints left on it after all this rain.

The linen cap was a good find. The man must have torn it off when he removed the corno. It would certainly contain some hair which held DNA.

Emma remembered little of the journey back to the palazzo. Marco's arms were closed round her and that was all that mattered. She wondered if she was dreaming and would soon wake up and find herself back in the ruin, wrapped in sacking.

But his voice was with her all the time. 'You are safe now, Emma. Try and sleep.'

Claudio returned to his small flat and found the water tank cold. He switched on the immersion heater, peeled off his wet clothes, drank coffee till the water was warm enough to get into. He boiled several kettles and tipped them first into the bath. He could not wait forever.

He was bone weary. He was always tired these days. Perhaps he should go to the doctor soon. But there was never a free hour and he did not like to waste their time. Too many people wasted doctors' valuable time with trivial ailments.

He sighed as he sank under the water, letting the warmth wash over his head. He was elated that they had found Emma. If she had become another victim, he would have failed with his investigations and been devastated. But she was alive. He doubted if she would have survived another night in the cold. It was all tied up together. The hacking of the Prosecco fortune and the three ruthless attacks, two of which had resulted in death.

He would go to the palazzo later that morning. It was already beginning to get light, sunrise creeping through the clouds with unsteady pink-streaked fingers. The different bells were tolling their unearthly wake-up calls. No one ever thought to complain. No one dared to complain. It was as if the doges still wielded their immense power over the citizens of Venice.

Wrapped in an old navy towelling robe, he began making a list of everything that had happened. It was not his usual procedure. He normally carried lists in his head. Somewhere there was a link, something that he had missed. It was hidden in this maze of information.

If he stared at the words long enough, one or two of them might begin to make sense.

Marco had not gone to his own bed. He slept on the floor in Emma's room, not wanting to wake her but not daring to leave her. Maria had fussed around in the bathroom with warm towels and more hot milky drinks. But Emma only wanted to sleep now and the comfortable duvet enveloped her like some heavenly cloud of warmth.

'Sleep well,' said Marco, kissing her lightly. But she had already fallen asleep.

'What shall I do with these clothes?' Maria asked, her arms full of sodden and torn clothing. They smelt of the sea, of rotting material.

'Bin them, but perhaps not yet. The police may find some fibres. Forensics are so clever these days.'

'*Si*, signor. I will put them in a bag but not the intimates. Those I will wash and dry for the signorina.'

Marco smiled at Maria's discreet wording. And her thriftiness. He always wanted to buy everything brand new for Emma. He wanted to buy her closets and closets full of beautiful new clothes.

He wanted to buy her everything she had ever wanted. How he would spoil her when she was his.

'*Grazie.*'

It was about ten o'clock when Marco awoke to the loud noise of his front doorbell. He knew instantly that it was the Commissario. Emma did not stir. Marco pulled on a black towelling robe and went downstairs. Maria was talking to the poliziotto.

'No,' she was saying. 'Signor Marco cannot be disturbed. He is still sleeping. The signorina is still sleeping. Please go away.'

'I will wait until they are both awake,' said Claudio Morelli patiently. 'I have urgent business with them.'

'This is not the time. Come back later.'

'It's all right, Maria,' said Marco, pausing at the top of the marble staircase. 'Show the Commissario to the sitting room and make us some coffee while I get dressed.'

'Si, signor.'

'Signorina Emma Chandler?' asked Claudio. 'She is all right?'

'She is well but still asleep. These British women are strong. I didn't say my full gratitude to you when you found her. But I say it now. I am forever in your debt.' Marco thought this was ironic when he had no ready money, not until he sold the next harvest of grapes. He hoped it would be a good harvest.

'It is my job,' said Claudio.

'And the young recruit?'

'He will not be forgotten. He will be commended.'

Marco went upstairs to shower and dress. Emma was still sleeping. The colour had returned to her face. He did not wake her even though he was tempted.

Maria bustled into the sitting room with a tray set with coffee and a dish of hot croissants. She knew the detective was always without food. It was no wonder he was so thin.

'*Grazie,*' he said. 'You make the best coffee in Venice.'

'Always the soft soap,' she said, but pleased.

Marco came back in black jeans, black polo-necked jersey. He had not stopped to shave. The bristles on his chin made him look like a member of the Sicilian Mafia.

'We have traced a stolen water taxi,' said Claudio. 'The licensed taxi drivers reported him. He has been stealing business from them. It may be the water taxi which took Emma to the island.'

'That's good.'

'I have more leads. But the only person who can help me is the signorina. Her evidence is vital. I need her statement.'

'So glad to hear I am needed,' Emma said, from the doorway. She was dressed in a blue tracksuit, her hair tied back with a ribbon, her feet in flip-flops.

Both men stood and made room for her. She went straight for a hot croissant and a plate. She was not wearing any make-up. She looked like a schoolgirl. She was as hungry as any schoolgirl.

'I dreamed of this kind of food on the island,' she said. 'I dreamed a lot about food. I didn't want to eat insects. Once I thought I might have to.'

Marco poured out coffee for her into the cup that Maria had laid for him. 'Start from the beginning,' he said. 'We need to know everything that you can remember.'

Emma curled up on the settee, tucking her feet under herself. She sank her teeth into the hot croissant, flakes round her lips, savouring the taste. It tasted so good. She would always savour food now, knowing what it was like to be without any.

'I thought Enrico had ordered the water taxi. I should have checked but there was no way of doing so. He had rung off. I remember the motorboat had lots of tinkling sounds, bells or something hanging.'

'Some of the taxis have hanging charms or tokens. What did the driver look like? Can you describe him?'

'The driver had a dish-shaped face, narrow eyes and a peaked cap. He had the usual yellow plastic jacket. He was not particularly pleasant and big, much bigger than most Italians. The other man was wearing very strange clothes because they were sort of medieval, like in the paintings of the medieval doges. I thought perhaps he had been to a party. He had a funny hat. He threw me on the deck and wrapped sacking round me, then rope. I lost my briefcase but I held onto my bag as it was tied against me.'

'Then what happened?' Claudio asked gently.

'I don't know,' Emma faltered. 'We drove over the sea for a long time. It was very choppy. I felt sick. Then the motorboat seemed to go up on a mudbank and stop. They heaved me over the side and onto the island. I only heard them go away, leaving me on the wet sand.'

'Can you remember anything they said?'

'They spoke in Italian, a different dialect I think. And loud and very fast. I could hardly understand a word.'

'Can you remember any names being mentioned?'

Emma scratched at her memory. Had she heard any names? None. Only *il marmo* and she did not know what that meant. 'Only *il marmo* and that means nothing to me. I remember it because it sounded like Marmite.'

'*Il marmo* means marble.'

'I don't know why they were talking about marble.'

'Describe the second man's clothes, the one you thought had been to a party.'

'He was wearing a big swirling black cloak with a high collar. And on his head was the horn-shaped hat that you see in the paintings of the doges. It was strange and weird.'

'The fancy-dress shops have these outfits. For the carnivals and festivals when everyone dresses up. The doge outfit is popular, especially with an elaborate cream brocade cape. But a black cloak is different. And the other man, the thug driver, the big man?'

'I don't remember. Jeans maybe, a jersey, the yellow jacket. I don't know. I'm sorry.'

'Do not be sorrowful, signorina. We have many clues now and you are safe.'

'That is the most important thing,' said Marco, interrupting. 'You are safe.'

Claudio fetched a loose-leaf folder from his briefcase. 'Do you feel strong enough to look at photographs? Perhaps you will remember the dish-shaped face?'

'Emma has had enough,' said Marco firmly. 'No more.'

'I'm all right, Marco,' Emma said gently. 'I can look at photographs while it's all fresh in my mind. Tomorrow I may have forgotten.'

Marco nodded. Emma was as strong-minded as ever and he loved her for it.

'Five minutes only,' he growled.

She leafed over the pages of photographs. The driver's mean

face was imprinted on her mind. She hoped his face would not come into her dreams. She wanted to wipe him from her mind, so it was best she looked at the photographs now.

Suddenly she went cold. The dish-shaped face and narrow eyes stared at her from the page. She said nothing but handed the open page to Claudio. 'This is the driver,' she said.

'*Grazie*, signorina. And the second man?'

'No more,' Marco said firmly. 'Enough. You will find both thugs if you know this man.'

'And this is the second man in the doge costume.'

'He is known to us. He is a nasty piece of work.' Claudio did not say that he was recently out of prison for assault, that Emma would have to come to the Questura to make a formal statement and attend an identification parade. He could see that Marco was getting impatient. So would he be, if Emma belonged to him. He would protect her night and day. Claudio knew this was foolishness on his part. Emma had eyes only for Marco.

If she would give him a small part of her day, a small part of her time, a few grains of affection from her heart, he would be satisfied. Claudio wondered if he was expecting too much.

'*Grazie*, Commissario,' Emma said, rising. 'Now I want to spend some time with Marco.'

'*Naturalmente*. I will see myself out.'

Marco watched Emma eating the last of the croissants. He wondered if he should suggest a lunch out, somewhere civilized, so that she could forget her terrible ordeal.

Emma was ahead of him. 'Lunch out would be great,' she said. 'I want to get back to being normal. I don't want to be treated as an invalid.'

'Tomorrow we will eat out, but today you will rest,' said Marco. 'I have no experience with invalids.'

Emma climbed off the sofa and sat on his lap, twining her arms round his neck. 'Firstly, you have to be very gentle with them.'

'I can do gentle.'

'And loving.'

'I can do a lot of loving.'

'And be patient if they ask for impossible things.'

Marco thought about this. 'What impossible things?'

Emma leaned forward and whispered in his ear. He smiled and nodded his agreement. He carried her upstairs to his bed where they lay together, entwined, and slept for a few more hours, their breath mingling.

The identification of Gatta Foscari was a big step forward in their investigations. His parents had named him after Gattamelata, a mercenary soldier, whose equestrian statue was famous. But the name was too long for anyone with time to pronounce.

Claudio alerted the system for sightings of Gatta Foscari and any known associates. The fancy-dress shops were being canvassed. One reported a recent break-in. A doge's horned hat was stolen and a black cloak. Also some white make-up.

They did not report it at the time as they were too busy.

'*Insolito*,' said Claudio, throwing up his hands. 'Unbelievable.'

He phoned the forensics laboratory. 'The linen cap from the island. You have found some DNA?'

'There are hairs. And sweat. It's very good.'

'But have you identified anything yet?'

'Commissario, *per favore*. You are so impatient. This is meticulous work. It is not done in minutes. We are professionals.'

'*Mi dispiace.*'

Claudio sat back, his head aching. As if he was not a professional. The lack of sleep, the lack of food, it was getting to him. The forensic team hadn't spent half the night in a police launch, wading through the shallows, searching one rain-lashed scrap of land after another for a terrified woman.

He took a painkiller. He wondered sometimes if he took too many.

twenty~four

Professor Windsor tipped back the chair and rubbed his face. He was bone weary.

He hadn't slept much either, waiting for news of Emma and now another long day sorting out the maze of complications in this computer system. But now it was done. It was finished. He could go back to his London town house, forget this world. He did not want to forget his new friends, especially Emma, but so much talking was tiring.

He wondered how he could explain it all in layman's terms. He did not relish what he was going to have to tell Marco. He wouldn't like it. But he had to tell him the truth. Marco was sitting opposite him, waiting for the verdict.

'Malicious attackers think like thieves, often exploiting a physical security weakness. In your case, it was not checking the credibility of the people you bought the new computer system from, and secondly, having an easy-to-access password.'

'I thought a password was just a means of getting into a computer,' said Marco, glumly.

'It's a protection,' said the professor. 'It should be a pass phrase really. They are far harder to crack. There are machines which will crack a password, even if it is a word mixed up with numbers, upper and lower case. Your easily remembered phrase could be: I often go 2 museums. Sixteen letters.'

'Or: Maria's fish soup is perfect.'

'Better to change *perfect* to something more unusual.'

'*Grazie*. I will think up something unusual about Maria's soup.'

'There are several well-known malicious hackers but in your case, these hackers were after the money. When you get your new computer system from a reputable firm, I will install security countermeasures. And you will need to educate your users.'

'*Si*. My staff will go on courses.'

'The hackers used your laptop and your phone to initially gain entry to your system. You discussed getting a new computer system, arranged payment with an electronic transfer. That's why the theft has been concentrated on the last two years' income.'

The professor's coffee was cold but he drank it anyway. 'There is a new type of invisible root kit that can steal bank account data.'

'A root kit? I don't understand.'

'It's the most malicious of its kind and has been detected all over Europe. It downloads malware that logs all keystrokes that the unsuspecting user types into the computer. It also has a watch-dog thread that was detected when I started to remove it. The root kit reinstalled itself.'

'So how do you get rid of it?' Marco wished he understood what the professor was saying.

'It's a very detailed procedure to overwrite the root kit's entry. I've completed this. Your current computer system is now free of malware but I suggest you throw it out anyway and start afresh with a read-only system.'

'I will take it out to sea to the deepest depth and drown it,' Marco said with feeling.

'We will also remove the hard drive and destroy it.'

Marco looked relieved. 'Your work is *fantastico*. I am forever in your debt. So where is the money now?'

This was the part that Professor Windsor was dreading and Marco would hate hearing the truth. He was going to give him the worst of bad news.

'The euros have been deposited in an account in the Cayman Islands. It's a favourite place for illegal financial transactions. It's also famous for its turtles.'

'Damn the turtles. Can I get any of the money back? In whose name is the account?'

The professor cleared his throat. 'The account is in three names: Harry Stone and Emma Chandler are two of them. It is true. I have seen her signature. She is a joint holder of the account in the Cayman Islands.'

Marco's face went pale. He was visibly shocked. 'I don't believe it. Not my Emma. She is innocent of all this hacking.'

'I suggest we ask her to her face, with Commissario Morelli present at the meeting. We must give her a chance to explain.'

'I will set up this meeting. This evening at five o'clock at my palazzo. Does this suit you? The Commissario should be free by then and Emma will be rested. I told Maria that she was to do nothing today, only sleep and eat.'

Emma had spent the day in a velvet languor. It had been therapeutic, a vital silence. She had washed her hair again, eaten several small meals, mostly soup, and slept a lot. Marco had phoned. He sounded a bit strange but said he would arrive at 5 p.m. with Commissario Morelli and Professor Windsor.

'How lovely,' said Emma. 'All my favourite people.'

'If you say so.' It was an odd reply.

But Emma didn't care. 'I'll see you soon,' she said happily.

Emma went into Francesca's bedroom to find something different to wear, something that Marco would like. She was feeling so much better. The tracksuit was creased and she had spilt a drop of soup on the front. Her hand had been shaking.

Francesca did not have many casual clothes but Emma found some crushed black trousers, a long-sleeved cream shirt and a padded waistcoat threaded with many silver and gold colours. Francesca had wonderful taste. Emma would never have bought anything so flamboyant. But then, Emma had worked all her life. And she dressed to work. Her London clothes were plain and classic.

Emma flew downstairs when she heard Marco arrive at the palazzo. She had to be careful on the marble staircase as she was still not too steady.

'Marco, Marco.' She went straight into his arms. He held her very close as if he never wanted to let her go. She pressed her face against his chest, breathing in the scent of his body.

'You would never let me down, my sweet Emma, would you?' he said, his voice almost choking in his throat. 'You would never do anything to hurt me?'

She leaned back, not understanding. 'Of course not, Marco. Never. I don't know what you mean.'

'We will go upstairs and I will explain. Professor Windsor will also explain. Commissario Morelli is joining us. He may have some news.'

'You look very tired.'

'I am very tired. It has been a long day. And it's not finished yet.'

Emma did not like the grave tone of his voice For a moment it frightened her, but then her good sense told her that Marco could never be frightening. He'd not slept yet, only snatched the odd hour. She had had the luxury of a whole day doing nothing.

'Come upstairs,' she said. 'I'll fetch your favourite brandy. You can sleep until the others arrive.'

'You always seem to want to look after me, Emma. But is it all an act?'

'An act?' Emma looked confused. 'Of course not. I am here with you, not acting.'

'Never mind, Emma,' Marco said, tousling her newly washed hair. 'Upstairs, a brandy and a sleep. I will worry about the rest tomorrow.'

Marco was asleep in moments. Emma took the half-drunk brandy from his hand before it spilled. He was exhausted. She hoped the others would be late. Marco needed this time alone with her, needed to heal whatever had hurt him so much.

They were both late. Commissario Morelli had a frantic and productive day. Professor Windsor had gone to his hotel to pack. He was flying back to London the next day, a generous post-dated cheque in his briefcase for his services.

On cue, Maria came into the sitting room with a tray of coffee and small snacks to eat. Professor Windsor and Commissario Morelli arrived, full of apologies. Strangely no one was hungry. No one ate anything. Not even the detective.

Professor Windsor recited his explanation of the hacking of Marco's computer system and the steps he had taken.

'It will not happen again,' he said. 'The system is safe now. But I have suggested the purchase of completely new equipment.'

Marco nodded his thanks. 'Commissario, have you anything to add?'

'We have arrested Gatta Foscari on several counts. He was

newly out of prison. The DNA of the hairs on the linen cap match hairs on the raincoat which Pia was wearing. This other villain was caught trying to sell the signorina's laptop. He is also known and can be hired. We have found the stolen water taxi and there is much evidence on the deck. Both men are on their way to Milan, under guard. They have both been charged.'

'Well done,' said Emma, her eyes bright. 'That's marvellous news. Isn't that wonderful, Marco? They have caught the two men who kidnapped me.'

'So good,' said Marco. He seemed incapable of saying anything more.

'And we have found the fancy-dress shop where Gatta hired the black cloak and the horned hat of a doge. He likes to be dramatic and disguised. He knew his face was familiar to us. The linen cap was worn under the hat. It is the custom. We will soon be able to link him to Brad's hanging under the bridge.'

'He was a good student,' said the professor. 'He didn't deserve to die.'

'So everything is all right now?' said Emma, relieved.

'Not quite,' said the professor. 'You see, I have traced the big sums of hacked money to bank accounts in the Cayman Islands. The accounts are in three names. They include the names of Harry Stone and Emma Chandler.'

There was a stunned silence. Emma looked from Marco's pale face, to Professor Windsor, who would not look straight at her, then at Commissario Morelli, who looked bewildered.

'I don't understand,' Emma faltered. 'My name? I don't know anything about funds in the Cayman Islands. It's not me. It's someone else pretending to be me.'

'Your signature is clearly on the documents,' said Professor Windsor wearily.

'It's not true,' said Emma, turning to Marco, her face aflame. 'I've nothing to do with this. Do you believe me, Marco? This isn't me.'

'I want to believe you,' Marco said.

'Harry Stone is a creep and I refused to go out with him. I turned him down, day after day, week after week when I joined the firm. It's his revenge …' She burst into tears, grabbing a napkin from the tray to staunch her tears. 'It's someone else using my name.'

'The signorina is right about the name Stone. She recalled hearing a word repeated when the two men seized her in the water taxi. We thought it was marble but it was the other meaning of the word which is stone. They were talking about their contact in London, the man who was paying them.'

'How do you know this?'

'We have their mobile phones and the same number recurs several times. It is also the same number which was used to contact Vikki Boccetta, the air hostess. We have also found a considerable amount of money in their rooms, used notes, but we may be able to trace them. We have also found wire which is similar to that used to throttle the student, Brad.'

'How do you know that Gatta Foscari murdered the girl and the student?' Marco asked. 'Is there evidence?'

'There is no honour among Venetian thieves. The other thug split on him. He told us everything, thinking it would get him a lighter sentence.'

'But what about the money in the bank account?' said Emma. 'The money that I know nothing about, that is deposited in my name.'

'I asked them to send me by fax a copy of your specimen signature,' said the professor, opening his briefcase. 'Is this your signature, Emma?' He laid a sheet of paper before her.

She nodded unhappily. 'Yes, that is my signature. But I didn't sign anything for this bank. Don't you have to show them proof of identity?'

'It is all done electronically these days. It merely has to be witnessed by some authority. I'm sure Irving Stone has plenty of contacts willing to witness.'

'You mean, Irving Stone is connected to this as well?' Emma could barely believe it. Irving Stone Chartered Accountants was a long-established firm in London with a reputation for the best work.

'The Cayman Island account is in three names. Two signatures have to be on every transaction. Irving Stone's wife, Brenda Stone, and his son, Harry, are the main signatories. But your signature has authorized several recent transfers.'

Emma sank back. All her worst fears were returning. It was a nightmare. None of this could be true.

'No, no, it's not true. They could have got my signature from anywhere in the office. I've witnessed many documents, accounts, signed letters. My signature is on many files. They could have lifted it.' Emma turned to Marco. 'Please believe me, please, Marco. I had nothing to do with this.'

'I want to believe you, Emma,' he said quietly. 'There must be an explanation. Some reason why you are involved in this conspiracy. It must be more than jealousy on the part of the rejected son.'

'A third name is often used in such transactions,' said Professor Windsor. 'It gives the business set up more authenticity. Emma was probably described as Harry's fiancée to make it seem like a family business.'

This was now another nightmare. Emma saw Marco's mouth tighten. 'Was this another reason why you would not marry me?' he said. 'Because you are already engaged to this Harry Stone?'

'No, no, it's nothing like that,' she cried. 'He's the most obnoxious person I've ever met. I had nothing to do with him. He was a pain. It took months to shake him off before he got the message.'

'So what is this message now for me?' said Marco with a steely glint. 'What am I to believe?'

Commissario Morelli saw the whole scenario unravelling before his eyes in chaos and disorder. He did not believe for a moment that Emma was involved. Somehow they had used her name and her signature. For her sake, he had to find out the truth.

'Signor dell'Orto, do not be hasty.' Claudio addressed him by his full name to add weight to his words. 'There is no proof that the signorina is part of the money fraud. She could be completely innocent. Let me see what I can discover. We have contacts all over the world. I have already passed on all my information to the CID, Scotland Yard. Remember what Emma has gone through. Remember that attempts have been made on her life.'

'They could have been the fake attempts, to pull the wool over my face.' Marco's English was going to pieces. He was clearly distressed. Emma was weeping openly. The professor was wringing his hands, wishing he had not discovered such disturbing information. Perhaps he should have kept his mouth shut.

Claudio did not know what to do. In view of the professor's evidence, he should take Emma to the Questura for further questioning. She must have a lawyer present. It was a dilemma. He began to feel ill. He was sweating. He stood up, uncertainly.

'If you will excuse me, I am feeling unwell. I will leave the signorina in your charge tonight, Signor dell'Orto, and send an escort for her tomorrow. Please assemble your documents for me, Professor Windsor, and deliver them to my office.'

'Sì, Commissario. You don't look too well. A long day and no sleep last night. I will accompany you to your home. Allow me,' said the professor. 'We'll leave now. Marco and Emma have much to talk about.'

Professor Windsor and the Commissario left the room. No one had touched the coffee or the snacks. Maria would think she had done something wrong. That it was her fault that everything had gone haywire.

Marco leaned over and took Emma's hand. The napkin was screwed up into a tight, wet ball. Her eyes were puffy, her nose red. She was trembling. Her grief could not be more genuine.

'I believe you,' he said gently. 'We will dig out the truth.'

twenty~five

Emma slept the sleep of the exhausted. Marco came to lock her into her room, feeling like a traitor. She understood that he had to do it. She was under suspicion.

'I'm sorry. It is wrong,' he said, the key in his hand. 'But you are in my charge. Claudio has let you stay here.'

'No, you have to do it. I promise I'll not jump out of the window.'

He groaned. 'Then I will stay with you.'

'No, Marco, you need to be in your own room and sleep in your own bed. You are desperate for sleep. Everything will be different tomorrow, you'll see.'

'Domain, si, domain.'

The day began with glimmers of sun. Perhaps winter had decided to fold up its mantle and escape to warmer climes. Emma stretched, wondering if this would be her last morning in a comfortable bed, this luxurious room. Would it be a prison cell from now onwards? But she was innocent. They had to prove her guilt.

It was a subdued breakfast on the balcony. Maria did not understand why. Emma was dressed in her own plain clothes. She would take nothing of Francesca's with her to the police station. Marco had shaved but did not look more rested. They ate a little brioche, drank juice and coffee as if dehydrated.

'We will go now,' he said, rising. 'If you are ready.'

'Do you want me to pack my things?'

'No. That is not necessary.'

'Grazie.'

Emma did not know what to make of that remark. She did not know what was going to happen to her. Before leaving, she went into the kitchen to reassure Maria that all would soon be well.

Maria looked up from the sink. She was already preparing vegetables for the lunch, her expression forlorn.

'There has been a terrible misunderstanding,' said Emma. 'We are now going to sort it out. Don't worry, Maria. I will be back.'

'I hope so, signorina. All this worry is making me older.'

Emma gave her a quick hug. 'No, not you, dear friend. Never.'

'That Vikki Boccetta was here this morning,' Maria went on. 'She wanted to speak to the signor, but I said no and to go away.'

'Quite right,' Emma agreed. 'She probably wanted money.'

The interview room at the Questura was the same as any police interview room anywhere in the world. Cold, cheerless, faded paintwork, a dead plant. Professor Windsor sat on a hard wooden chair. He had delayed his flight home till the evening.

'Please, professor, record for the tape,' said Claudio, switching on the machine. 'Your findings of the hacking.'

Professor Windsor launched into his observations of the hacking and the transfer of money from the dell'Orto account. He kept it as brief as possible. No one understood a word he was saying. It was all technology.

'It was at first small amounts which Signor Bragora did not notice. Then the amounts got larger. Finally the dell'Orto bank accounts were cleared and all the money transferred to the Cayman Islands.'

'And where is the money now?'

'We don't know. The Cayman Island accounts have also been closed.'

'So the money has disappeared?'

'The vineyard workers and factory staff who work for me will all be paid,' said Marco. 'No one will go short. But maybe the Inland Revenue will have to wait.'

'The Inland Revenue is another matter,' said Emma, back in her accountant's role. 'I can deal with that. I'll write and explain.'

'If you are not in prison,' said Marco.

There was a stunned silence.

Commissario Morelli shuffled his papers. 'Please, not to be hasty, signor. I have been in contact with CID, Scotland Yard. I sent them all my information. They are at this minute investigating

Irving Stone Chartered Accountants. There is evidence of big purchases and transfers of large sums of money. Brenda Stone has bought a property in the South of France and Harry Stone has bought a villa in Spain. Also past big debts have been paid off: Harry's gambling debts, and debts to the Inland Revenue.'

'What does that mean about me?' Emma asked, stunned.

'You were involved in the setting-up of the Cayman Island account four years ago.'

'But I only began working for them four years ago.'

'I know. I have the date of when you began working for them. It was only a few weeks before your signature and identity were sent to the Caymans and your name registered. You were someone new, someone innocent, someone who would not know what was going on or what you were signing.'

Emma groaned. 'What an idiot. I certainly didn't know what was going on.'

There was a knock on the door. 'Commissario Morelli. There is someone to see you. She says it is very important.'

Claudio switched off the tape recorder. '*Un momento, per favore.* Please ask her to wait. I am busy.'

'She cannot wait, she says. She is flying to Hong Kong this evening from Milan. It will be some days before she returns to Venice. It is something about her mother.'

'How I hate demanding women,' Claudio said. 'I will be out in five minutes. Give her a cup of coffee.'

'*Si*, Commissario. It will be a pleasure.'

'What did he mean by that?' Claudio switched on the tape to resume the recording. 'Irving Stone and his son, Harry, have not been arrested but they are being questioned. They say that the money has come from wise investments.'

'Can this be proved or disproved?'

'Scotland Yard is working on this now. The matter is in the hands of the Fraud Squad. I have every confidence in their work. But it is slow, *naturalmente*. Financial investigations are like a needle in a corn stack.'

'Haystack,' said Emma. They all looked at her. It was as if they had forgotten she was there. 'What will happen to me?'

'I regret that I shall have to ask you to stay here. I should prefer that you stay voluntarily and that I do not have to detain you in custody.'

'I'll stay,' said Emma in a small voice. 'Of course, whatever you say.'

'I will stay with her,' said Marco sharply.

'This is not a hotel, signor,' said Claudio, equally sharp. 'I will make sure the signorina is comfortable and she will have a female companion.'

They heard raised voices outside in the corridor. One was clearly female. There was a rap on the door and it opened. A tall, slim vision walked in, her uniform immaculate, her make-up flawless, her hair golden and superbly cut. Emma recognized her immediately. It was Vikki, the airline hostess.

'I shall lose my job if I am late at the airport. If you don't want my information then I shall go. *Mia madre* says I must give it to you. It is my duty. I don't care if it is my duty. I care more if I lose my good job.'

'*Benvenuto*, Signorina Boccetta. Please do sit down. You will not lose your job. I will make sure that a car is available to take you to the airport,' said Claudio, pulling up a chair for her. 'You have some information from your mother?'

Vikki Boccetta sat down, crossing one silk-clad leg over the other. She was mollified, now that they were taking her seriously.

'Can I offer you a drink?'

'No, *grazie*, your coffee is terrible.'

'*Si*, I agree. There is nothing I can do about it. Please continue.'

'It is not from my mother. I am giving the information. Some years ago, my mother was in danger of losing her apartment. We were behind with the rent and I was not yet earning good money with the airline. This man offered to pay me for a day's work. It was nothing, really. I had to present this passport and answer a few questions. I signed nothing. The signing was already done and witnessed, they said.'

'What passport?'

'This passport. I kept it because it is a good photograph of me.' She fished in her capacious bag and produced a maroon-covered British passport. She handed it to Claudio. 'I had forgotten all about it.'

Claudio opened the passport. It was indeed an excellent portrait of Vikki Boccetta. But the printed details were for Emma Chandler, address, date of birth, occupation, passport issue and expiry and her signature. Everything was correct, except the photograph.

'And where did you go with this passport?' Claudio asked. But he already knew.

'I flew to the Cayman Islands, to some office, a bank, I think. I didn't take much notice of the arrangement. It was nothing. I fly everywhere. Then I flew back the same evening.'

'What was the date of this transaction?'

'It's the date stamped in the passport.'

Claudio looked at the dates. 'Of course. Four years ago, I see.'

Marco drew in his breath. He looked at the passport details. 'So you impersonated Emma Chandler, said that you were she.'

Vikki shrugged her shoulders. 'How was I to know? I didn't know her. The name meant nothing to me. But *mia madre*, she remembers everything. She said this Emma Chandler was now lost and the police were searching for her. She said I must come and tell you. She said it was my duty.'

'How did your mother learn that the police were searching for Emma?'

'She had lent Maria some buckets when the palazzo was flooded. She called by to get them back and Maria told her. *Mia madre* does a lot of washing and needs her buckets.'

'*Grazie*, signorina. We are most grateful. I have to keep the passport but I will have a copy made of the photograph for you because it is, indeed, most beautiful. Your statement will be printed and I will ask you to sign it, then you may leave. A car will take you to Marco Polo Airport so you will not miss your flight.'

Vikki looked at Emma. Emma's hair was tied back with a ribbon. She wore no make-up. Her dark suit was severe. 'You don't look a bit like me,' said Vikki with some satisfaction as she turned to leave.

Marco took Emma's hand and raised her fingers to his lips. 'Forgive me, *caro*. I have been a fool, thinking more of my fortune and not enough about you. How can you ever trust me again?'

'It will be easy,' said Emma. 'Because I've never stopped loving you.'

'I am mortified. I should be flogged. Commissario Morelli, thank you. I cannot thank you enough. You and the professor. You have given me back my life and given me back Emma.'

'But not your money.'

'I don't care about the money. Emma is more important.'

'Will you have to charge Vikki Boccetta?' Emma asked anxiously. 'What she did is against the law, isn't it? Using a false passport? But her mother sounds quite poor and she would be devastated.'

'I may forget to charge Vikki. I have such a poor memory,' said Claudio vaguely. 'Instead, I will send her mother some flowers. Maybe she will have to stand them in a bucket.'

The laughter lifted the atmosphere. It was a moment for everyone to remember. Claudio opened the passport. He would scan it immediately and send details to Scotland Yard. The professor could catch his plane back to London. As for Emma and Marco, they had the rest of their lives.

'What would you like to do?' Marco asked, wondering how he was ever going to make amends to Emma.

'I would like to go home.'

'To London, with the professor?'

'No, home with you.'

'To the palazzo?'

'Wherever you are is home,' said Emma.

epilogue

Marco and Emma were married in the dell'Orto vineyard. It was a glorious May day with spring flowers everywhere around the house and up the outside stairs, and already the blossom was heavy on the vines.

'It is going to be a good harvest,' said Marco, taking Emma for an early-morning walk among the vines.

No superstition here about not seeing the bride on the wedding morning. Emma had woken with Marco's dear dark head on the pillow beside her, his breathing sweet and even. It was what she wanted. It was what they both wanted. They had waited long enough. It had been an intense pleasure with waves of ecstasy. They floated down to earth, equally spent.

'Yes,' said Emma, quietly. 'It's going to be a very good harvest.'

It had started off being a small, private wedding, but it had grown.

The accounts staff, Rocco and Luka and the secretaries, were being driven over from Venice, along with Maria and Professor Windsor, who was delighted to return to Venice. Many of the plant staff were also coming, in their own cars, as it was not far. Marco also had some business friends he wanted to invite.

'What about you, *mia caro*?' he asked tenderly. 'Have you no one you want to invite?'

'No one,' said Emma. 'I've never had anyone. No family. Even my little cat died. My foster parents put him to sleep. I would like a cat.'

'You will have a small kitten, but promise it will not go on a lead and collar like a slave. A cat should always have his freedom.'

Marco took her in his arms in the vineyard, amongst the vines, his lips warm and passionate on her mouth. 'Soon this will be legal. Today you will be Signora dell'Orto, my wife.'

'Your wife,' breathed Emma. 'It's like a dream.'

'A dream coming true.'

There was nothing remotely suitable in Francesca's wardrobe for a wedding. Emma also thought it would be tactless to remind everyone of what had happened to that poor, hapless young woman.

So Emma shopped in London, on her trip back to vacate her flat and put some of her possessions into storage. She visited the London office and handed in her resignation to the new partners.

The names of Irving Stone and his son Harry had been removed from the office doors, from the stationery. The firm would have a new name.

'Now you can promote someone else,' she told the new partners. 'I am going to work for my husband. Signor Bragora is about to retire and I shall take over his workload. But now that Professor Windsor and the Japanese expert have traced the hacking back to the installation system, and black-walled it, all will be well. The system is going to be modernized and there will be no more problems. All that is lost is two years' income.'

She did not say that this amounted to many millions of euros. Marco said he could absorb the loss. She believed him.

'You're already starting to sound like an Italian,' said one of her colleagues, noting the elegant navy and red trouser suit, the flamboyant red blouse. 'And to look like one.'

'I feel Italian,' said Emma. She grinned. 'It's all the good wine I have been drinking. And the pasta I have been eating.'

Her couture London wedding dress was gossamer cream silk, low cut but with long medieval sleeves, tiny pearls sewn along every seam. It was ankle length so that it would not get dirty walking outside in the vineyard. Her cream shoes had kitten heels so that she could walk over the rough ground.

Paola had said that there was grandmother's lace veil stored away and by tradition it should be worn. Emma did not argue. It was easier not to argue. She would have worn a tea cosy on her head, if that was what Marco wanted.

But the lace veil was beautiful, almost falling apart with age. It might last the ceremony. Then it could be put away, carefully folded into tissue paper for another generation.

'I suppose we should return to the house. I think our guests are beginning to arrive,' said Marco, curving his arm around her slender waist.

'Do we have to?'

'A wedding is a family duty.'

The yard was being decorated by the vineyard workers' children with flowers and garlands and streamers everywhere. Another group were enthusiastically blowing up silver balloons and hanging them from trees.

'Very ... rural,' said Emma, laughing, unable to find the right word.

'Not your posh wedding in the palazzo in Venice,' said Marco.

'I didn't want a posh wedding.'

'Neither did I. But when we return to Venice, we will have a grand party in the palazzo and a blessing in a church. You can choose the church. So many to choose from.'

He left her, as he always would, to greet his business friends and offer them refreshments. Emma did not mind. Marco would never change. But he would always be hers, in body and soul. They were soulmates. Nothing could change that.

Emma went to greet Claudio Morelli. He had had an emergency operation for an ulcer in Milan but was recovering well. His skin had a good colour and he did not look tired any more.

'It was a very small growth,' he said. 'But it was benign so all is well.'

'I'm so glad,' Emma said. 'We were all worried about you. I don't think I have ever thanked you properly for saving me from the island.'

He shrugged his shoulders, smiled. 'It was my job.'

Maria and Paola began fussing over her. She must shower, she must change, the hairdresser had arrived to do her hair. Emma let them fuss around her. In a way this was their day too. They had waited a long time for a bride to fuss over and would talk about it for months.

'But first a glass of Prosecco,' they said, bringing in a tray of the crystal flutes already brimming with the sparkling liquid. 'We must have Prosecco.'

'To the bride,' they laughed, toasting her and each other. It was going to be a very merry wedding. They were both smiling. 'To Signor Marco's bride.'

The ceremony was in both Italian and English so that Emma could understand what she was saying. Marco stood, tall and solemn at her side, unbelievably handsome in a pale grey suit, white shirt and white satin tie. Emma had managed to pin his grandmother's lace onto her piled-up hair and somehow felt that the old couple were here, beside them, nodding approvingly and happy.

Professor Windsor gave the bride away. It was an honour that almost brought tears to his eyes, but of course, highly professional computer experts don't cry.

Marco slipped the gold ring on her finger.

'Ti amo,' he whispered.

'Ti amo,' she promised.

The wedding feast was of gigantic proportions. There was so much food on long tables laid in the courtyard. Wedding guests sat everywhere, out in the yard, in the garden, in the formal dining room. All the doors were open so guests could wander where they pleased, glass in hand, food on a plate.

Professor Windsor was getting on very well with one of the young secretaries from the Venice office, enjoying her admiration. Enrico was helping to serve the feast, like a butler. His job was secure. He could also think about marriage to his girlfriend.

'So soon we shall leave for our honeymoon,' said Marco in her ear. 'Shall we slip away while everyone is enjoying themselves?'

'Where are we going?' Emma asked. It had been a closely guarded secret. So close Marco had refused to tell her.

'To Lake Garda. I have a villa there but I have rarely used it. What is the point of going alone? I am worried that you will not like it. It is ver' secluded.'

'Lake Garda?' Emma could not believe her ears. 'It'll be perfect. Of course I will like it. You will be there.'

'Then let us slip away like mouses in the dark. My car is at the back where no one can see it. Shall we say, in half an hour?'

'Twenty minutes.'

But suddenly Marco's attention was diverted. He was looking

at a solitary figure standing alone at the edge of the crowd like a statue, holding no glass, no plate. It was a thin, gaunt, dark-haired young woman, in a grey dress, swaying as if the spring breeze would knock her over. She looked lonely and forlorn.

Marco left Emma swiftly, but she followed him. She had already recognized the lone beauty, recognized the desolation on her face.

It was Francesca. She had not died, alone with painkillers and a bottle of cheap brandy in some lonely French hotel. She was here at her brother's wedding, still beautiful but pale and desolate. She smiled, hesitantly, as Marco came over to her.

'Francesca? Is it you?' Marco swept her into his arms. 'We thought you were dead. Oh my dearest sister, we have grieved for you so.'

'Marco, my beloved brother. I had to come to your wedding. I could not miss it.'

'Where have you been? We searched for you everywhere.'

'I'm so sorry, Marco. Am I forgiven? I did not know what to do. I wanted to die but I did not have the courage. I was a coward. At the last minute, I could not do it. I threw the pills away, but I drank the brandy and slept for many days.'

'No, no, you were very brave. But you are here now. You are here at my wedding and we are never going to let you go away again. This is your family and this is my wife, Emma. We will always look after you, both of us.'

Emma came forward, smiling, still in her wedding dress, veil thrown back, hoping her eyes were saying that she knew how much Francesca had suffered.

'Francesca, my new sister,' she said. 'Please stay with us. I want you, I need you. We could be such friends.' Emma did not say why. Then she added, because it seemed right, 'I have been wearing some of your lovely clothes, thank you for letting me. Such beautiful clothes, thank you.'

Francesca smiled. 'Nothing would fit me now. I am so thin.'

'Please don't vanish, away into the night,' Marco was saying, urgently. 'Stay here at the vineyard with Paola. She will look after you. There is plenty of room. We will be back soon. I have to work, of course. Emma and I must go because this is our honeymoon. We have waited so long.'

Francesca looked between them but there was something that she recognized in Emma, who was smiling and nodding. Emma did not know the right words to say in Italian, but she was desperate to make Francesca stay, not to disappear again.

'I need someone to teach me to speak Italian,' she said. 'Will you teach me? *Per favore*. Be my sister, help me to become Italian. For Marco's sake. Because I love him so.'

Francesca reached out for Emma's hand. Her hand was thin and cold, like a bird. 'I will teach you. I will be your sister.'

Emma was ready in thirty minutes, in blue jeans and a white T-shirt, a travel bag of essentials, nothing else. The pale-green convertible was waiting, Marco at the wheel. He drove away slowly. It picked up speed without a sound. Behind they could hear music, the local band having arrived to add to the festivities.

Paola and Maria had been told of Francesca's sudden appearance. Already they were taking care of her, making her feel at home and safe. Francesca hugged Emma before they left. She was smiling and some of the forlorn look had left her.

'You will be my student,' she said, her eyes already glowing. 'And we will have coffee and go shopping? We will be friends?'

'I promise,' said Emma. 'Good friends.'

Some way from the farmhouse, Marco slowed down. 'I have a special wedding present for you, Emma,' said Marco, his hands firm on the wheel. 'Look on the back seat.'

There was a basket carrier on the back seat. Emma lifted it forwards carefully because Marco was still driving quite fast, the countryside receding in lines of green.

She opened the end hatch. Inside was a tiny crouching kitten, very pale fur, looking bewildered. Emma lifted him out and cradled him under her chin. He was so small, so lost but longing for comfort.

'He's a darling,' she said, loving him immediately. 'Thank you, Marco. I'll love him forever, sweet baby.'

'He is a farm kitten from the vineyard. The mother cat, she has many kittens to look after. I know how you like to rescue small things. So will you rescue him?'

'He's the perfect wedding present, thank you,' said Emma. 'And

I have a present for you, Marco. Something special. But I will give it to you tonight.'

Then she would tell him that she was already pregnant and the illustrious dell'Orto line would continue. She was so happy with the news. Marco would be pleased. Maybe more than very pleased. Maybe elated, always very Italian.

The fluffy grey kitten fell asleep in her arms, half curled up on her lap. She would call him Miracolo. Mira for short, because Emma's life had now become a miracle.

acknowledgements

My gratitude
To
The Venice Tourist Office
for their kind help

To
Dr D. C. Thomas
for medical details

To
Donna Leon
who lives in Venice, for her friendly guidance

To
Oxted and Worthing Library staff
for information about computer hacking

To
Gill Jackson and all her staff at Hale
for their patience and support,
especially Esther, my editor,
and the art department for that
eerie and mysterious cover.
Grazie!